sammy keyes

AND THE search for snake eyes

Also by Wendelin Van Draanen

How I Survived Being a Girl
1. Sammy Keyes and the Hotel Thief
2. Sammy Keyes and the Skeleton Man
3. Sammy Keyes and the Sisters of Mercy
4. Sammy Keyes and the Runaway Elf
5. Sammy Keyes and the Curse of Moustache Mary
6. Sammy Keyes and the Hollywood Mummy
Flipped

sammy keyes
AND THE search for snake eyes

by WENDELIN VAN DRAANEN

ALFRED A. KNOPF
New York

THIS IS A BORZOI BOOK PUBLISHED BY ALFRED A. KNOPF

Text copyright © 2002 by Wendelin Van Draanen Parsons
Illustrations copyright © 2002 by Dan Yaccarino
All rights reserved under International and Pan-American Copyright Conventions.
Published in the United States of America by Alfred A. Knopf, a division of Random
House, Inc., New York, and simultaneously in Canada by Random House of Canada
Limited, Toronto. Distributed by Random House, Inc., New York.

www.randomhouse.com/kids

KNOPF, BORZOI BOOKS, and the colophon are registered trademarks
of Random House, Inc.

Library of Congress Cataloging-in-Publication Data
Van Draanen, Wendelin.
Sammy Keyes and the search for Snake Eyes / by Wendelin Van Draanen.
p. cm.
Summary: When thirteen-year-old Sammy finds herself with an abandoned baby on
her hands, she sets out to find the young mother, who may belong to a gang, and
accidentally jeopardizes her position on the softball team.
ISBN 0-375-81175-3 (trade) — ISBN 0-375-91175-8 (lib. bdg.)
[1. Babies—Fiction. 2. Abandoned children—Fiction. 3. Gangs—Fiction.
4. Softball—Fiction. 5. Mystery and detective stories.] I. Title.

PZ7.V2857 Sap 2002
[Fic]—dc21
2001050236

Printed in the United States of America
May 2002
10 9 8 7 6 5 4 3 2 1
First Edition

Dedicated to those who stand up to terrorists, both big and small.

◆ ◆ ◆

Thanks to the following for their help with research:
Sergeant Gregory Carroll of the Santa Maria Police Department;
Cathy DeCaprio-Wells at Santa Barbara County
Child Protective Services

Also, sincere gratitude to:
Mark and Nancy for their help, support, and, yes, ruthless edits;
Honey Beth Felter, bibliographer extraordinaire;
Kathleen Dunn, Isabel Warren-Lynch, Michelle Gengaro-Kokmen,
and the Gang of Goodguys at Knopf who are helping
Sammy fight the good fight

sammy keyes

AND THE search for snake eyes

PROLOGUE

I'm embarrassed to say that I didn't see it coming. She just passed off the bag, and suddenly there I was, stuck. And even after I felt how heavy it was, I *still* didn't know what was in it. How was I supposed to know? I'd never touched one before—never even been that *close* to one before. But the minute I looked inside, I knew I was in trouble.

Serious, heart-stopping trouble.

ONE

I don't generally hang out at the mall. It's full of biting shoes, shrinking clothes, and useless knickknacks. It's also crawling with poseur kids who think it's their private stage for rehearsing public coolness. Please. I get enough of that in junior high.

But the Santa Martina mall also has a video arcade, and if you know anything about my best friend, Marissa, you know that video games are the only thing that'll make her quit talking about softball. And since we're in the middle of gearing up for the Junior Sluggers' Cup tournament, softball is *all* Marissa's had on her mind. For *weeks*. She's working up plays, she's practicing after practice, she's even talked Coach Rothhammer out of her home phone number so she can run ideas by her in the middle of the night. You have to know Ms. Rothhammer to understand the significance of this—nobody's got her number, and I mean nobody. She teaches P.E. and eighth-grade science, and she's got a reputation for being really strict and really private. Like, is she married? We don't know. Does she have kids? Dogs? Horses? Flower beds? Nobody knows. I'll bet Vice Principal Caan doesn't even know, that's how good she is at being private.

What I do know about Ms. Rothhammer is that she's the one person who wants to bring home the Junior Sluggers' Cup as much as Marissa does. Probably for different reasons—like, I know Ms. Rothhammer couldn't care less about us winning the school a party day. More likely it has to do with showing up Mr. Vince, who told her she'd never get her hands on the cup. Of course, that was last November, after our team beat his team in our school's playoffs, so maybe she's forgotten all about that.

Then again, maybe not.

Anyway, the point is, Marissa McKenze has been the Softball Czar for weeks, and the past few days it's been driving me batty. And maybe I should've just said, "Marissa, enough! There's life beyond softball!" but I *do* live in Santa Martina, a town where everyone from Heather Acosta, Princess Prevaricator, to Mayor Hibbs, Sultan of City Hall, is *into* the game. So much so that people play year-round. Rain or shine, mud or flood, people play.

So instead of telling Marissa something she'd never buy into anyhow, what I said was "Hey, you want to go to the mall and play some video games?" And since I'm *never* the one to suggest it, she said, "Are you kidding?" and off we went.

Now, I'm not big on playing myself. I don't have the quarters to spare. So while Marissa's seriously invested in the skill of electro-badguy annihilation, I'm more an observer than anything else. Sure, I'll play a few games just to keep her happy, but pretty much I'm a peanut gallery of one.

Good as she is, though, I get bored and wind up looking around at other stuff. People, mostly. And let me tell you, there are some pretty strange people in the arcade. I'm not talking about the kids, either. They just strut around, cussing and stuff, acting like they'll take you down if you look at them wrong. Like they could actually *catch* you with the way they wear their pants halfway down their butts.

No, the *adults* are strange. It's men, mostly, and mostly they look the same—scraggly hair, faded band T-shirts, dirty jeans, and work boots. They come in alone, park themselves at the gun games, and shoot. They don't look at anyone or anything else, they just shoot. And good luck cutting in if you want a turn. I've seen kids try it, and let me tell you, it's *dangerous*.

Anyway, there I was, at four in the afternoon, surrounded by the noise of electro-fire, checking out the arcade clientele, when this girl with a big red-and-white Sears bag backs right into me. Hard.

Does she say, Sorry? Or, Excuse me? Or even turn around and *look* at me?

No.

She whimpers, "Jesus! Oh, Jesus!" and drags that bag in close, between her feet. Her eyes are glued to the arcade entrance, and she's shaking. First it's just sort of a shiver, then a rumble; then she starts having her very own internal earthquake.

"What's the matter?" I ask her, but she still doesn't turn around to look at me. She just paws through her Sears bag and rearranges a yellow towel that's on top, then weaves the bag's cord handles together, shaking the whole time.

I look between the two video games we're standing in front of so I can get a clear shot of the entrance, but all I see is a bunch of people milling around outside.

This girl is melting down about something, though, so I say to her, "Are you all right?"

"No! Oh Jesus, no!" She turns to me, her eyes full of terror. "What am I going to *do*? He'll kill me! He'll kill us both!"

"Who?" And I'm thinking, Whoa, now! Why would he want to kill *me*?

She doesn't answer. She just stays behind cover while she checks out the entrance.

"Do you want me to call the police?"

"No!" She turns back to me, looking even more scared than she had before. "No!"

"But—"

"Whatever you do . . ." Her shaking goes up a notch. "Oh Jesus, there he is!"

"Where?"

"Right over there!" she says, looking out into the halls of the mall. Only there are about thirty people roaming around out there. "Oh Jesus, what am I going to do? What am I going to *do*?"

"If you're that scared, why don't you let me call the police?"

She whirls around and says, "No! You hear me! They mess everything up. They put him away and now he's out! He's gonna kill me!"

"But if he's going to *kill* you . . ."

"Oh Jesus, here he comes." She looks around frantically. "Is there a back door to this place?"

I shake my head.

"How am I going to get *out* of here?" She goes back to looking outside, practically shaking herself to death.

Then I see him. I can just tell. It's the way he's walking. Slow, but, I don't know . . . *tight*. Like every step is for a reason and nothing better get in his way.

He's wearing a tight white tank T that shows off his muscles, and his hair is short on the sides, but a little longer on top and gelled forward. There's a heavy gold cross around his neck and a beeper on the waistband of his baggy jeans, and there's no doubt about it—he's headed straight for the arcade.

She slumps down at my feet. "Hide me. You've got to hide me!"

"Hide you?" I look around and say, "There's no place *to* hide!"

"Is he in?"

I look at the entrance. "He's hanging right outside."

"He'll be in. He can smell me."

"*Smell* you?" I hadn't noticed any perfume or anything on her, and the way she said it was weird.

"It's his way."

"Now he's in. He's . . . he's going down the first aisle." I squat down beside her and say, "Why don't you let me get security? Or we could get a bunch of people together and tackle him if he tries to hurt you. . . ."

She gives me a sad little smile, then closes her eyes and

mouths a quick prayer as she makes the sign of the cross on her chest. And that's when I notice these weird sort of slashy scars on the inside of her left arm. Not down by her wrist, up higher. One zigzags side to side and the other overlaps it a little, zigzagging up and down. And I want to ask her if the guy she's so afraid of cut up her arm, but all of a sudden she stops shaking, slides her Sears bag toward me, and says, "I'll meet you back here at . . . at seven. *Be* here, you hear me? Everything you need's in the elevator—go get it. And don't let nothing happen to him!" She grabs me by the shoulders and says, "Do not, do *not* call the cops. You hear me? Promise me!"

Everything was happening so fast. First she's scared to death of this guy; then she doesn't want anything to happen to him. And what was that about the elevator?

But her eyes were so intense. It was like they hypnotized a nod out of me. And before I could ask her any questions, she said, "If I'm not back right at seven, *wait* for me, you hear me? I *will* be back." In a flash she's gone, crawling around the corner, then darting out the door.

I look around for the guy who's stalking her, and there he is, coming my way. I do my best to act cool, but let me tell you, this guy's creepy, and the closer he gets, the more I shrink back until I'm practically hugging a video game backward.

When he's right beside me, he sniffs the air. Three times really fast, then slowly three times. And while he's sniffing, I'm noticing the tattoo on the top part of his left arm. It's the head of a cobra with eyes like *dice*. They're popping out, with the ones facing forward. Real "snake eyes." And the mouth of the snake is open—like it's in midstrike, coming right at me.

Now, the tattoo's plenty scary, but when the guy turns and looks straight at me, my knees practically buckle. I'd never seen a face like his. He had hatred for eyes. Steel for a mouth. He almost didn't look human.

And while I'm dissolving into the front of a video game, he keeps looking right at me, then sniffs the air again and heads slowly out the door.

I had chills running all through me. Hard as she ran, that girl would never get away from him. He'd hunt her down until he found her. I could just tell.

"God, Marissa, what are we going to do?" I looked over my shoulder. "Marissa?"

"What?" Her finger's just a blur, punching the shoot button.

"Don't tell me you didn't see any of that...?"

"Any of what?" Her finger's flying, fast and furious.

"Marissa!"

She looks at me for a split second. "What?"

"There was a girl in here, scared to death that this creepy guy was going to kill her!"

"Hang on a minute, I've just about... Yeah!" She turns to me. "Okay, what?"

I shake my head at her. "You didn't see *any* of that?"

"Any of what?"

"What I just told you! About the girl and the creepy guy."

"So where are they now?"

"They *left*."

"So...?"

"So do you think we should call the police?"

"About *what*?"

"Marissa!"

"Look, I don't know what you're talking about! I was in the middle of a game. It's noisy in here. I didn't even know you were talking to someone." She points to the Sears bag and says, "What's that?"

"She left it with me. I think she couldn't run with it. It looks kind of heavy. And I'm supposed to get some stuff of hers out of the elevator and meet her back here at seven."

Marissa squints at me. *"Why?"*

I shrug real big and say, "I don't know! That's just what she said!"

"How *do* you get yourself into these things?"

"Hey! I just asked her if she was all right, and it turns out she *wasn't*. She was scared to death!"

"So why come in here? Why not call the police?"

"Marissa, I don't know! She was hiding, okay? And she was real clear about not calling the police. *Real* clear. She seemed, you know, *allergic* to the idea."

"What did she do? Break out in hives?"

"Pretty much, yeah."

"Well, I'm not hanging around here until seven...."

"Neither am I! Grams would kill me." I reach for the Sears bag and say, "I'll just take this home and bring it back after... dinner."

"What's wrong?"

"It weighs a ton...!"

"What's in it?"

I put it back down and say, "Feels like a bowling ball!" and when I look inside, what do I see?

A brand-new Barbie giving me a bubble-head smile through a bubble pack.

Obviously that didn't weigh much. And neither did the puffy yellow towel underneath it. So I pull back the towel, muttering, "There must be something else...." And that's when I see it. "Marissa," I gasp. "Look!"

It was bigger than a bomb.

Scarier than a bomb.

And it wouldn't be long before shrapnel went flying.

TWO

I grabbed the bag and charged out of the arcade. In a panic I flew around the whole central courtyard, looking up the escalator, looking down the corridors. It hadn't been *that* long. Where had she gone?

Marissa was right behind me, dragging our backpacks along. "Do you see her?"

"No!"

"What does she look like?"

"Long black hair. Curly. Pulled back in a scrunchie." I spun around and whimpered, "I can't *believe* this!"

Marissa leaned over to look in the bag. "You don't think it's . . . *dead* . . . do you?"

I peeked in, too, and there it was—the scariest thing I'd ever seen.

A baby.

I got in a little closer and said, "It doesn't *look* dead."

"I can't believe it slept through all that *noise*. Don't you think you should pick it up and find out?"

"No!"

"Why not?"

"I'm not touching it! I'm going to find that girl and give it back!"

Marissa looks around and shakes her head. "Sorry to break it to you, but she is long gone."

"But...I can't believe she'd..." I looked in the bag one more time. "Marissa, it's a *baby*."

"Exactly. Now make sure it's all right, would you?"

"Why am *I* the one who's always got to investigate? Why am *I* always the one checking pulses and—"

"Because *you're* the one who accepts unidentified packages from strangers, that's why. She could've been handing you a *bomb*, Sammy. Why didn't you look?"

"A bomb I could handle! And it happened so fast! One minute she's shaking and quaking like she's about to *die*, and the next she's shoving this thing at me and running out the door! This is not my fault!"

Marissa gives me a closed little smile, then says, "It never is."

In a flash she's squatting beside the bag, digging under the towel to check out the baby. "Look," she says to me. "He's fine! He's moving."

I looked in at the little head with the wispy black hair. It had such tiny ears. Such a tiny nose. Such a tiny mouth. And sure enough, it was moving. "Great," I whispered. "So now what?"

She didn't have time to answer. That tiny mouth let out an enormous *"Wwwwwaaaaaaaahhhhhh!"*

"Marissa! You woke it up!"

"It would've woken up anyway. Now pick it up, would you?"

"Wwwwwaaaaaaaahhhhhh!" went the bag, and you

better believe I picked it up! I grabbed those Sears-bag handles and made a beeline for the elevator.

"Sammy! Where are you going?"

"She said something about leaving stuff in the elevator. I'm gonna go find it!"

"Sammy! Sammy, that is *not* how you carry a baby!"

I held the screaming bag out to her. "Oh, really? Well, here! You hold it!"

She just stood there, her eyes wide open.

I resumed my dash to the elevator with Marissa chasing after me. "Sammy, *I* didn't take the baby—"

"*Wwwwwaaaaahhhhhhhhhh!*"

"—and *I* didn't—"

"*Wwwwwaaaaahhhhhhhhhh!*"

"—promise to meet some stranger back here at seven—"

"*Wwwwwaaaaahhhhhhhhhh!*"

"—and *I* didn't—"

"*Wwwwwaaaaahhhhhhhhhh!*"

She blocked my path and cried, "Would you just pick up the baby!"

I dodged around her, and believe me, people were staring at us. When I reached the elevator, I punched the button about five hundred times and stood by with a screaming bag on one side and a bossy friend on the other.

Finally Marissa says through her teeth, "I just don't understand why you aren't picking it up!"

I spin around and say, "Because I don't know *how* to, all right? I've never even *touched* one before! I keep asking *you* to do it, but you're too focused on whose *fault* all of this is to help me out."

She pulls a little face and says, "Well, *I* don't know anything about it, either!"

"Then why are you acting like you do?"

By now the baby's kicking and punching the sides of the bag. Marissa shouts over the crying, "I *do* know you're not supposed to carry a baby around under towels and a Barbie in a Sears bag, though! And when they cry, you're supposed to pick them up and feed them or change their diaper or rock them or, you know, do *something*. You're not supposed to leave them to punch a hole in the side of a sack!"

Just then the elevator door opens and an elderly couple steps out. They frown at us and our Sears bag as we scoot past them to get on board. And from their whispers and gasps, I can tell it won't be long before they notify security about two teenagers on the loose with a wailing, flailing Sears sack.

So I smile at them as the doors close and call, "It's a Dolly Scream-A-Lot. The switch is stuck!"

Marissa rolls her eyes and says, "A Dolly Scream-A-Lot?" But then she points and cries, "Look!"

Propped in the corner is a stroller. A collapsible stroller, all folded up so it looks like a double-handled umbrella on wheels. The corners of a blue knitted blanket are peeking out the sides, and there's a rubbery-looking bag wrapped over the handles.

"This must be what she was talking about, don't you think?" Marissa asks me.

The Sears bag is still wailing, and the elevator's cruising up to the second floor. "You know how to work it?" I shouted.

She fumbles with the stroller, then screams, *"Would you take the baby out of the bag!"*

"Okay! Okay!"

I started to. Really, I did. But then the elevator came to a stop and the door opened up and a herd of kids shuffled in. So I grabbed the bag and bolted, leaving a screaming *"Wwwaahhhhahhhh"* in my wake.

Marissa struggled out behind me with the stroller, yelling, "Where are you *going*?"

I just marched down the corridor, around a bend, and blasted straight through an Employees Only door.

"Sammy! Sammy, stop!" She knew where I was headed. We'd been there before.

"I can't think, all right? And I don't want to figure this thing out with everyone staring at us!"

Down a maze of back corridors we went, right, left, then right again. Then up some cement steps, through the roof access door, and into the sunlight.

Marissa drags the stroller and plastic bag and our backpacks up with her, yelling, "If you don't pick that baby up *now*, I'm going to..."

She never did say what she would do, but I could tell she was serious. And I wanted the thing to shut up as much as she did, so the minute we were on the roof I reached in, grabbed the baby under the arms, and lifted.

So there I am, holding a baby for the first time in my entire life, and what's it do?

Screams even louder.

Marissa says, "You can't hold it *out* like that, Sammy! You've got to hold it close to you. On your shoulder!"

I put it on my shoulder and look at Marissa like, Well?

"It's not a sack of potatoes! *Hold* it."

I yank it off my shoulder and give it to Marissa. "*You* hold it!"

She did. One hand under the rump, one hand on the back, the baby's head against her shoulder. And after about a minute of bouncing up and down, the wailing quieted into gasps and hiccups.

I let out a huge breath and said, "Oh, *thank* you. How did you *do* that?"

She shrugged. "Haven't you ever seen someone hold a baby?"

I felt pretty much like an idiot. I mean, sure, I'd seen women with babies. They're everywhere. And I can't really explain why this one felt like a bomb instead of a baby, but it did. That's *exactly* what it felt like.

"I think he's hungry," Marissa was saying. "He's rooting around like crazy! Is there a bottle in that bag? He also needs a new diaper—pee-yew!"

I dug through the bag. "Bottle, check!" I held it out to her. "Diaper, check!"

"Let's feed him first."

She sat down cross-legged on the graveled tar paper and held the baby in the crook of her arm. The baby grabbed the bottle with both hands and sucked like it hadn't been fed in days.

"Wow, look at that," I said.

Marissa grinned. "He was just hungry."

I sat down next to her. "Why do you think it's a him?"

"Looks like a him, don't you think?"

"It looks like an it. And there's a *Barbie* in the bag."

"Yeah, but the blanket's blue. And his outfit's mostly blue. Mothers are very blue and pink oriented at this stage."

"Is that so." I shook my head at her. "For someone who doesn't know anything about babies, you're sure sounding like a pediatric pro."

"Well, *here*. Have some experience."

Before I could stop her, she'd transferred the baby into my lap. "See?" she says. "It's just a baby."

Nuh-uh, I thought. This thing's a *bomb*. But I sat there and watched it chugalug the bottle, and when there were all of two drops left, the baby pushed the bottle aside and started fussing again. "What?" I asked it. "What do you want *now*?"

"I think you're supposed to burp him now."

"How do I do that?"

"I don't know. Hold him on your shoulder and tap his back?"

I tried, but it started fussing even more.

"Maybe bounce a little?"

So there I am, cross-legged on the roof of the mall, bouncing and patting and sort of trying to shake the bubbles out of him, when all of a sudden he goes, *"Aaaarp!"*

"Yeah! You did it!"

I was about to say, "Hey, I did!" but before I got the

chance, he *bombed* me. Half that bottle came up. And it was *hot,* too. It spread all over my shoulder and down my back, and all I could say was "Oh! Oh, *yuck!*" I held the baby away from me and cried, "Why'd you do *that?*" And you know what that little monster did? He smiled. Smiled and *cooed*.

"Oh, great. Just great!" I practically threw the Bomber to Marissa and dug through the bag. One small package of Kleenex, a can of baby formula, a tube of baby wipes, a plastic mat, five diapers, and a thin flannel towel.

I sacrificed the towel, but it was hopeless. I had baby barf all over my shirt and it wasn't coming off. And I'm barely coming to grips with the barf when Marissa says, "We'd better change him and go, Sammy. What if they lock that door or something?"

I was more worried about Grams worrying about why I was so late than I was about the door getting locked. So I decided, All right. Let's change this puppy and get a move on. Pit stop at home for dinner and then back out to the mall at seven. It'd be over before my shirt was done tumbling dry.

I opened up the plastic mat and said, "Let's do it."

She laid him down and said, "Smell that? This boy's pretty poopy."

"Oh, great." I unsnapped the jumper, ripped the side tabs of the diaper open, and it turns out Marissa was right. It was stinky. It was poopy.

And it was, indeed, a boy.

"I told you so," Marissa said with a grin.

He starts kicking and cooing, and the more I tried to

clean him up, the more he giggled and pumped those legs. Finally I grabbed both his feet with one hand and cleaned him up with the other. And as I'm shoving a new diaper under his bouncing bottom, he suddenly stops struggling, looks right at me, and opens his eyes real big.

"What?" I ask him. "Why are you looking at me like that?"

He holds my gaze, then lets loose.

Not with a wail.

Not with a burp or barf.

No, this time he shoots a fountain of *pee*, straight up in the air.

And since what goes up must come down—down it came. All over him, all over the new diaper, all over the changing mat, and all over me.

So I'm kneeling there with pee on my hands, pee in my hair, pee *every*where, when he starts kicking again. And cooing. Like, Whipee! Wasn't that fun!

Marissa's trying hard not to, but she can't help it. She just cracks up.

I grab the flannel towel and clean everything the best I can; then I wrap him in his diaper, snap up his jumper, flip open the stroller, and strap him in. I stuff everything else into the Sears bag, whip on my backpack, and say, "Let's go."

Marissa holds open the door and helps me carry him in the stroller down to the back-corridor maze. Then we jet out of the mall and over to where Marissa's parked her bike. She looks at all the stuff I've got and asks, "How are you going to get into the apartment?"

Now, this is a very good question, seeing how I'm living in a seniors-only apartment complex where kids are not allowed to live. But for once, I don't have to give her a plan that involves the fire escape and bubble gum in the doorjamb. For once I get to say, "I'm going to walk right in."

"Oh, of course," she says. "That way you can walk right back out."

"Exactly. And after I give this baby back, *then* I'll sneak in for the night."

I should have known it wouldn't be that easy.

THREE

I backed the stroller through the lobby door of the Senior Highrise and called "Hi, Mr. Garnucci!" over to the manager's desk. "How are you?"

"Samantha. How nice to see you," he yelled. "Haven't seen you in ages!" Mr. Garnucci always yells, even when he's standing right next to you. Comes from dealing with old people all day, I suppose. What's funny is, I find myself yelling at him, too. I guess it's kind of contagious.

"I'm fine!" I called to him. "I thought my grandmother might like seeing this baby I'm taking care of! You don't mind, do you?" I turned the stroller his way. "Check him out. What do you think?"

Mr. Garnucci coochie-cooed the baby for a minute, then said, "It's fine with me, and it's sure to brighten her day." Then he smiles at me and says, "Your grandmother's new neighbor moved in today. Her name's Mrs. Wedgewood and she seems much more "—he clears his throat—"*agreeable* than your grandmother's old neighbor."

"Well, that's good," I said, then pushed the stroller toward the elevator. "I'll see you in a little while."

"Have a nice visit!"

I rode up to the fifth floor and zipped down the hall, but as I got close to our apartment, I started slowing down.

Our door was open.

Wide open.

Now, Grams is very quick about coming in and going out, and her lock is always snapped in place, *presto*. Before you're even done coming in, you're locked in. That's the way she runs her door, and there's no arguing with her about it. And with the way our old neighbor, Mrs. Graybill, was always trying to prove that I live there, it's been a good thing. A *necessary* thing.

But even after Mrs. Graybill was gone, Grams was still very quick about the door. Until now. Now the door was hanging there, wide open.

The minute I poked my nose in the apartment, I knew why. "Samantha!" my grandmother says as she hurries toward me. "What a nice surprise. Come in! Come in!"

A very large woman is planted on the couch. She's got the blackest hair I've ever seen on anyone, and arms that are *way* bigger than my legs—maybe even bigger than my *body*—and they're covered with bruises. Big blue and black and green bruises. They look like a gorilla's been using them for punching bags.

She smiles at me real big, and my grams scoots me in, saying, "Rose, this is Samantha, the granddaughter I was telling you so much about. Samantha, this is my new neighbor, Mrs. Wedgewood."

"Pleased to meet you," I tell her as we shake hands over her metal walker. And I do try to look her in the eye, but it's hard with her arm moving back and forth in big fatty waves, distracting me.

She lets go of my hand and says, "Your grandmother has been telling me what a big help you are to her." She smiles. "And who is this little doll?"

"I'm baby-sitting him and I thought, you know, that Grams might like a visit."

Now, through all this I'm smiling and trying to act normal, but Grams' radar is in full scan, and I can practically hear her thinking, Baby-sitting? *You?*

"Well, how nice of you," Mrs. Wedgewood says. She leans over a little to get a better look, and that's when I notice long, scraggly strands of gray hair poking out at her neck and around her ears. And it's just dawning on me that all that big bouncy black hair on her head is a wig when she says, "And what's the little fellow's name?"

I quit staring at her wig. A name! Wild names start flying through my brain: Screamin' Joe. Flailing Frank. Peein' Pete. Poopy... "Pepe," I tell her. "His name's Pepe."

They both look at me like, *Pepe?* but I just smile and pretend it's a name that every little boy should have.

Mrs. Wedgewood takes a deep breath and says, "Well, it's been nice chatting with you, Rita, but I really should be getting home now so you can have a little time with your visitors." She scoots to the edge of the couch, grabs the walker, then rocks forward and pulls herself to a standing position. Well, almost standing. She's leaning on the walker so hard that she looks a lot like a humpback whale trying to push around a gurney, her arms flapping from side to side like flabby, bruised fins.

She winks at the baby and says, "Your ride looks like more fun than mine, Pepe!" Then she shuffles out the door with a "Nice to meet you both. We'll be seeing lots of each other, I'm sure."

Grams locks the door behind her and says, "Well. She seems very pleasant." Then she turns to me, plants her hands on her hips and zeros in on me. "Why are you so late, and what is the real story with this baby?"

"I'm so late because, well . . . it's sort of a long story."

She gives me a closed little smile, then says, "It always is."

I couldn't believe my ears. "Have you and Marissa been talking?"

"No. . . . Why do you say that?"

"Because she said something just like that when I told her it wasn't my fault I got stuck with this . . . this . . . *monster*."

"Monster? He doesn't look like a monster to me."

"Yeah, well, just wait until he barfs on *your* shirt and pees in *your* hair!"

She grins. "Ah, the joys of motherhood." Then she heads for the kitchen, saying, "So what *is* the long story? I haven't even started on dinner yet, so we have plenty of time."

So I told her. Everything. And by the time I'm done, she's not only stopped making dinner, she's also practically stopped breathing. "You mean to tell me," she whispers from the kitchen chair she'd sort of crumbled into, "you have no idea whose baby this is?"

Poopy Pepe's squirming in the stroller, twisting around and starting to squawk. "Well, sure, I know whose it is, and I'm going to give it back to her at seven."

"What if she doesn't show up?"

"It's her *baby*. Of course she's going to show up."

She looks at Pepe and says, "Samantha, you've got to take that baby out of his stroller. And when did you say you fed him?"

"He *just* ate. Like an hour ago."

"But you said he spit half of it up."

"Well, yeah, but there's no way he can be hungry yet...is there?"

"Babies that age eat every couple of hours. Is there formula in that bag?"

"Yeah. There's a small can of it in there."

"Well, let me see it." The whimpering was getting louder. "And get him out of that stroller!"

I handed her the can and pinched the clip open on the stroller straps. "What do I do with him?"

She was reading the label. "Hold him. Or put him down on a towel to let him get some exercise."

I liked the towel idea. I laid him on the floor and ran off to get the one out of the Sears bag.

"Samantha! You don't just put a baby on the floor. It's cold!"

"I'll be right back!"

"Oh, and close that cat of yours in my room. He is *not* going to like this baby."

She was right. Dorito would *hate* Poopy Pepe.

And people wonder why I love my cat.

Anyway, I locked Dorito in Grams' room and came flying into the kitchen with the towel. "Here."

"Put it on the carpet in the front room."

I did.

She looks up from reading the formula can. "Samantha Jo, what are you waiting for? Put the baby on the towel!"

Pepe was not looking or sounding too happy. A sure sign he was about to bomb me with something. I picked him up and held him out at arm's length, then ran him over to the towel.

Grams mutters, "You are terrible with that baby, Samantha."

"Well he's . . . he's scary!" I said.

"Why?"

"I don't know. . . . He just is."

"You're reminding me of your mother, child."

Ouch. I inched back into the kitchen. "Don't say that."

"Well, it's true," she said with a frown.

I looked over at Pepe, kicking away at the air above him, making little slobbery throaty noises. Had I been this scary to my mother? No way. Nuh-uh. That baby had done more to me in an hour than . . .

"You were a screamer."

"What?"

"A screamer. Night and day. The doctor said it was colic, but that's just a nice way of saying you were a screamer."

"But—"

"That over there is a good baby." She stood and took the baby bottle out of the bag and said, "Now here. Clean the bottle and mix up some formula. Two scoops, tap water'll have to do. I'll get a pan going for you to warm it in—oh, never mind. We'll just be careful with the microwave. And don't mix it with the nipple on. You'll plug it."

I did manage to do all that and feed Pepe. Even burped him halfway through because Grams told me that's what you're supposed to do.

It didn't stop him from spitting up all over me again, but this time it was only about a quarter of the bottle. And this time I didn't mind so much because, hey, I was already coated. Barf away, baby.

But two minutes after he'd finished re-barfing me, he starts turning beet red in the face and I can tell—Poopy Pepe's piling up a big one.

Grams laughs at the expression on my face. "They do that, Samantha."

"Every time you feed them?"

"No . . . but often enough. And you have to change him right away or he'll get a rash."

Twenty minutes later I finally had a new diaper on him. I didn't fall for the ol' fountain trick again, either. I wadded up practically a whole roll of toilet paper and laid it across him, and even though Grams' eyebrows were flying up and down a lot, she didn't actually *say* anything.

Then before you know it I'd shoveled down dinner, packed Pepe into his stroller, and hit the hallway. "Bye,

Grams!" I called for the world to hear, then hurried to the elevator. Down we went, and out through the lobby. "Bye, Mr. Garnucci! See you soon!"

"Bye, Samantha!" he yelled back. "You take care!"

The mall's only a few blocks from the Senior Highrise, so I actually got there five minutes early. I stood right outside the arcade, keeping one eye on the wall of glass doors leading to the parking structure and the other on the tower clock, which sticks right up through the escalators in the central courtyard. Seven o'clock. Seven-oh-five. Seven-ten.

There weren't a whole lot of people milling around, and even though I wasn't too worried yet, I couldn't help wondering what I was going to do if she *didn't* show up. Seven-fifteen. Seven-thirty. By now I was having to roll the stroller back and forth to keep Pepe quiet.

Then, just as the big hand clicked up to the Roman numeral nine, I saw something that made my heart stop. It wasn't the guy with the snake-eyed cobra. It was worse. *Way* worse.

Coming right at me was the Queen of Mean.

The Mistress of Misery.

The Baroness of Brattiness.

That's right, it was the one and only Heather Acosta.

And flanking her like a couple of court jesters were her wanna-bes, Tenille Toolee and Monet Jarlsberg.

I ducked behind the stroller, but it was too late. They'd spotted me. So I retied the shoelace on my high-top, took a deep breath, and stood up to face the firing squad.

Heather came right up to me and said through her sneer, "Hey, loser. What are you doing hanging around the mall with a *baby*, huh?"

I told myself to ignore her. I told myself to look right through her. But my mouth shoots off with, "I was about to ask Tenille and Monet the same thing."

Tenille didn't get it. Neither did Monet. But Heather did. She wobbles her wicked red head, hissing, "Don't *even* think you can harass me here. There's no administration building for you to hide in, and I don't see Ms. Rothhammer around anywhere to bail you out." She shoves me and says, "So don't start with me, stupid."

Her even touching me was enough to make my skin creep right off my body, but her *shoving* me practically vaporized my self-control. I wanted to knock her flat! I didn't care that it was three against one. Monet and Tenille would be easy to scare off, and Heather, well, I'd taken her down before. Right here in the mall.

But then Pepe started whimpering and twisting around in the stroller, and I realized that I couldn't exactly run if it came to that. I was in charge of a *baby*.

So I took a deep breath, took a step back, and said, "Look, Heather, I'm baby-sitting. Don't insult me, I won't insult you. Okay?"

She snorts and says, "Just having to *look* at you's an insult, loser." She smirks at my high-tops, then gives my shirt a pitiful little shake of the head. "Like, what *is* that all over you?"

Pepe's still squawking, so I roll the stroller back and forth to quiet him. "Look, do you mind? Just go away."

All of a sudden her eyebrows go up and her lips curve into an evil oval. "It's baby barf!" She looks at Pepe and cries, "Look! It's all over him, too!"

I whip the stroller around so he's facing me, and sure enough, there's spit-up running down his jumper.

"How cute. Mommy and baby have matching outfits!"

I pull out the same old flannel towel and try to wipe him up with it, but the towel's already pretty gross and it's not helping matters much. And with Tenille and Monet snickering and saying stuff like "Dis*gu*sting," and "Who'd ever trust *her* with a baby?" and "Like, it's probably sitting in a diaper full of doo-doo, too!" well, it took everything I had not to punch their little lemon lips shut.

By now Pepe's crying, so I take him out of the stroller and move away from them a few yards, saying, "Will you please just back off? Go. Go play video games. Just leave me alone."

It came out sort of quiet because I was trying real hard to rock Pepe and hold it all together, but it must've sounded like I was scared—or at least intimidated—because Heather's head inflates on the spot. She'd won and she knew it. "C'mon, guys," she says to Monet and Tenille. "Like we want to be seen anywhere *near* this loser."

They slithered into the darkness of the arcade, which was almost worse than having them out where I could see them. There was something really creepy about knowing they could see me through the arcade windows when I couldn't see them at all.

So I moved into a corner near the wall of doors that led to the parking lot. Heather and her friends could still see me if they tried, but at least I wasn't right out in front. I had a clear shot of the corridors and the clock, and there's no way Pepe's mom could miss *me*. I was bouncing her baby like crazy on my shoulder, trying to keep him quiet.

And the longer I bounced, the more panicked I got. Where *was* she? Pepe needed another bottle. He needed another *diaper*. He needed a clean shoulder to barf on!

But the clock ticked on, and at closing time Heather and her pip-squeak posse did a strut-by, shooting off with "Ooo, baby!" and "Sammy the Nanny!" and "Hot date, huh?"

I didn't even look their way. I had bigger problems than being the brunt of their jokes. It was late. It was dark outside. I didn't know who Pepe's mother was, and yeah, it had finally sunk in that no, she wasn't going to be taking over her motherly duties. Pepe's mother had made it real clear that I shouldn't go to the police, but I couldn't exactly go *home*. I mean, if *I* wasn't allowed to live there, imagine how welcome Pepe would be!

As the lights inside the mall started going off and cars zoomed away from the parking structure, I just stood outside, frozen to the sidewalk.

What in the world was I going to do with this baby?

FOUR

There's only so long you can stand outside in the cold watching a mall go dark before you make a move. Especially when the baby you've been stuck with is wailing like his diaper's on fire. And maybe his bottom did need some attending to, but I just couldn't *think* straight with all the noise he was making.

So the move I made was to strap Pepe back in the stroller and run up and down the sidewalk looking for a water fountain. I needed to mix some formula and hush that puppy up!

Pepe's having none of it, though, kicking and wailing louder than ever. And since there's no water fountain or working spigot *any*where, I decided to go across the street to the police station.

Now, I wasn't going over there because I was thinking I could turn Pepe over to the police. I was going over there because I knew the police station had a hose coiled up behind a bush right by the front steps. So I charged through the parking structure, jaywalked across Cook Street, and parked Pepe on the police-station lawn. And right behind the bushes, there it was! Spigot, crank, hose, water!

I probably should have run the water a minute to clear the hose, or even just taken the hose off. I mean, you know what hose water tastes like, and it sure wasn't purified like the formula label directed. But I couldn't *think*. It's weird. A baby crying is not like a vacuum cleaner running, which actually *helps* me think. A baby crying *bites* your eardrums. And really, what I wanted to do was yell "SHUT UP! I'm working on it!" but instead, I threw in some formula, blasted it with water, shook the bottle like mad, then stuffed it in that big boy's mouth.

The formula was cold, but he didn't even seem to care. And the hose flavor must've seemed mighty tasty to him because he guzzled that bottle like there was no tomorrow.

I let out a sigh of relief, then sat down on the bottom step and helped him hold the bottle up. Finally. I could think. What was I going to *do* with this little chugalug? I glanced over my shoulder at the police station. Why had his mother been so afraid of the police? Not that I haven't felt that way myself a few times, but still. Instead of going to the police, she'd left her baby with me.

Me.

With her *baby*.

Plus, to me the guy with the snake-eyes tattoo was way scarier than the police. And why hadn't she shown up? Had Snake Eyes found her? Had he kept her from coming back?

As a certain big-bellied cop would say, I was *way* out of my jurisdiction. If only I could just go in the station and turn Pepe over. But they'd want to know a whole lot of stuff that didn't have anything to do with Pepe. Like who I was and where I lived, and how to contact *my* parents.

No, if I was going to talk to the police, there was only one man I could talk to. One man who thought he knew me plenty well already—even if half of what he knew wasn't true. One man who was sick enough of seeing me that seeing me *leave* was a welcome sight.

Yeah, the one guy on the force I could hit with a dump-and-run was Officer Borsch. But would he still be here this late?

The bottle was empty enough for Pepe to manage it on his own, so I ran up the steps to the police-station door and tried the handle. To my surprise, it opened.

The clerk's window was rolled down tight and there wasn't anybody around. But there was a courtesy phone on the wall. I picked it up and listened to it ring on the other end—like I was calling home or something.

On the third ring a man picks up saying, "Detective Draper here. How may I help you?"

"Uh," I said in a real intelligent fashion, "does, um... does Officer Borsch happen to be around?"

"No. He's working day shift. Is there something I can help you with?"

"Uh, no. That's okay." Then I added, "Does that mean he'll be in in the morning?"

"At oh-six-hundred hours. Do you want to leave your name? Or a message?"

"Uh, no. But thanks. Thanks a lot."

I hung up and jetted out of there, and the minute I got outside I thought something terrible had happened to

Pepe. The bottle was lying on the grass and Pepe's head was bent completely forward. He wasn't moving at all. I raced down the steps with wild thoughts flying through my head. I hadn't burped him! I'd just let him guzzle. Had he spit up and choked? Had he died from a burp getting stuck in his throat?

Can hose water kill?

I propped his head back and said, "Pepe? Pepe? Hey! Are you all right?"

He didn't open his eyes, but he did move. Sort of twisted in the stroller and arched his back. Then he let out a huge burp, smacked his lips a few times and hung his head again.

I got down and said, "Pepe?" But that was it. He was out like a light, sound asleep.

I looked around. Cook Street was wet with fog, and deserted. What was I going to do? It was too late to knock on Marissa's door. Same with Holly and Dot. Besides, showing up in the middle of the night with a baby would provoke as many questions from their parents as from the police.

But I *could* go to Hudson's. His house was only a few blocks from the police station, and he would know what to do. Hudson *always* knows what to do. Maybe it's from being around for seventy-two years, I don't know, but if there's one person on earth who knows something about everything, it's Hudson Graham. He's not bossy about it, either. Or grumpy. He's just, you know, calm and *wise*. Like nothing's too big to handle; nothing's too tough to solve.

And that, I decided as I started pushing Pepe along, included what to do with an abandoned baby.

I was expecting to find him on the porch. Morning, noon, or this hour of night, that's where he hangs out. Usually with a glass of iced tea and the newspaper or a book, with his wacky cowboy boots propped up on the railing. But as I raced Pepe up Hudson's walkway, the only thing I saw on the porch was the porch light. It was glaring away in the fog, while the rest of the house was pitch-black.

"Oh, no!" I said as I ran up the steps. "He's not even home!"

I rang the bell anyway and waited. I rang some more in case he was in there asleep, but he didn't come stumbling to the door. "Hudson," I whispered to the door, "where *are* you?"

I waited on the steps for a while, trying to decide what to do, but I couldn't wait there all night. It was really late and I knew that by now Grams would be wringing her hands off.

So I got up and flipped a U-ie with the stroller. There was only one place I could go.

Home.

I did what I always do when I come in for the night. I snuck over to the fire escape and headed up. Only this time, instead of just a backpack, I had the Sears bag with the Barbie and all Pepe's paraphernalia, plus the stroller and a baby. I clamped Ol' Droopyhead onto one shoulder with one arm, put the bag over my other arm, and fumbled around until I'd collapsed the stroller with my foot.

Then up we went. And let me tell you, it is hard enough to climb stairs with a baby on one shoulder. Throw in a bag that's cutting your arm in two and a stroller that's dragging behind, bumping against every stair, and you've got the makings of a human avalanche.

And to top it all off, well, whiff-of-jiff, boy! Pepe needed a new diaper.

Then all of a sudden I hear sirens. *Loud* sirens. And my heart practically jumps out of my chest because I can't help thinking that they're coming after *me*.

So I crouch the best I can in the shadow of the stairs zigzagging above me, but I feel like a tubby toddler trying to hide behind Tinkertoys.

The sirens are getting louder. I peek down below to Broadway. Maynard's Market looks locked up tight, and so do the rest of the businesses along the street. There are a few lights on at the Heavenly Hotel, but it looks quiet. Calm.

Still, the sirens sound like they're coming my way, and I can't help it—I'm starting to shake. What am I going to do if they spot me? How am I ever going to explain being on the third floor of a fire escape with a baby this late at night?

Then the sirens cut. Just like that. I wait a minute, then peek out from beneath the stairs and scour Broadway in both directions. I lean out to get a glimpse of Main Street. And what do I see?

A whole lot of nothing.

So I tell myself that it's probably just trouble out at the Red Coach again. Or maybe my friend Madame Nashira needs a customer escorted out of her House of Astrology. Whatever; no one's charging the fire escape, so I make myself take a few deep breaths, then start clomping my way up to the fifth floor.

The higher I get, the heavier Pepe seems and the harder the stroller bangs the steps. But when I finally reach the fifth floor, it's no problem getting inside. I'd jammed the jamb with a nice fat wad of bubble gum, so the door just swings right open. The *problem* is there are other doors open, too. My grams', for one, and right next door, Mrs. Wedgewood's.

Now, I know I shouldn't go forward, but I sure don't want to go back, either. So I just stand there like an idiot, going nowhere.

Then all of a sudden Grams' head appears through Mrs. Wedgewood's apartment doorway, only she looks down the hall in the opposite direction—toward the elevator.

"Pssst!" I call. "Grams!"

She looks my way and her eyes get about as big as her owl glasses. Then, before she can say anything about the baby on my shoulder, the elevator dings. She frantically waves me back outside, whispering, "They're here!"

"Who?"

"The paramedics, now go!"

I must have gotten back out on the fire-escape landing before anyone else noticed me, because no one came out to bust me. And I wound up standing out there for*ever*, wondering what was going on.

Finally Grams' head pops outside. But she doesn't say "Coast is clear" or "Come on in" or "You must be freezing out there!" No, she looks straight at me and whispers, "This is too much, Samantha. I cannot have a baby staying here!"

"What happened to Mrs. Wedgewood? Is she okay?"

"Yes, and don't think you can change the subject. I knew this was why you were so late, I just knew it! But how could you bring that baby back here?"

"What else was I supposed to do?"

"What about the police? What about Social Services? What about Hudson?"

"I went to the police station. Officer Borsch won't be working until tomorrow morning and anyone else is going to ask me too many questions. And I tried Hudson's—he's not home!"

"He's not?" She looks at her watch, and for a second she looks more disturbed than angry. Then she shakes her head a little and says, "Well, this is certainly no place for a baby. Babies cry!"

Like this is news to me? "Grams, I'll keep him quiet, I promise. Look, he's asleep!"

"They will evict us, Samantha!"

"No one'll know. I promise! What else can I do? I'll turn him over to Officer Borsch first thing in the morning."

She stares at me a minute, then checks over her shoulder. And suddenly she's grabbing my arm and dragging me inside and down the hall.

The minute we're safe inside the apartment, she lets go and collapses into a chair. "What a night! Between what happened with Rose and you not coming back...I was worried sick about you!"

"Grams, I'm sorry. Really I am. I didn't want to leave the spot I was supposed to meet her, and then, well, I ran over to the police station, I ran over to Hudson's...It just got late. I'm sorry."

She shakes her head and says, "We cannot let that baby make a peep tonight."

"He won't, Grams, I promise." I take the yellow towel and work at laying it flat on the floor by the couch with my free hand. "What happened to Mrs. Wedgewood, anyway?"

Silence.

So I turn to her and ask, "Grams?"

She sighs and says, "She fell off the toilet."

I stopped struggling with the towel. "What?"

She sighs again. "She fell off the toilet and got stuck between the wall and the...and the bowl."

"You're kidding, right?"

"No, I'm not. And wipe that silly grin off your face!"

"But Grams, how do you fall off a *toilet*?"

Grams mutters, "Apparently she's quite good at it."

It didn't even sound like her. "Grams!" I laid Poopy Pepe on the plastic mat and ripped his diaper open. "And you're telling *me* to straighten out?"

"You're right, Samantha, that wasn't very nice of me. But really! The woman beats on the wall and cries for help like the world's coming to an end, and when I finally get Mr. Garnucci to unlock her door, I find her... in that state. Of course, she didn't want Mr. Garnucci to see her, and I certainly couldn't lift her alone. She's rather...well, she's quite heavy."

"But still, why's that make her *good* at it?"

"The fellows from the fire brigade all knew her! They went right in, heaved her up and back onto the seat, and said, 'See you next time, Rose.' "

"Do you think that's why she's got all those bruises on her arms?"

"I wouldn't be at all surprised. It wasn't an easy... uh...maneuver."

By now I've got Pepe cleaned up and changed. And since I don't want Grams to notice that I'm down to one diaper, I try to distract her with "But *how* do you fall off a toilet?"

"Let's not get into it, okay? People have more physical challenges as they get older—someday you'll understand that." She looks at Pepe and whispers, "He's waking up!"

I pick Pepe up and lean him back on my shoulder and start bouncing.

"Slower," she says. "No one can sleep on a jack-hammer."

I stoop down, get the bottle out of the bag, grab the can of formula, and head for the kitchen, trying my best to do the bouncing thing a little better.

"Here, I'll do that for you," Grams says, and mixes up a bottle. When it's warm, she tests it on her wrist and says, "Are you sure she meant seven P.M.?"

I blink at her. "I...I *think* so. I mean, the mall isn't even open at seven in the morning."

Grams hands me the bottle and frowns. "I was just grasping, I suppose. It's a very worrisome situation. I hope the mother's all right." She kisses me on the forehead and says, "I'll keep Dorito in here with me. You wake me up if you need some help," then off she goes to bed.

I turned off all the lights and decided to feed Pepe *before* he started screaming. And as I sat there in the dark on the couch with this stranger's baby in my lap, I played the whole afternoon back in my brain. The things Pepe's mother had said, the way she'd been shaking with fear, and everything that had happened after that.

By the time I was laying Pepe down on the towel on the floor, I was kicking myself for having listened to her at all. I should have gone straight to the police. I should have tracked down Officer Borsch and told him what had happened. I mean, you don't just leave your baby with a stranger.

Not unless you're in something dangerous.

And in it deep.

FIVE

I've now got a whole new definition for "sleeps like a baby." I was up all *night*, changing and rocking and feeding that boy. And around three A.M., when the last real diaper was on beyond soaked and his clothes were completely wasted, I wound up stripping him down and cutting up the yellow towel to use as a diaper. And since I couldn't find any safety pins, I held the sides together with paper clips.

It was like wearing tissue-paper trousers in a thunderstorm—the first towel diaper was soaked through in about two seconds and wound up leaking all over me.

So I tried again, only this time I got a gallon-sized Ziploc bag, slit some leg holes in it, and stuffed his little yellow tush inside that.

By the time the clock said five, I'd given up on getting any sleep. He was up, he was wet, and he was hungry. Again.

I really had to go, though, and since he was barely fussing around, I made a dash for the bathroom. Trouble is, the second I'm out of the living room he starts crying. So I run back in there, pick him up, and drag his leaky little Ziplocked bottom into the bathroom with me.

Now, I'm holding him the whole time, so he's really got no excuse to start crying, but the minute I sit down, boy, that's just what he does. And let me tell you, it's big fun relieving yourself when you've got a baby bawling on your shoulder. Big, *big* fun.

Anyway, I got out of there as fast as I could, fed him, changed him, ate breakfast, got ready for school, and snuck out of the apartment before Grams was even awake. By six-ten, I was pushing through the police-station door.

I went right up to the courtesy phone, and ten rings later it was finally picked up inside. "Sergeant Nuñez here, how can I help you?"

"I'd like to speak with Officer Borsch, please."

"He's out on rounds."

"*What?* Already?" This was too much.

"Is there something I can help you with?"

Pepe was starting to cry. "No. I need to talk to Officer Borsch. It's an emergency, okay? Not a nine-one-one emergency. Just a regular…emergency! Can you radio him to come back or something?"

"Well…"

Then something hit me. "Listen. Radio him and have him meet me in front of the mall, okay? The entrance by the arcade. Right across the street."

"Miss, I don't understand why…"

Pepe was at full throttle now. "*Because*, okay? Would you just do that for me? Radio Officer Borsch. Tell him to meet Sammy over by the mall."

"Sammy? Is that *your* name? Sammy?"

45

I crossed my eyes at the video camera and said, "It's short for Samantha. Now, would you mind? I'm out of formula, I'm out of diapers...I need to see Officer Borsch!" I slammed the phone down, whipped Pepe out the door, and jolted him down the station steps. Then I zoomed him across the street and through the parking structure with my eyes peeled. Maybe she *had* meant seven A.M. Maybe she'd show up and this whole nightmare would be over!

So I waited. And I waited. I could see the mall's tower clock through the glass doors. Finally it was seven, then seven-oh-five. No girl, no Officer Borsch. Seven-ten. No girl, and where was Officer Borsch? Had they even radioed him? And Pepe was letting the whole wide world know that he was not happy, sitting in a towel that he'd made way yellower than it was to begin with.

Then at seven-fifteen a homeless man scared me half to death, coming out from behind some bushes where he'd been sleeping. I almost apologized for Pepe's having woken him up, but he didn't even look at me. He just sat on a bench and lit a cigarette, staring off into the distance.

Then, just as I'm about to go back to the police station to find out why Officer Borsch hasn't shown up, a squad car comes putting along the mall road. And I know it's Officer Borsch, all right, because he's going all of two miles an hour, checking me out as I'm bouncing Pepe on my shoulder.

He pulls over but leaves the motor running as he gets out. And when he's finally done hiking up his gun belt and twitching at the mouth, he moseys up and says, "Well. Don't you look like a wretched river rat."

The homeless guy yells from his bench, "Hey, copper, I'll sue! You can't degrade me like that!"

"Take it easy, Teddy. I'm talking to this girl over here."

The homeless guy eyes me and says, "Oh." Then he takes a deep drag off his third cigarette and says, "Disturbin' the peace. Get her for that. That brat of hers is worse than your siren, man!"

Officer Borsch motions me aside and says, "I'm almost afraid to ask, you know."

"I know and I'm sorry, but I don't know what else to do!"

He squints at Pepe. "And what *is* that he's wearing?"

I wrap the baby blanket back over his bottom. "I ran out of diapers, okay? And formula, too, which is why he's crying so hard."

"What about a pacifier?"

"A pacifier?"

"You know...a binky?"

Normally, I would've busted up. I mean, big ol' Officer Borsch saying the word *binky*? But I was too wiped out to laugh. So I tell him, "No. She didn't leave me one of those."

"She," he says. Just, She. Like I'm already irritating him. But then he sticks his arms out and says, "And here. You're doing that all wrong. He's going to need a chiropractor if you keep that up."

I stopped bouncing and stared at him. I mean, I'd heard that sleep deprivation can cause hallucinations, but this was beyond that. This was no hallucination, this was *impossible*.

I blinked. Probably fifty times. But he didn't go away, he just stood there with his arms out and a twinge of softness in his eyes.

So I passed that puppy over, boy. One wailing, flailing, soaking-wet kid shoved right into the Borschman's arms.

Now, Pepe knows something's going on, so he hushes up for a second while Officer Borsch cradles him in the crook of one arm. And where for me Pepe'd been like a sack of squirmy cement, in Officer Borsch's meaty arm he looks light. Like a fluffy little teddy bear. And where I've got bones sticking out, Officer Borsch, well, he's got *padding*. Nice, soft padding.

Officer Borsch touches Pepe's chin and smiles at him, saying, "Hey, little fella, what's your story, eh?" And then, when Pepe starts fussing again, Officer Borsch sticks the end of his little finger in his mouth and says, "Don't worry, champ. We'll get you some breakfast."

Pepe grabs Officer Borsch's finger and starts sucking like he's actually going to *get* something out of it, and while he's busy with his little pinky pacifier, Officer Borsch looks me over with a sigh, then says, "I don't think I've ever seen you looking this...uh...desperate. So let's hear it. What's the story with this baby?"

So I tell him the whole thing, from the top. Well, except for the part about sneaking home and having to wait forever outside on account of Mrs. Wedgewood falling off the toilet. I mean, as far as Officer Borsch knows, I live with Marissa, so I couldn't very well go and tell him about having to keep Pepe from making a peep all night or any of that.

"So your folks just dropped you off here at six this morning with no diapers and no formula, looking like *that*?"

"Uh, well, no. I . . . I walked."

He frowns at me. "From East Jasmine."

"It's not *that* far. And I . . . I didn't want to wake them up, you know?"

"Hmm" is all he says. Then he takes a deep breath and nods to himself a little. And I'm sweating it out because even to me, I sound like a liar. A big fat sneaky liar.

He lets it go, though, and asks, "You think you could ID this Snake Eyes guy?"

"You mean if I saw him again?"

"Or if you saw a picture of him?"

"Yeah. Yeah, I do."

"Well, come on, then." He opens the back door of his squad car and says, "We'll get someone from Child Protective Services to come get this baby, I'll get your statement, have you peruse a few mug books, and see what we can do."

So I scoot into the backseat and he hands Pepe to me. And of course, right away Pepe starts wailing. He doesn't want anything to do with *my* finger, either. He just wails like a siren, no matter what I do.

Officer Borsch tisks and shakes his head at me in the mirror. "Sounds like you're torturing that baby!"

"He's torturing *me*. I've been nothing but nice to this kid!"

He shakes his head some more. "Well, take my advice—don't become a mother anytime soon."

"You can count on that!"

We go inside and Officer Borsch takes my statement. He takes about two hours doing it, too. And somewhere in the middle of that, some very nice lady from Child Protective Services comes and rescues Pepe. Gives him a clean diaper on the spot, pops a bottle in that big ol' mouth of his, and tells me, "We've lined up a shelter-care home for him, so don't you worry. He'll be just fine." She coos at him a minute, then looks my way. "They tell me your name's Sammy?"

I nod.

"And his is Pepe?"

"Oh, well, no. Probably not, anyway. That's just what I wound up calling him."

One of her eyebrows arches up, but there's a little twinkle in her eye. "Well, then, Pepe it is. For now, anyway." She nods at the stroller and Sears bag and says to Officer Borsch, "You'll be taking those into custody?"

Officer Borsch hesitates, then bobs his head. "S'pose we should."

"Well, then," she says as she stands, "we'll be off." She takes one of Pepe's hands off the bottle and waves it at me. "Bye-bye, Sammy, thank you," she says in a little-kid voice. Then suddenly she's gone. *He's* gone. Whoosh, out the door. Out of my life. And the funny thing is, it felt strange. Kind of, I don't know...uncomfortable.

'Course, I *was* in a room with Officer Borsch, so what was I expecting, right?

Officer Borsch gets back to quizzing me about everything that's happened, and even though I tried my best to tell him what Snake Eyes looked like, he didn't want to hear how he had hatred for eyes and steel for a mouth or about the way he walked. He just wanted to know the facts. Height, weight, color of hair, approximate age ... that sort of stuff.

And he *was* real interested in the snake-eyed cobra, but then he starts asking me about the guy's clothes. Real detailed questions about his clothes. And that didn't make any sense to me because, what? The guy can't just go home and put on something else?

But he wanted to know the color of everything. And really, there wasn't much to say. No stand-out colors or flashy designs. Everything was either blue or black or white.

And then what's he start quizzing me on?

Shoelaces.

*Shoe*laces.

So I had to break it to him that no, I hadn't noticed the guy's shoelaces; that I'd been too spooked by his *face* to look at his feet.

But then he starts on about what colors the *girl* was wearing, and was I *sure* she was wearing a gray sweater and tan pants, not blue and black, or blue and *purple*.

"I'm sure," I told him. "Positive."

"Well, what about her shoelaces? Did you get a look at those?"

"Officer Borsch, what is with the shoelaces?"

He just looks at me says, "Did you notice them?"

I close my eyes and think. "Yeah. They were white. She was wearing, you know, little white sneakers with little white shoelaces."

He frowns, then takes a deep breath and lets it out as he shakes his head. "Okay, then. Anything else? Distinguishing features? Moles? Scars?"

"Oh, yeah! She had these weird slashes on the inside of her left arm. Scars. Like she'd gotten in a little saber duel with Zorro or something."

"A saber duel with Zorro," he says, like I'm giving him gas.

"Officer Borsch, I don't know how else to describe it. It wasn't a burn, and it wasn't, you know, a *scratch*. It was slashy. It went zig-zag-zig . . . zig-zag-zig-*zag*." My finger zips through the air, drawing it for him, but he's still not getting my picture. "Here," he says, shoving a piece of paper and a pencil my way.

So I close my eyes and try to picture it. Then I sketch it the best I can and pass it back to him.

He takes one look at it, and suddenly the slits he sports for eyes double in size. "Ah!"

"What?"

"Is this to scale?"

"Uh, I think the scar was even bigger than that. Maybe an inch and a half high and two inches wide."

"And it was on the left side, you say?"

"Yeah, but—"

"Was it healed up? Any blood or redness?"

"No, it was just, you know, a scar."

"But she wasn't wearing anything blue or black, or blue *and* black?"

"Officer Borsch! No! And what's that got to do with anything?"

He takes a deep breath, then leans forward across the table. "S," he says as he traces my drawing with the tip of the pencil, "W."

I just blink at him.

"S, W. South West."

I keep right on blinking at him.

He leans back. "It's a street gang, Sammy. They claim Cook down to Morrison and basically out to Blosser. Their main rival, North West, claims everything on the west side, north of Donovan."

"What do you mean, they claim it?"

He shrugs. "They say it's their territory. Their turf. Their hood. Don't tell me you haven't heard about any of this at school."

"Well . . . *no*. Just that if there's gang graffiti, we should report it right away so they can paint it over."

He scowls and mutters, "Your tax dollars, hard at work."

"What?"

"Never mind. Listen. I'll bet this girl is in a gang. South West. She probably got that scar when she was jumped in."

One look at me and he knows I'm not following. "You know, initiated? And the guy who was after her, he's got South West written all over him. Besides that snake tattoo, he's probably also got South West or SW and his moniker tattooed on him somewhere."

"His...moniker?"

"His street name. Like Ace or Stoney or Li'l Stinky."

"Little *Stinky*? Someone would tattoo *that* on themselves?"

"Oh, yeah. But the obvious thing—and the point I'm trying to make if you'd let me—is that this fella was also wearing South West colors."

"Blue and...black?"

"That's right. And North West's colors are..."

"Blue and purple?"

"You're catching on. And you don't want to be caught wearing the wrong colors on the wrong turf. It can get you killed."

I thought about this a minute and said, "But if Snake Eyes and Pepe's mom are both in the South West gang, then why was she so afraid of him?"

"Good question. And why wasn't she wearing colors? Maybe she's trying to get out. Maybe she's breaking it off with him. Hard to say. But the fact that she didn't want you to come here indicates to me that she's got something bigger than her gang affiliation to hide."

"What do you mean?"

"Well, being in a street gang is not in and of itself against the law. Committing misdemeanors and felonies is. Inevitably, one leads to the other." He chews the inside of his mouth a minute, then says, "There may be a warrant out on her, I don't know. What I do know is if that fella served time, we'll have a mug on him. You got time to look through a few books?"

I checked the wall clock and said, "Can I use the phone? I need to call home and...school. I don't want to get in trouble for ditching or anything."

"You want to come back and do this after school?"

"Well, don't you think you ought to try and find the guy? I mean, what if he's hurt her or something? Besides, I can't come after. We've got practice."

"Practice?"

"We're in the Junior Sluggers' Cup tournament this weekend, and it's like *death* if I miss practice."

He grins, a boyish, almost mischievous grin. Like he's remembering something from a long time ago. "You made the playoffs? Atta girl." He clears his throat and says, "Okay, then. Let's call your, uh, folks, and let's call the school."

Now, his words made me a little nervous. Especially that "uh." But he was smiling at me almost *kindly*, so I tried not to worry about it. I just used the phone he led me to and called Grams.

She was real relieved to hear that I'd turned Pepe over to the police and wanted to know all about it. But since Officer Borsch was standing right there, I promised I'd fill her in on everything after I got home from practice, and got off the phone.

Then I let Officer Borsch call the school for me so they'd believe it right off instead of after half an hour of me trying to explain things.

And then I went into a back room and started looking through mug books for Snake Eyes. I'd find him, I told myself. His face was branded in my brain.

Hatred for eyes.

Steel for a mouth.

This would be easy.

SIX

Two hours later, my eyes were blurry and my brain felt like sawdust. I hadn't found him. Or her. And I was really concentrating, too. But practically every face I looked at had hatred for eyes and steel for a mouth. I guess having your mug shot taken doesn't exactly make you want to sit up straight and say cheese, but still—it was creepy.

Officer Borsch checked in every once in a while to see how I was doing, and finally he comes in, sits down, and watches me as he mixes chunky-looking creamer into his coffee. "Had enough?"

"I can't even tell anymore. It's like all of them are him. Or *none* of them are him."

Officer Borsch nods and takes a gulp of coffee. "Well, you did your best. And you've been here a long time, so I think I'd better get you off to school."

"Let me look just a little longer...please?"

He shrugs, "Suit yourself," and leaves the room.

So for the next fifteen minutes I flip through pages as fast as I can. And I'm just starting to think that finding ol' Snake Eyes is like looking for a repeating pattern in pi when all of a sudden there he is. His hair's not gelled forward, it's buzzed completely off. But from the chills running down my spine, I know it's him.

Definitely him.

I charge the door and call, "Officer Borsch! I found him!"

Officer Borsch hurries in, and looks at the face under my finger. "Raymond Ramirez," he says. "I remember him. I thought he was doing time." He looks at me and says, "Sit tight. I'll call up his rap sheet."

When he finally comes back, I ask him, "Well?" and he sits down across from me, saying, "He's no Boy Scout. Quite a few drug-related infractions—finally put away for armed robbery about a year ago. He's been out for about three months." He scowls. "Time off for good behavior and an appeal by his mother."

"His *mother*?" Somehow I couldn't picture Snake Eyes with a mother. "How old is he?"

"He was just shy of eighteen when he held up Peg's...."

"Peg's?"

"A donut shop on the west end."

"He held up a *donut* shop?"

"It doesn't matter what you hold up, you stick a gun in someone's face, you go to jail."

"But a *donut* shop?"

He leans back a little, his face getting red around the edges. "Oh, I get it. You think donut shops are exempt because *cops* hang out there. You think all we do all day long is sit in cars and donut shops, eating sugar and drinking coffee."

"Officer Borsch! I didn't mean anything *like* that! I meant, how much money can you possibly get holding up a *donut* shop? It seems like the stupidest place in the world to rob!"

"Oh," he says, and I can see his blood pressure start to drop. "Sorry. I guess you'd say I'm a little sensitized to donut humor." He clears his throat. "Anyway. That was a year ago."

"So he's what—nineteen now?"

"That's right. And his parole officer says he's had no problem with him."

"But that doesn't mean he doesn't know anything about Pepe's mom."

"Right. I got the address from his parole officer, and after I drop you at school, I think I'll go have a little chat with the boy. And his mom."

When we pulled up to my school, we were greeted by BRUSTER'S #1, sprayed in red paint across the front steps.

Officer Borsch shakes his head. "Crosstown rivalry at its worst." He stops for a closer look, saying, "Might be able to steam it off—probably needs methanol, though." He tisks. "Red's tough."

Now, seeing this BRUSTER'S #1 stuff is sort of making me mad. I mean, a) they're not number one, and b) this stuff on our steps looks ugly. And what right do they have doing something like that to our school, anyway?

Actually, it kind of surprised me how mad it made me. I kept looking back at it as we walked into the administration building. What a bunch of jerks!

Officer Borsch made sure I'd be excused for missing so

much of the school day, then took off, saying, "I'll let you know what I find out."

The minute he's gone, the school's secretary, Mrs. Tweeter, whispers to me, "Are you sure everything's all right, dear? You haven't gotten yourself into trouble again, have you? You look like you've been dragged through a knothole."

Now, the last time I'd had any kind of conversation with Mrs. Tweeter, I'd lied to her. Tricked her, actually. It had to do with catsup and blood and Heather Acosta. It also had to do with . . . well, with taking the school's P.A. system hostage. And sure, I served *twenty* hours of detention for what I did, but debt to society aside, I never expected Mrs. Tweeter to talk to me again, let alone be nice to me.

So I stood there blinking at her while she looked at me over the tops of her reading glasses.

"Dear?" she finally asks. "Are you feeling all right?"

"Yes. I'm . . . I'm fine. I just thought that you probably, you know, *hated* me."

She laughs. A tinkly little laugh. Then she leans forward across the counter and says, "You may think I'm old, dear, but I remember the seventh grade." She laughs again. "Do I ever!" She leans even farther forward and whispers, "The thorn in *my* side was named Paula, and to this day I wish I'd found a way to stand up to her." She straightens a little and adds, "So no, my dear, I don't hate you. Just next time, try asking."

Asking? Like she would have just turned over the P.A. system to me?

I was still blinking at her when the passing bell rang. She looks up at the clock and smiles. "Nice timing. That's the lunch bell." I'm *still* standing there like an idiot, not knowing what to say, so she says, "Go *on*, dear. Go be young. And remember to steer clear of those nasty thorns!"

I laugh and say, "Thanks. And believe me, I will!" then hurry out to the lunch table where Holly, Marissa, Dot, and I always meet.

Holly's already there, digging through her sack lunch. "Hi!" I say as I sit down across from her.

She stops with her hand in her sack and says, "What are you doing here?"

"I just got here. I kinda got stuck with a baby all night and—"

"Well, you better get to the softball meeting."

"What softball meeting?"

It's like she finally heard what I said. "A *baby*? What baby?"

"I'll tell you about it later. What softball meeting?"

"They announced it this morning. All the Junior Sluggers' Cup players are supposed to meet in the locker room at lunch."

"Why?"

"I have no idea, but that's where Marissa and Dot are, so you'd better go."

I grabbed my backpack and said, "Next year you're playing too, okay?"

She laughs, "Okay, okay!"

So I jet over to the locker room, where the team is

already straddling benches. Ms. Rothhammer looks up from her clipboard and says, "And there's Sammy, which makes everybody."

I scoot in next to Marissa, who whispers, "Where have you *been*? God, look at you. You look like you slept in a Dumpster."

"Sssh," I tell her. "I'll explain later."

Then Becky Bork says, "Hey, Dawn's not here yet."

Ms. Rothhammer nods. "Actually, she's the reason we're having this meeting."

Cindy Salazar takes a bite out of her apple. "What do you mean?"

"Well...," Ms. Rothhammer starts, but then she takes a deep breath and looks down at her clipboard.

Now, she's not looking at notes or anything else. It's more like she's looking at *it* because her eyes are too heavy to look at *us*. Everyone's quiet until Xandi Chapan says, "She's all right, isn't she?"

"Oh, yes. Absolutely. I'm sorry." Ms. Rothhammer straightens a little, then says, "She just can't play in the tournament."

"Her hand?" Becky asks.

"That's right. We thought she'd recovered from her surgery last November, but she hurt it at practice yesterday and her mother's putting her foot down."

Xandi says, "But Dawn said it didn't even hurt that bad! She didn't *break* it again, did she?"

"No, it's not broken. And Dawn *wants* to play, but her mother got a scare yesterday and doesn't feel she should take the risk." Ms. Rothhammer puts a hand up, stopping our protests. "I understand Mrs. Wilson's concern. If Dawn's hand gets damaged again, it probably means they'll have to put a pin in it, and it *isn't* worth the risk. It just puts us in a very bad spot this late in the game."

The five eighth-grade players start whispering together, and Marissa, Dot, and I put our heads together and start buzzing, too.

"Girls! Girls! This is not all I have to tell you. Actually, it gets..." Her eyes fall back to the clipboard.

"It gets *what*?" Cindy Salazar asks. "Worse?"

Ms. Rothhammer scratches her head and puts up a smile. "Let's just say it gets...interesting." She takes another deep breath and says, "We need to replace Dawn. Unless you want to just withdraw from the tournament, that is."

"No!" we all say together.

"Well then, we need a new shortstop."

"Hey," Marissa says. "We have a friend that plays pretty well. She's—"

Ms. Rothhammer shakes her head. "The administration has already met, and a decision has been made."

"What do you mean? Without talking to us?" Cindy asks, then Xandi chimes in with, "Yeah, shouldn't we have some say in this?"

Very slowly Ms. Rothhammer nods. "*But* a decision has been made, and although I don't *agree* with it, there is a definite logic to it that's difficult to argue against."

We all look at her and say, "Well...tell us!"

She looks back at us. "Heather Acosta will replace Dawn at shortstop."

63

I jump up and cry, "You can't be serious! You just *can't* be!"

"She's the number-two shortstop on campus. She might even be better than Dawn, if she'd get out of her own way."

"But she's . . . she's like poison! She'll *ruin* our team! I can't play with her. I *won't* play with her!"

Like ice, Ms. Rothhammer says, "I brought that up, and their response was, they'll replace you with Babs Filarski."

"But I can't play with Babs!" Marissa cries. "I *won't* play with Babs! She is the most obnoxious catcher I've ever known!"

"Then they'll replace you with Emiko Lee."

"What?"

"I'm serious, Marissa. Emiko's a great pitcher and you know it." Ms. Rothhammer shakes her head and says, "And they view this as a wonderful opportunity for all of you to bury the hatchet and field the strongest team for the school."

"Who's *they?*" Xandi asks.

"The administration," she says, but she says it real hesitantly. And I know, just *know*, that there's more to it than that. Then it hits me. "Mr. Vince!" I cry. "He's pushing for this, isn't he!"

She takes a deep breath, then lets it out and says, "He pushed it until they bought it."

"But couldn't you have . . . couldn't you have done *some*thing?"

"No, Sammy, because the truth is, I don't have a better suggestion for shortstop."

"*Nobody* would be better than Heather! Can't we just play without a shortstop?"

"You know that's not an option. We're just going to have to make the best of it, and this is where all of you come in." She looks directly at me. "I don't care *how* you feel about her, welcome her. Adopt her into the team *to-day*. We have three days to make this work, and if we are indeed going to bring home the Cup, you *have* to do it together."

Cindy Salazar chimes in with, "Hey, if *I* quit, are they going to replace me with Tenille *Toolee*?" which makes everyone bust up, because Tenille was the lamest player on the number-two team. Then she says, "Just kidding, Coach. I'm cool with Heather."

I grumble, "Yeah, 'cause you're out in right field and don't have to *deal* with her."

"Enough. We'll all meet right here after school, and I want each of you, *all* of you, to act like the winners that you are. You hear me?"

Everyone says, Yeah, they hear her, and piles out of the locker room. Marissa, Dot, and I hang back, though, and when the others are gone, Ms. Rothhammer says, "Sammy, I know how you feel, and I'm sorry."

Marissa says, "It's not your fault, Coach, but we might as well kiss that cup good-bye."

I point at myself. "On account of *me*? No way!"

Ms. Rothhammer gives me a little smile. "Now that's

what I like to hear. And who knows, maybe you and Heather will come to some kind of understanding."

I snicker and mutter, "Yeah. Like what would happen if you and Mr. Vince got put on the same team, huh?"

"Hmmmm," she says, then changes the subject with, "The good news is, the tournament *is* going to be held at the high school."

"Seriously?" Marissa asks, her eyes popping open. "Cool!"

"We're on the lower field against Bruster for round one, winner moves to the upper field against either Wesler or El Rancho, and then next week the winner from South County plays our region's winner under the lights."

"That will be us," Marissa says, "under the lights!"

I look up at Ms. Rothhammer. "Does she already know?"

"Heather?" she asks me, then checks her watch. "Yes." She puts her hand on my shoulder and says, "Don't worry, Sammy. This is *my* team, and she will play by my rules. Besides, she's an outsider coming in. Maybe she'll . . . behave."

I shake my head and say, "Yeah, and maybe there's ice-skating on the Lake of Fire and Brimstone."

The minute I walked into science, there it was, written all over Heather's snotty little face—IIIIIII'M SHORT-STOP!

God, I tried to ignore her. And if her snotty little face had said I'M RIGHT FIELD! well, maybe that would have been easier. But *short*stop? It's one of the most coveted positions. It's *important.*

Not that playing catcher isn't—playing catcher is crucial—but how many people want to be team turtle? It's hard on the legs, it's dusty or muddy, depending on the weather, and you're constantly getting hit with something. Bats. Balls. Cleats. And now, dirty looks. And my strategy of pretending she didn't exist would not cut it on the playing field.

Turns out I couldn't ignore her in class, either. She volunteered to collect homework, and when she got to our table, I pretended to look for mine while everyone else handed theirs over. She just stands there with her hand on her hip and a catty smile on her face, and says, "Too busy playing mommy to do it?"

"Shut up," I tell her, but it was true. I'd been so wrapped up with Pepe that I hadn't done homework for *any* of my classes.

Then she whispers, "You look even worse than usual, you know that? Ever heard of a hairbrush? And I swear you smell like a toilet."

I stop rustling through papers and look at the ceiling with my hands up. "*How* am I supposed to play softball with her?"

"You won't have to," she whispers as she walks to the next table. "They're gonna trade you out with Babs."

"What!"

She just smiles her evil little smile and walks on.

I tried to tell myself it wasn't true. That it *couldn't* be true. But she'd sure said it like she knew something I didn't, and it was making my heart pound angry blood through my body and my mind race from one crazy conclusion to the next.

I also tried to beg an extension off Mr. Pence, but he wouldn't listen. Told me to sit down and be quiet. No extensions, period.

After science I ditched Heather by going to my next class a way I'd never gone before. Trouble is, I wound up plowing right into someone I try to avoid even more than Heather.

Her brother.

"Casey," I gasped.

"Sammy?" he asked.

I don't think I've ever blushed so red in my life.

He just stood there, blinking. "What happened to *you?*"

I just shook my head and tried to scoot around him.

"Hey, are you all right?" he asked, stepping right in front of me.

I kept looking down. "It's a really long story, okay? But in a word, no." I looked up at him. "*Heather's* taking Dawn's place at shortstop."

His whole face seemed to fly apart. His eyebrows shot up, his mouth dropped down, his nostrils flared wide, and his voice croaked out, "Seriously?"

"Yeah. And it's just got me, you know, freaked out."

"No kidding," he says. "I'd be freaked out, too!"

That made me smile. I said, "Thanks," but my cheeks were still burning, and I got out of there as fast as I could.

By the time school was over, I was wishing I'd missed the whole day instead of just the morning. I was behind in all my classes, *everyone* said how bad I looked, and now I had to go face Heather at practice.

And then as I'm heading over, I see her cutting across the grass toward the locker room. She isn't alone, either. On one side of her there's Mr. Vince, waving his hands around as he's drilling her with instructions.

And on the other, listening real intently, is Babs Filarski.

SEVEN

Practice was a nightmare. Ms. Rothhammer tried to make Mr. Vince and Babs leave the field, but they wouldn't go. They stayed on the sidelines whispering the whole time.

Heather was the Kiss-up Queen, too. Not to me or Marissa or Dot. Noooo. To the eighth graders. She went around saying stuff like "Hey, Xandi, Jennifer! I am, like, so honored to be on your team." And "Becky, Kris, Cindy! Wow! I am going to work so hard to be worthy. You guys are awesome!"

Gag me.

She tried it on Ms. Rothhammer, but she got shut down cold. "Don't think for a minute I suffer from selective memory, Heather. You've got a lot to make up for."

"Aw, Coach . . . we were rivals before. But now I'm, you know, *with* you."

"Well then, I expect you to treat *all* of your teammates with respect and kindness. *All* of them."

Heather gives Ms. Rothhammer one of her better innocent looks. "Of *course,* Coach. C'mon, all that stuff's ancient history as far as I'm concerned."

Ms. Rothhammer studies her carefully, but doesn't reply. Instead, she calls, "Two laps, everybody!"

And of course as we do our laps, Heather runs beside me for as long as it takes to whisper, "You are on the menu, loser, and there's nothing she can do to stop it!"

Which made me nervous, okay? I mean, there was Babs on the sidelines with Mr. Vince, acting all, you know, conspiratory, and there I am, fumbling balls and missing calls and just *blowing* it while Heather plays smooth and confident.

Afterward, Heather goes off with the eighth graders like she's one of them, while Ms. Rothhammer tries to give me a pep talk.

"Look," I finally tell her, "Heather's saying that Babs is going to replace me."

"What?"

"That's what she's saying, okay? And did you see her and Mr. Vince? They looked like they were plotting to take over the world."

"Listen, Sammy. I don't want you to give that another thought. Heather is trying to psych you out again. You should be used to this tactic. Don't let it get to you! This is *your* team, and Babs Filarski is not in the wings as your replacement."

"They weren't out there talking about the weather! They were drawing out plays and stuff. Mr. Vince wouldn't do that unless he had something planned. It's like he's horning in on our team."

"Well," Ms. Rothhammer says, "I don't like it any better than you do, but Mr. Vince is right in that I have no authority to say he can't watch practice." She takes a deep breath. "I have to pick my battles with him carefully,

Sammy, and whether or not he sits in on practice is not a battle I think is worth fighting. I prefer to just ignore him, and that's exactly what you should do with Babs."

She eyes me and says, "That *is* a battle worth fighting, and one I'd win. So don't give it another thought, okay?"

That was hopeless, but I said, "Okay," anyway.

Dot's dad was waiting in his big green DeVries Nursery delivery truck, ready to take Dot home. He offered Marissa and me a lift too, but Marissa had her bike and well, as far as I knew, Mr. DeVries didn't know about me living with Grams. Besides, Marissa and I always walk as far as we can together, and since I hadn't had the chance to tell her about what had happened with Pepe and Officer Borsch and everything, I didn't *want* a ride. I wanted to walk and talk.

So we waved bye to Dot and Mr. DeVries and headed out on foot. And we were trucking along Cook Street, me running a million miles an hour at the mouth about seeing Heather at the mall and how Pepe's mom hadn't shown up, when Marissa says, "Hey! Let's go check out the fields at the high school!"

"What? *Now?*"

"Sure! It won't take that long. Just a quick look? It's been forever since I've been there."

"But—"

"Come on! I'll give you a ride on my handlebars."

I took a step back from her. "That's okay. I'll walk. And in case you hadn't noticed, I was in the middle of telling you how I got stuck with that baby. All night."

"Right, right. So go on. What happened after you

decided to go home? And why didn't you just go to the police?"

"If you would *listen*..."

"Okay!"

So I picked up where I'd left off, only all of a sudden Marissa decides she wants to take a shortcut to the high school.

I used to be big on shortcuts. And maybe it's because I've been down one too many slimy alleys, but a shortcut to the high school seemed unnecessary. I mean, Santa Martina High isn't *that* far from William Rose Junior High. Basically, you go up Cook, hang a right on Broadway, and there it is on the right, taking up an entire city block.

Marissa, though, insisted on taking a right on Thornton. "Why go clear out to Broadway?" she said. "The fields are at the back end of the school—this'll be quicker!"

Now, in the back of my mind, I knew we were walking through a sort of poor part of town—there was barbed wire and beer bottles and graffiti everywhere—but I wasn't really thinking about it. I was more wrapped up in telling Marissa about my endless night with Poopy Pepe.

But then Thornton dead-ended. And my story sort of dead-ended, too. We looked up and down the street that T-ed off of Thornton, trying to decide which way to go. "Right or left?" I asked her.

"Uh, left," she said. Like the coin had come down tails. So we took a left and then the first right, and pretty soon I'm back on track with my story, too. And I'm just getting to the part where Officer Borsch comes up to me in front of the mall when Marissa interrupts me with "Why do people *do* that?"

"Do what?"

She nods at some graffiti on a wall and says, "That. You can't even read it." She keeps walking, but I slow down, because for the first time in my life, I'm seeing more than the hieroglyphics I usually see when I notice graffiti. I'm seeing letters. Fancy, spiky letters. And in the back of my mind I'm hearing Officer Borsch's voice: "They claim Cook down to Morrison...." Cook down to Morrison... Cook down to Morrison.

"Marissa," I whisper.

"What? Hey, why are you stopping? Come on!"

"Marissa, come here."

"What?" She backtracks to me. "Why are you staring at that?"

"Because—look over there. That's an S and a...W. Marissa! That's an S and a W!"

"So *what*?"

I look around and whisper, "It stands for South West, Marissa."

"It may *stand* for South West, but it's vandalism, Sammy. Van-da-lis-m. Just like that stupid stuff Bruster sprayed on our school."

Suddenly I get a very creepy feeling. Like every house on the block is watching us, wondering what we're doing. I check myself and Marissa over real quick, and Marissa says, "*Now* what are you doing?"

"I'm looking for purple," I whisper. "You're not wearing any, are you?"

She squints at me. "*Purple?* God, Sammy, sometimes I don't know about you."

"Oh yeah?" I tell her. "Well this little shortcut you've taken us on cuts right through gang territory."

"Oh, please," she says, then nods down the street. "There's the only drive-by you've got to worry about."

It's a police car. And as it gets closer, the passenger window powers down and the Borschman calls, "Couldn't resist a tour of Tigertown, huh?" across the front seat.

"Tigertown?" I ask him.

"Uh-huh. Our little urban jungle." He parks along the curb and gets out. "And why is it," he says as he's hiking up his gun belt, "that when I say left, you go right?"

"Officer Borsch, really! We were just taking a shortcut to the high school to check out the fields. I didn't know where we were until I saw *that*."

He nods across at the graffiti and says, "Last night's roll call. A unit's supposed to be by to paint it over, but—"

"Roll call? Like that's a list of everybody in the gang?"

He chuckles. "Not exactly. See the *Viva la Buena?*"

We both nod.

"What you see there is the roll call of the Buena Park set of the South West gang."

Marissa says, "The Buena Park *set?*"

"Clique. Group. Faction. Specifically, the Buena Park neighborhood in the South West territory. They claim Buena Park, so we police it a lot. Try to keep the activity low. Especially after school, when trouble tends to start brewing."

Marissa's eyes have been getting wider and wider, and I can tell, softball is finally *not* the only thing on her mind. "So this is really the middle of gang territory?"

"That's right."

"Are you *serious*?"

"As a heart attack."

"What's the thirteen all about?" I ask him, because I'm starting to make out more on the wall. Some places it's a spiky 13, some places it's a Roman numeral XIII, and in one place it's a combination—X3. "Does it mean bad luck?"

He laughs. "No. It stands for the thirteenth letter of the alphabet."

"M?" Marissa asks.

"Which stands for...?" He looks from Marissa to me and back again, waiting for us to fill in the blank. Finally, we both shrug, so he says, "Mexican. South West is a Mexican gang." He points at a different spot on the wall. "R means rules. So X3R means Mexicans rule."

"Wow. How'd you know that?"

He shrugs. "You learn to read the walls." He points to another one—13 P/V. "Can you figure that one out?"

I study it a minute, then shake my head.

"Know any Spanish?"

I shrug. "Not much."

"Por vida?"

"For life?"

"That's right."

"So that means Mexican for life?"

He nods. "How about *vato loco*?"

"Crazy dude?"

He smiles. "Right. So that one right there," he says, pointing to a fancy B.B.V.L., "was probably put up by someone with the moniker B.B. who's trying to get a rep as being gutsy." He points to a spiky, overlapping CZR sprayed on a diagonal with RIFA written under it. "That's some homie saying he rules. *Rifa*—or usually just R—means rules."

"Wow." I said. "It's always looked like hieroglyphics—or just a mess—to me before."

"What about H?" Marissa asks. "What's that stand for?"

Officer Borsch frowns. "Heroin. So don't get too fascinated. There's a lot here about drugs and threats that you don't want to be able to read."

Marissa looks around over both shoulders. "But...I mean...we're not like, in any *danger* here, are we? They don't have, you know, drive-bys and knifings and...and stuff like that...do they? It's more like they just hang out and, you know, *van*dalize, right?"

He makes a little sucking sound. Like he's vacuuming pastrami from between his teeth or something. "I take it you don't read the *Santa Martina Times*? Or watch the news? It doesn't reach up to your oasis on East Jasmine, but wake up, kid. It's a growing problem—one you and your, uh, sister want to stay away from."

Now, a) I didn't like the "uh" in Officer Borsch's

sentence *again,* and b) he's starting to act pretty hostile toward Marissa, so I just want to cut it short and get a move on. And this whole conversation *is* making Marissa do a bit of the McKenze dance, squirming from side to side, biting a nail, but does she say, Yes, sir, and now I'm getting *out* of here? No. She says, "You mean, people have actually gotten *killed* around here?"

"More than once," he says, then adds, "South West has no beef with you per se, but it still would be wise to avoid this area. They might flash a sign that you don't get, might mistake something you do or say as a challenge, might even think you're from North West."

"What would we be doing *here* if we were from North West?" I ask him.

He shrugs. "Casing. Carrying. Serving as decoy…"

Marissa squints at him. *"Us?"*

"You."

"But—"

"I can't frisk you, now can I? And no, you're not too young. We've got all sorts of kids in juvee that are younger than you."

"But—"

"Look, just be smart and stay out of this area. Good chance nothing'll happen, but why risk it?" He sucks at his tooth some more, then says, "This is not make-believe, girls, or me trying to scare you. It's reality, so deal with it accordingly." He looks at me, saying, "By the way, I visited Ray Ramirez's mother out on Las Flores. She claims her son's being a perfect angel, and Ray himself says he doesn't know anything about anything.

Doesn't know *who* I'm talking about. Was just cruising the mall yesterday for fun."

"But...you don't believe him, do you?"

"I don't believe anyone with eyes like that."

"See?"

"Oh yeah." He heads back toward the car, saying, "No one's come to claim Pepe yet, but I've put out an APB for his mother based on your description. The scar should help."

He zooms off, and we head out of there as fast as we can, cutting through the park and across Morrison to the high school. And while we're running, I'm filling Marissa in on all the stuff I hadn't told her about before Officer Borsch had shown up. And when I've finally gotten it all out, she pants, "Wow," and then, "Do you think she could be...dead?"

I didn't want to think that way. I mean, what if it was true? What if I'd doomed Pepe to a life without a mother because I hadn't gone straight to the police? What if I'd ruined his life? I could just see his epitaph:

POOPY PEPE

CRADLED IN A SEARS BAG

SOILED IN A ZIPLOC

SCARRED FOR LIFE

BY A REFUGEE TEENAGER

Marissa was saying, "All that stuff Officer Borsch was talking about—it doesn't even feel real. It's like we've walked into the middle of some movie."

"Yeah. Only there's no theater to walk out of."

"Well, at least we're out of *there*," she said, nodding back across the park. "Ready to check out the fields?"

Marissa McKenze is one of the few people on the planet who can find beauty in mowed weeds and gravelly dirt. I swear she even thinks chain-link is beautiful. Well, as long as it's in the form of a backstop. Ask her to climb it when it's in fence form and she'll cower like it's a big clanky monster out to rip the clothes right off her bottom.

Anyway, there were practices going on at the top two diamonds, so we watched for a few minutes, then went down to check out the lower field. Marissa got on the mound and tossed a few pitches, and you could tell—in her mind she was already under the lights, pitching a no-hitter.

I let her throw about a dozen pitches before calling, "Have you seen enough? I've got a lot of homework to catch up on!"

"I could stay out here all night, but yeah, we should go."

So we headed up past the other fields and hung a right on Morrison. And as we're hiking along toward Broadway, Marissa's jabbering away about how having at least one practice on the high school field before the tournament might really give us an edge. And I'm listening, but I'm also noticing these three girls walking toward us on the sidewalk.

Marissa sees them coming, too, because she steers her bike onto the high school lawn and moves out of the way, but she's still jabbering away about softball like they're not even there.

And I know *they* know *we're* there because they sort of shift to the side to pass us by, but they're not seeing us, if you know what I mean. They're more looking through us.

They're not saying anything to each other, either. They're just shuffling along, kind of stony-faced. Two of them are wearing baggy jeans and strappy tops, and the other one's got on camouflage pants with pockets everywhere and a tight white T-shirt that doesn't even come close to covering her stomach.

Then as they pass us, I notice their shoes.

Their shoe*laces.*

They're blue. And black. Doubled up; laced together.

And all of a sudden it hits me—these girls are gangsters.

Gangsters from South West.

And before I can stop myself, I've turned around to talk to them.

EIGHT

I didn't know what I was going to say. And even though one side of my brain was screaming, Let it go, Sammy! Let it go! the other side was saying, It's okay. . . . What are they going to do? *Shoot* you? So before you know it, there I am, walking alongside three South West gangsters, saying, "Hi."

They look at me like, Who let you out of your cradle? then look at each other and bust up.

Now, to me this no big deal. This is the way most kids in high school treat kids in junior high. And even though I can hear Marissa running up behind me saying, "What are you *doing*?" between her teeth, I just smile at them and say, "You guys from South West?"

All of a sudden everyone stops walking. The Gangster Girls line up to face me; then one by one they hold both hands up in front of them, near their waists. The pinky, ring, and middle fingers of their left hands are spread out, facing up, with the first finger and thumb pinched together, while the fingers of their right hands are curved around like they've suddenly developed some sort of painful cramp.

And they just stand there, caught in a giant finger spasm, giving me really hard looks.

"I . . . I'm not trying to fight or anything, I'm just looking for someone."

They keep right on glaring.

"I've . . . well, I've got something of hers. Or I *did* anyway. And actually, I'm pretty worried about her because she never came back to pick it up."

One by one they drop their hands. Then the girl in the camouflage pants says, "What's her name?"

"Yeah," says the girl to her right, who's wearing really white makeup and brown lipstick. "And what makes you think we know her?"

"I . . . I don't know her name. But she's about five six and, you know, normal weight, and she's got long kinda curly black hair and . . . and she's got a scar on her arm." I tap the inside of my left forearm and say, "Right here."

They just stare at me. Hard. And as I look from one to the other to the other, I realize that *they're* all about five-six and, you know, normal weight, and they've all got long kinda curly black hair.

Then one at a time they turn their left arms outward, and I see that they've got something else in common, too.

SW scars.

I cringe and ask them, "Do you do that to your*selves*?"

The one in camo pants sort of snorts and says, "You can't just walk in, y'know. You gotta prove you're down."

"Yeah," says the one with the brown lips. "Down for life."

Now, Marissa's standing by, sort of doing the McKenze dance, whispering, "Sammy, come on. Sammy...?" but I couldn't just leave. I had a million questions zooming through my head, most of them revolving around the word *why*. And since this connection was better than *no* connection to Pepe's mom, I tried to act as casual as I could when I asked, "Well, is anybody, you know, *missing* from your gang?"

The girl in camo pants says, "This ain't no *girls'* club, you hear what I'm saying?"

"I...I know, but, I mean...how many of you *are* there?"

She snickers and says, *"Somos pocos pero locos,"* then leans in and says, "Enough, okay? There's enough of us to bust on any and all of you."

Now, she's getting pretty up close and personal. And I'm scrambling through my limited list of Spanish words to figure out what she said. I know *poco* is small, and *loco* is crazy, so I try, "Well, if there aren't many of you, then you *must* know who I'm talking about. I mean, she has to be older than you, but—"

The girl in camo pants steps forward and snaps one wrist like she's shaking off water. "This here's a cemetery for the ignorant, and you, *hina,* are ignorant. You get my meaning? You don't go quizzin' up gangstas, girl." She flicks her wrist again and says, "Today I'm cuttin' you slack. Tomorrow I'm in your face, you hear me?"

Well, let me tell you, she was already in my face. I took a step back and tried not to let my voice shake as I said,

"Look, there was this guy named Raymond Ramirez after her."

Their faces smooth back into blanks.

"He's got a snake tattoo with dice eyes on his arm and he was wearing South West colors. Do you know who I'm talking about?"

More blank stares.

"Well, she seemed really afraid of him, but she's got a South West scar, too, so I don't know what to think."

The Gangster Girls' eyes shift back and forth, and then they start muttering stuff to each other, partly in English, partly in Spanish. And Brown Lips and Camo Butt are being really quiet, but then the third girl says, "It's gotta be her, Puffy—who else?"

Camo Butt gets right in the third girl's face and points at me, saying, "You think this snow bunny's got no ears? She ain't down with us! What are you thinking!"

The third girl kind of cowers back, but Brown Lips steps up and says, "Stall it out, Puffy."

Puffy-butt doesn't calm down, though. She stays right in the Quiet One's face, saying, "You gotta learn to watch your mouth, *chola,* or that *vato loco*'s gonna bust a cap in *you.*" She glances at Marissa and me and hisses, "What if they're trying to mess us over, huh? Then what?"

"We're . . . we're not trying to mess you over," I tell her. "We're just trying to find her so we can—you know—*return* something."

"Oh yeah," says Camo Butt with her hands on her hips. "What?"

Now my brain is screaming, Don't tell her. Don't tell

her! But really, I'm confused. I mean, what's left to lose? Pepe's mother's missing and no one's got any idea who she is or where she is, and Officer Borsch is never going to be able to find her from my description.

But Pepe's mother's face flashes through my mind. She hadn't wanted Snake Eyes to know—not at any cost. So I say, "Something...valuable." Then I add real fast, "To *her,* anyway."

"Well," says Camo Butt, "we're not missin' none of our homegirls, so we can't do nothin' for you."

She turns to Brown Lips and mutters what sounds like, "Let's go check the palace," then they all shuffle off across Morrison.

Very slowly, Marissa lets out a deep breath, one that I think she'd been holding the whole time we'd been talking to them. Then she whispers, "I don't want to go to high school."

"What?"

"Ever. I swear, I thought junior high was scary, but this is over the top. Can you imagine being on campus with *them?*"

"Seems kinda like dealing with Heather Acosta to me. Only those guys were nicer."

"*Nicer?* Sammy, that Puffy girl was like Heather times ten! Did you see that little wrist action of hers? Any minute I was expecting her to slice you up with a switchblade!"

We headed up Morrison, along the high school grass toward Broadway. And we were just about *at* Broadway when I got an idea. "Marissa?"

She looks at me. "Oh, no. What."

"Well, I was thinking."

"I knew it. I'm never going to get home tonight, am I? I'm never going to get to pitch in the Sluggers' Cup tournament because you've got some harebrained scheme that's gonna get me sliced and diced and left for dead, am I right? Why don't I just step out in traffic now and get it over with?"

I laughed at her. "Marissa!"

"Well? Am I right? What do you want to do? Go *back* through gang territory?"

"No! I just want to go to the library."

"The . . . library?"

"Yeah. The high school library. Do you think it's open?"

"This late? I don't know, *may*be. Why do you want to go there?"

"I've got an idea, that's all. It won't take long—come on."

"But Sammy . . ."

"Look, I checked out the fields with you, and we wouldn't be doing this at all if you hadn't decided to take that wonderful shortcut through Tigertown."

"All right," she grumbled. "All right!"

So we ran across the grass and onto the high school campus and asked the first person we saw where the library was. "Right over there," he said, pointing.

"Is it open?" I asked him.

"Yeah."

"Thanks!" I said, running toward the library.

"Wow," Marissa whispered, pushing her bike beside me. "He was cute!"

I laughed. "You're never going here, remember?"

We thwonked through the library turnstile and headed straight for the librarian's desk. Right away I knew the man reading a newspaper behind the counter was not a librarian, or if he was, he wasn't a very good one. First off, he wasn't old enough. I mean, to be a good librarian, you need to be, well, old enough to know about books. Lots of books. And he also had this look about him—not like he was shy a few pages, more like there were whole chapters he hadn't bothered to read.

Then the clincher—this guy wasn't reading the front page, or the obituaries, or even the funnies. He was soaking up the sports page.

I said, "Hey, Coach, where do they keep the yearbooks?"

He glanced at me, and for a split second I could see him trying to place me, but then he just flashed a smile and hitched a thumb behind him. "Back there." He turned around a little. "On that last shelf."

"Thanks!"

On our way over, Marissa whispers, "You think Pepe's mom went to school here?"

"Yeah, I do. But I'm also looking for those Gangster Girls. I want to know their real names." I pulled the previous year's book off the shelf. "Start with juniors and work back through sophomores—that would make them seniors or juniors this year. They can't be any younger than that, right?"

"They looked pretty old to me."

I pulled down a book from the year before for myself. "I'll go through this one."

Two minutes later, Marissa had a hit. "Here's one!"

It was the quiet girl. Real name: Sonja Ibarra. And she looked positively sweet in the picture. Happy eyes, friendly smile.

I pulled my school binder out of my backpack and wrote down her name. "Is that the juniors section?"

"Yeah."

"So she's a senior this year."

"Right."

I took Marissa's book and flipped to the index. "Ibarra...Ibarra...here it is! Sonja Ibarra, pages fifty-one, ninety-three, and one eighty-two." I jotted down the numbers and started digging though the book. "Fifty-one. That's her mug shot. Ninety-three. Here we go." It was a spread of candids, some dress-up, some from rallies. "You see her?"

"Yeah! Right there!" Marissa planted her finger under Sonja's face and whispered, "And look who's right beside her!"

It was Puffy, the Camo-butt Queen.

We flew through the captions, reading names. "Margie Hernandez!" we said together, then looked at each other and whispered, *"Margie?"*

I jotted it down and said, "Let's finish with Sonja first."

Marissa flipped over to page 182. "Softball?" she said.

"You're kidding."

"No, look! She played varsity last year."

I studied the picture. "Wow. What position?"

We both started skimming the article and captions, but Marissa found it first. "'Returners Sonja Ibarra and Christy Spry had the corners covered, with Sonja on third and Christy on first.'" She looked at me and said, "She played third base."

While I jotted this down, Marissa flipped to the index and found two pages on Sonja's homegirl Margie. "There's only one other on her—page one ten."

The page was another collage of candids, this time under the heading Friends. I spotted Miss Puffy right away. And two days ago I wouldn't have paid any attention to her hands, but now they jumped right out at me. In the picture, they were casually pulled back to her sides, but the fingers stretched and spazzed into the same shapes I'd seen her make on the street. This time, though, I could tell what those hands were doing. "Look," I said as I pointed it out to Marissa. "That's an S and that's a W."

Marissa whispers, "They're flashing gang signs? In a *year*book?"

"I guess so."

"Hey, look!" she says. "Right there. Isn't that the other girl?"

Sure enough, there she was, brown lips and all, way in the back, flashing her sign. I muttered through the caption, "'Friends in need are friends indeed; from left to right, friends for life...' She's the fourth one over?"

"Right."

"That would be...Gizelle Menendez."

I wrote it down while Marissa flipped back to the index. "Just her mug on fifty-four."

So we'd found them. Puffy the Camo Butt was Margie Hernandez. Brown Lips was Gizelle Menendez. And the Quiet One was Sonja Ibarra. All seniors at Santa Martina High. "Okay!" I said. "We've got the Gangster Girls. Now to find Pepe's mom."

"We don't even know that she went to school here."

"But her scar tells us she lived in the neighborhood, right?"

"I guess." She hesitated, then said, "How old do you think she is?"

"I don't know...twenty?"

"So she would have graduated two years ago?"

"Maybe three?"

Marissa closed her book. "So she probably wouldn't be in this book. And I'm not going to be much help—I don't even know what she looks like."

"Okay, look. You can go if you want to, but I've got to try."

"No, I'll stay, but—"

"Hey, would you call Grams for me? Tell her I'll be home as soon as I can?"

"Sure. I ought to check in, too, just in case Mom's actually home on time."

So while she was off tracking down a phone, I began scouring the books. I started with a yearbook that was two years old, and I made myself focus on every picture. By the time I'd made it through the seniors, juniors, and sophomores in the first book, Marissa was back.

She slides in next to me and says, "Your grams says thanks for the message. She was starting to get worried. She also says be careful when you come home—she's got to talk to you about Mrs. Wedgewood."

"Uh-oh. Wonder if she fell off the toilet again."

"What?"

So while I went through more pages, I explained to her about Mrs. Wedgewood and having to stand out on the fire-escape landing while the paramedics hoisted her up.

"Tell me you're joking."

I flipped a page. "Nope. Beats Mrs. Graybill, though. Any day of the week."

Marissa looks at what I'm doing and says, "These are freshmen here? Why not just go to the next book? Their pictures get bigger, don't they?"

She was right. The freshmen mug shots were tiny, even smaller than the sophomores. It wasn't until the juniors section that the pictures were a decent size. So I pulled down a book two years older and started all over again. And when I didn't find her in *that* one, Marissa says, "Well, maybe she didn't go here. Or maybe she's older than twenty."

It was beginning to feel like my morning at the police station, looking through page after page of mug shots. Not as bad, though, because almost every picture had someone smiling instead of glaring.

But still, after the next book, I'd about given up. And I was kind of mad about it, too, because in my gut I just *knew* she had to be in one of these books. *Some*where. And as I'm putting the yearbook I'd just gone through away, Marissa says, "Maybe she's younger than she looks. Ever think of that?"

"Well, how young could she be?"

Marissa shrugs, "How should I know? If you look through this book, you've covered the last four years. You've already gone back, what—four books? That's eight years, right? Is she older than twenty-two?"

"I don't know—I'm terrible at ages!"

Just then, from over by the librarian's desk, we hear the coach guy call, "We're out of here in ten! Start cleaning up!"

"Rats!" I grabbed the book Marissa had and pushed through the pages to the beginning of the seniors section. As fast as I could, I looked at every single picture. Then I looked at the juniors. Then the sophomores. And finally I'm down to the freshmen section, just waiting for Coach to blow the whistle, when all of a sudden I spot her. "Marissa!"

"What?"

I put my finger on the page. "That's her!"

Marissa looks real close and says, "Lena Moreno. She looks nice! And she's very pretty. Are you sure that's her?"

"I'm positive. But Marissa . . . this is last year's book and she was a *freshman*." I look at her and whisper, "That means she's only . . ."

Marissa's head bobs up and down as she says, "About sixteen."

I blinked at the picture, not quite believing it. I checked the year on the spine, the section in the book, but there was just no getting around it.

Pepe's mother was only a few years older than we were.

NINE

I was still having trouble believing what we'd figured out about Pepe's mom as I waved good-bye to Marissa at the police station. I mean, after the one night I'd spent with Pepe, there was no way I could see raising a baby. Not now, not in three or four years, not even in *ten* years. Talk to me when I'm thirty—maybe I'll be ready to never sleep again and to live my life in spit-up, changing diapers and mixing formula, but for now I've seen enough of babies to know that they're not cute little coochie-cooey dolls. Demanding little demons, that's what they are. And I plan to stay miles away for a long, long time.

Anyway, I went inside the police station, figuring I'd have to track Officer Borsch down via courtesy phone seeing how it was after five o'clock. But the counter's roll-up window was still rolled up, and there behind the counter was Debra the Dodo.

Now, it's not that Debra *is* a dumb dodo. She might actually be smart. I just haven't been able to get past that big ratty nest of bleached hair she wears on top of her head to check out her brain. I can't imagine why she wears her hair like that—or why she doesn't either chip the orange nail polish on her claws completely off or coat it over. And then I get distracted by her nose. I mean, I know she's trying to hide it, but putting that much powder on it is like shoveling snow on top of Mount Everest. Every time I see her, I get this urge to strap on skis and cry, "Geronimo!"

Anyway, to me she's always just looked like some kind of freak dodo bird carrying a nest on her head. Officer Borsch, though, doesn't see her like I do. You can just tell. He's *friendly* with her, and if you know the Borschman, you know this is weird. Extremely weird.

Anyway, Debra the Dodo was right there behind the counter, and the minute she sees me, she breaks into a big-beak smile. "Hey-ya, Sams. I heard you were back makin' trouble. Here to see the big guy, I suppose?"

"Uh, yeah."

"Well, hang on. You're in luck. I know he's around 'cause he was just up here borrowing my tweezers."

"Your...tweezers?"

"Yeah, now hang on. I'll go round him up."

Two minutes later she was back, and she practically had him by the ear. "Here you go, Sams. At your service."

Officer Borsch comes out to the foyer, saying, "You've got something, I can tell. What is it?"

So I tell him about the Camo-butt Queen and her West Side Posse. And after he gets done berating me for talking to gangsters, I show him my notebook and explain everything Marissa and I had figured out at the high school library.

Officer Borsch interrupts me a lot, like he always does, and frowns a lot, like he always does, but for once he jots stuff down in his notebook like he actually cares. And when I'm all done he says, "Now *this* ought to get us somewhere, and you didn't have to stick your neck into gang territory to get it. Nice work, Sammy."

I just sat there blinking, not believing my ears. I mean, Officer Borsch's idea of showing appreciation is the Grunt. The God-it's-killing-me-to-consider-this Grunt. So I didn't know what to say to his Nice work, Sammy.

Then the Dodo says over the counter, "Can you take a call, Gil? Line two," and off he goes, grumbling, "I'll contact you if something breaks," over his shoulder.

So off *I* go, to home sweet home. And on the way there I'm thinking, Okay. Now he'll find her. Or her family, at least. But then I start wondering, If she has a family, wouldn't they have called in a missing persons report? 'Course, maybe she didn't live at home. Maybe she'd been kicked out because of the baby. Still, her family had to be able to tell Officer Borsch *some*thing. They probably even knew Snake Eyes.

By the time I started up the fire escape, I was feeling pretty good. I'd earned myself a nice long shower and a good night's sleep. No baby to feed or change or *worry* about. After homework, I could just flop down and zzzzzzz, sleep!

When I got up to the fifth floor, I opened the fire-escape door a crack, like I always do; checked to make sure the coast was clear, like I always do; zipped down to Grams' door and let myself in, like I always do; and I'm about to toss my backpack down and call out "Hi, Grams," like I always do, only Grams comes flying out of the kitchen and drags me into the living room by the arm, whispering, "Did she see you?"

"No! Of course not." For a split second I thought she was talking about our old neighbor, Daisy Graybill. But then I realized that that couldn't be, so I just shook my head and said, "Did *who* see me?"

"Rose!"

"Mrs. Wedgewood? No. Grams, what's wrong? You look like you've seen a ghost."

Grams collapses onto the couch and puts a hand to her forehead like she's feeling for fever. She takes a deep breath and holds it, then lets it out all at once. "Perhaps I have. Perhaps Daisy's come back to haunt us in the form of that...that...woman!"

"But...but Mrs. Wedgewood doesn't seem anything like Mrs. Graybill."

Grams sits up a little and whispers, "At least with Daisy I knew where we stood. With this one, I can't tell. I just can't tell!"

I sit down beside her and ask, "What happened?"

"She heard, Samantha. She heard the baby last night."

"She couldn't have, Grams! I kept him so quiet!" Then I remembered. "He did cry a little when I went to the bathroom, but it was only for a minute. Grams, I couldn't help it—I had to *go*."

"I'm not blaming you, Samantha, I'm just not sure what to do."

"Well, what did she say?"

Just then there's a knock at the door. And after Grams and I look at each other with bug eyes, I do what I always do when there's a knock on the door. I pick up all my stuff, check the place over to make sure I haven't left something around that'll give me away, and head for Grams' room.

I really wanted to hear who was at the door, so I thought about hiding under Grams' bed, but the bed was stripped and the comforter was wadded in a heap on top. No cover there! So I made for the closet, but I left Grams' bedroom door wide open and the closet door open a few inches, too.

I could hear Grams answer the apartment door, and then I recognized the sound of Mrs. Wedgewood's walker creaking along and her voice saying, "Now, now, Rita. It's all right. We're *neigh*bors."

I couldn't hear Grams' end of the conversation very well because she was keeping her voice down, but ol' Mrs. Wedgewood was talking loud—like she wanted someone in another room to hear.

It took me longer than it should have to realize that that someone was me.

I shifted a little on Grams' shoes and strained to hear more. Mrs. Wedgewood was saying, "Honestly, Rita. I'm glad about it. Truly I am. All I'm asking is for her to run an errand for me now and then. Maybe take down my trash, or run to the market—nothing big." Then she calls, "Samantha? It's okay, sugar. You can come out now."

I held my breath and froze. Then Grams' voice shoots through the air, loud and clear. "Mrs. Wedgewood! This is not acceptable. Mrs. Wedgewood? Mrs. Wedgewood, stop! Where do you think you're going?"

The creaking and thumping of the walker is getting louder and louder, so I slink back in the closet, hiding the best I can behind Grams' dresses and pants. Then I hear Mrs. Wedgewood say, "Rita dear, if we're going to be neighbors, we need to trust each other. The rest of my body may be falling completely apart, but my hearing has always been superb." The thumping stops and I can practically see her turn to face my grams. "I can hear biscuits rising in my oven, I can hear ants march inside walls, so you'd better believe I can hear young girls coming home from school." She knocks twice on the closet door and says, "Now please, can we help each other out?"

"Mrs. Wedgewood, honestly!" Grams cries.

"Rita, she's either in here or under the bed, and from the way you're fighting me back, I'd place my money on...," the closet door swings wide open as she says, "...here."

Through Grams' hemlines I can see Mrs. Wedgewood's ankles, swelling over the tops of her rubbery black shoes. And as hard as I try to hold my breath and wish myself away, I can just *feel* that she knows I'm there.

"Of all the nerve!" All of a sudden Grams is latching on to her, *swinging* on her back, trying to pull her away from the closet. But Mrs. Wedgewood is like a beached whale, and finally she just twists Grams off. Then she jabs my foot with the rubber tip of her walker, and says, "Samantha, I can *see* you, sugar. Come *out.*"

What could I do? It was all over. I pushed out through the clothes while Grams stuttered and sputtered excuses that were even lamer than some of my very worst. ". . . and the headaches get so severe that she can't take the light. It's torture for her!"

Mrs. Wedgewood and I both look at her and sort of shake our heads. Then Mrs. Wedgewood says, "Rita, I won't tell a soul. She seems like a fine young lady, and I'm sure our arrangement will be mutually beneficial." And before Grams can start an argument, she wags her nose at the closet and asks, "So where do you hide the baby?"

"The *baby*?" Grams asks.

She nods. "Samantha's baby."

"It's not *my* baby!" I cry. "I really was baby-sitting!"

She looks at me suspiciously. "Well, it wouldn't be the first time a girl your age got in trouble, you know."

Grams throws her hands on her hips. "Mrs. Wedgewood!"

"Oh, Rita. Take a Valium."

Grams' eyes bug out so far they almost hit the lenses of her glasses. And while she's standing there with her mouth gaping, Mrs. Wedgewood hobbles out of the bedroom, saying, "The plain truth is that I'm not supposed to be living here, either. Anyone can see I've got Assisted Care written all over me, but I don't want that. I can't *afford* that. And since I managed to get in here, I intend to *stay* here as long as is humanly possible." She stops and looks at us over the beef of her shoulder. "With your help."

"But . . . ," I blurted. "What do you want me to *do*?"

"Nothing much, sugar," she says with a smile. "I'm just

asking you to be a little neighborly." She shrugs and pushes toward the front door, saying, "Run to the store for me now and again, help me around the apartment when I need it, and if I should fall again like I did the other night, help me up so's they don't have to call in the fire department." She clanks out into the hallway, nodding that great wiggy head of hers. "So glad we got that all straightened out. Good night!"

Grams slams the door behind her and fumes, "The *nerve* of that woman! Daisy, for all her flaws, would never have done that!"

"Grams, look. It's going to be okay. I don't mind helping her out."

"Samantha, it's blackmail!"

"But she never said if I didn't help her she would tell people I was living here."

"She didn't have to. It was perfectly clear." Then she mutters, "'Help each other out'—how is *she* helping *us*?"

I just shrug, so she says, "That woman is trouble with a capital T. In all my years I've never met anyone so brash. She may not look like a fox, but that one's crafty, believe me." Then she grumbles, "'Take a Valium'... the *nerve*."

"Well...what do you think we should do?"

"There's nothing we *can* do but keep her happy." She went to the refrigerator and pulled out a package of red snapper, a head of lettuce, and some carrots. She stopped suddenly and said, "Before I start on this I've got to run down to the basement and get the laundry. I didn't want to risk missing you earlier, so it's all still down

102

there." She scowls. "That is, if someone hasn't already run off with it."

"Run off with it? Who would want to do that?"

"Audrey Brown was telling me she got her nightclothes and towels stolen just the other night."

"Wow. A nightie-napper."

"It's not funny, Samantha, it's theft. Now would you mind making some rice while I run downstairs?"

I would've gone to get the laundry for her, but there was that whole being spotted problem. So I just said, "Sure," and pulled down a box of rice while she grabbed her keys and left the apartment.

And I'm busy reading the directions and measuring water, when I decide that if I hustle, I can surprise Grams and make everything. The snapper, the rice, the salad— everything. So while the water's heating up, I whip around the kitchen washing the fish, patting it dry, putting it in a glass pie dish with a little water and a lot of soy sauce, getting it ready to wrap and zap, just the way Grams likes it. And while I'm working, my mind kind of wanders around, thinking about Mrs. Wedgewood and whether she really is trouble with a capital T or just a lady who falls off toilets and needs a little help every now and again.

And then I remember how she thought Pepe was mine. *Mine.*

Please.

But that gets me thinking about Pepe's mom and how young *she* is, and I start wondering all over again about what in the world happened to her. Where *was* she? And after Officer Borsch went off duty, who'd be looking for her? Anybody? And I'm in the middle of imagining the very worst when I yank open the drawer with Baggies and plastic wrap and see something that puts the brakes on me making dinner.

The phone book.

It's sitting there, right next to the plastic wrap, chock-full of information. *Important* information.

I stare at it for all of two seconds before deciding—it can't hurt. Just one little flip through the M's—see if there are any Morenos listed.

What could it possibly hurt?

TEN

"Moreno . . . Moreno . . . Moreno," I muttered as I flipped through the white pages. And when I found the Moreno heading, I started counting. One, two, three, four . . . good grief! There were about thirty Morenos!

I skimmed through the addresses. Some lived in Sisquane, some in Pomloc, some in Santa Luisa . . . only about half of them were in Santa Martina. I took a pencil and started marking the possibilities. Some of the streets listed were clear across town—there was even one on East Jasmine. Those had to be out. I couldn't see someone with a South West scar being from Marissa's neighborhood.

When I was done, I had twelve names, two with no addresses, just S Mra.

Now what? The water was boiling like crazy, so I threw in the rice and stirred. Then I went to the phone and started dialing.

The first number picked up. "Hello?"

"Is Lena home?"

"Who?"

"Lena."

"You got the wrong number."

"Sorry," I said, and hung up.

The next number had an answering machine. "If you want to leave a message for Sara, Tim, Eddie, or Sophie, please speak after the beep. If you want to leave kibble for Tudor, just come on over! Have a great day!"

I hung up and dialed the next one. *"Hola?"* a woman answered.

"Uh . . . is Lena home?"

"Que?"

"Lena?"

"Que?"

"Is Lena *en su casa*?" I tried.

"No. No Lena here," she tried back.

"Gracias," I said.

She hung up.

I tried the next two numbers. No answer, no machine.

The rice water was spattering out of the pan, so I turned down the flame, then tried the next phone number. "Yeah," a man answered. Not a question, not really a *greeting,* just "Yeah."

"Is Lena there?"

Silence.

"Hello?"

"Who's this." Again, not really a question.

I could feel my heart speed up. "Uh, a friend."

He snorted—an airy, disgusted snort—then said, "A friend."

I didn't want to blow it by saying something stupid, so I just said, "That's right."

Finally he says, "Well, Lena ain't here."

"When do you expect her?"

All of a sudden I hear a woman's voice in the background saying, "Let me talk to them!" but then the line goes dead. Just *hmmmmm,* dead.

I clicked off and waited a minute. The voice in the background hadn't *sounded* like I remembered Lena sounding. The accent was heavier. It was probably her mom—and she'd wanted to talk. I pressed Redial, hoping the woman would get to the phone first.

The phone rang twice, three times, four times. And on the fifth ring it got picked up, but right away it got disconnected.

I tried again. Busy.

I rinsed the lettuce, shook it out, shredded it into a bowl, and thought about calling the police. Instead, I called the Morenos again.

Still busy.

Okay. So he'd taken the phone off the hook. I'd show him! I ripped a corner off a half-blank government page and scribbled all the information down—Tito Moreno, 410 S. Pinos, 555-3741. Maybe he doesn't want to talk to me, I thought as I tucked the paper away in my back pocket, but he'll be wishing he had when he sees Officer Borsch on his porch in the morning.

And I was in the middle of tucking the phone book back in its drawer when the phone rang, scaring the daylights out of me. I jumped back and stared at it all bugeyed. Did Moreno Man have Caller ID? Star 69? Why would he be calling *me* back? Did he want to find out where *I* lived?

On the fourth ring I picked up. "H-hello?"

"Are you doing your homework?" the voice asked. It was a grown-up. Female. No Mexican accent. And I recognized it—sort of.

"Wh-who is this?" I stammered.

"Your coach."

"Oh! Ms. Rothhammer, hello. And no, I'm making dinner, but of course I'm going to do my homework."

"I heard you didn't last night."

"But...that's because there were, you know, extenuating circumstances."

"Make up last night's."

"But...but most of my teachers don't accept missed homework."

"I don't care. Do it anyway. And don't miss another assignment."

"Ms. Rothhammer, you sound so...so *mad*. Did I do something wrong?"

Her voice softened. "No, Sammy, not at all. And I'm sorry to sound that way. Just make sure you get your homework done, all right? Don't compromise your eligibility."

"My eligibility? But my grades are fine!"

She took a deep breath, and when she finally spoke, all she said was "Just do your homework, all right?"

"Yes, ma'am."

"See you tomorrow," she said, and then hung up.

I barely had the phone down when Grams came through the door. I jumped again, squeaking, "Hi!"

Then I tried to compose myself and nodded at her basketful of clean clothes. "I see the nightie-napper wasn't on the prowl tonight!"

She eyed me suspiciously. "What have you been up to?"

"Making dinner! Look!" I said, putting the red snapper in the microwave, punching it like crazy to get it going, "Dinner's served in four minutes."

"Well!" she said, breaking into a smile. "Isn't this nice?"

I flew around, setting the table and fluffing the rice and in general acting way too hyper. Then during dinner, I answered all Grams' questions about how I'd finally turned Pepe over to the police, and tried not to shovel my food or act like a freak. But between Mrs. Wedgewood and Ms. Rothhammer and Madman Moreno, my brain felt completely overloaded—like I had to *do* something or I was going to explode.

But what? There was nothing I could think *to* do.

Except homework, that is. So after we ate and did the dishes, Grams went to make up her bed while I tackled my missing assignments. But I had trouble "staying on task," as Mr. Pence would say. If I wasn't thinking about the Moreno phone calls, I was thinking about school. How'd Ms. Rothhammer hear about my science homework, anyway? Were the teachers talking? Was Mr. Vince trying to dig something up to make me ineligible? What was going *on*?

Then the phone rang, which made my pencil go shooting out of my hand and through the air. And when it came clanking down on the linoleum floor, Grams eyed me but didn't say a thing. Instead, she picked up the phone and said, "Hello?"

In an instant I knew it was Trouble calling. In what form, I couldn't tell right off, but I knew it involved me because Grams scowled, put her free hand on her hip, and looked at me, shaking her head.

I crept over to my pencil, picked it up, and waited, while Grams just stood there, listening. But then, when she said, "It's much too late for her to be going out. I'm sure you can manage until morning," I heaved a sigh of relief.

It was only Mrs. Wedgewood.

Grams talked to her for a minute, but then there was a long silence. A *very* long silence, and finally my grams says, "Very well," and hangs up the phone.

She looks at me. "I knew it."

"Grams, I don't mind. What does she need?"

Grams sort of wobbles her head. "Tylenol. I offered her mine, but she insists on Tylenol PM. The gelcaps. And a quart of half-and-half."

"A *quart* of half-and-half?"

She goes into her bedroom, calling, "To wash it down." She comes back out with her coat and umbrella. "So it doesn't upset her stomach."

I cringed and then realized what Grams was doing. "Hey, you're not going out—this is my job."

Grams gathered her purse and said, "You're still busy with your homework, Samantha, and besides, it's just not right. You shouldn't have to go out this late at night."

"Come on, Grams. It's no big deal. I'll be back in no time." I wrestled the purse off her arm and made her hand over some cash; then I threw on my sweatshirt.

"Wear your jacket, would you?"

"I'll be fine!"

"Well, take this," she said, handing me the umbrella. "It's drizzling outside."

"Really? Darn!"

"What's wrong?"

"The fields'll be all soggy tomorrow."

"It's just a light rain, Samantha. I'm sure they'll be fine."

I put up the hood of my sweatshirt and tried leaving the umbrella on the table, but Grams would have none of that. She forced it on me, then checked the hallway, and before you know it I was pounding down the fire escape, on my way to Maynard's Market.

It felt great to be outside. Great to be *moving*. And it *was* drizzling, but I didn't mind. Grams' umbrella is one of those big black old-fashioned jobbies that really works. The sky can be dumping buckets and it doesn't matter. It's like a cone of dryness guiding you through town. I cut across the grass, jaywalked across Broadway, and basically just swooped into Maynard's without feeling a drop.

Maynard's is your average ma-and-pa corner store during the day. And I don't know if it's the location or the fact that the *son* is running the ma-and-pa, but the people who seem to converge there at night act a little off. Like they've left the majority of their marbles in their fridge, or in an ashtray, or just scattered around their house. And maybe if they'd collect them all and stuff 'em back in their heads, you could actually have a conversation with them, but with the way they show up at Maynard's unassembled, well, it's best to just shop around them.

So I don't like Grams going there at night. She takes it all a little too seriously. Gets wigged out if some guy's talking to himself with his head in the cooler or something.

But T.J.—who's Maynard's son—seems to know all the drifty people who pop in. And since they don't seem to faze him, I don't let them faze me, either. T.J.'s more worried about kids in his store. Thinks we're all out to shoplift the bubble gum. I've given up trying to show him he's wrong. Hating kids is his religion, and there's no converting him.

Anyway, I shook out Grams' umbrella under the awning, then collapsed it and ducked inside. There was a middle-aged man digging a six-pack out of the cooler, so I just do-si-doed around him and started looking for Tylenol PM.

Right away, T.J.'s radar goes off. "Hey!" he calls. "What'cha doing back there?"

"Just lookin' for some pain relief, T.J. Something to survive the experience of being in this store." You gotta talk to T.J. that way. Either that or just forget about shopping there if you're under twenty. Besides, it's good for him. Gives him a reason to pump blood, if you know what I mean.

"Sassy brat," he mutters from behind the counter, but he quits harassing me after that. I find the Tylenol, no problem. And while I'm digging through the cooler for two pints of half-and-half because Maynard's doesn't stock quarts, he rings up Six-Pack's Budweisers and pulls down a pack of cigarettes for him.

So okay. I'm on task. No sidetracks, no checking out the ice cream cooler for Double Dynamos or anything like that. I get my stuff, go to the counter, and wait politely.

Six-Pack puts out some rumpled bills, which would've gotten my head bitten off if I'd done it. But T.J.'s Mr. Nice to him about it, straightening them and saying, "Did you catch the fight on Pay-4-View tonight? I heard they were *floggin'*."

Six-Pack snorts. "Don't need to *pay* to see a fight. I get plenty of that from my old lady."

Now, all of a sudden I'm zooming in on the guy, because his snort sounds a *lot* like the snort Tito Moreno made when I said I was a friend of Lena's. And I know the chances of this guy being Tito Moreno are like, zilch, and besides, his voice doesn't really sound the same. But still, I can't help staring at him.

T.J. bags the beer, then gives Six-Pack his change, saying, "Take it easy, man."

"Yeah. Likewise," he says, then takes off.

Now, since T.J.'s the kind of guy who likes to impress you with how much he knows even more than he likes to tell you how much he can't stand you, I plop my stuff on the counter and risk asking, "Is that guy's name Tito?"

"What, you got the hots for him?"

I just stare him down, saying, "Guess that means you don't know."

"Sure I know his name. And it ain't no Tito, either. It's Kenny." He starts ringing me up. "I know all my customers, even the ones that are pains in the rear." He throws me a look, but I ignore it and pull the government page scrap out of my jeans. "Well, how about South Pinos? Do you know where that is?"

"Two—nah, three blocks thataway." He hitches his thumb behind him. "Something like that."

He starts to flip open a paper sack, but I stop him. "Can I have plastic?"

He scowls at me with the sack midair.

"It's raining out, T.J., come on."

He puts it in plastic, grumbling the whole time.

"I need the receipt, too."

Grumble, grumble.

I take the sack from him and say, "Thanks, T.J. Can't wait for next time."

"Scram, kid. You're giving me a headache."

I take the Tylenol PM out and rattle the box at him. "Aisle four."

"Scram!"

I zip out of there, all right, because I've already decided. It's only two, three blocks thataway. I'll be home before Grams even *suspects* I took a detour.

So I tie the plastic bag closed around Mrs. Wedgewood's medical supplies and ditch it behind the first bush I can find. Then I *whoosh* open the umbrella and dash down the sidewalk, wondering just what I'll find at 410 South Pinos.

ELEVEN

I know I should have known better, so don't even tell me about it, okay? And everything *was* going along fine. I mean, 410 South Pinos was a decent house. And a pretty friendly-looking lady answered it, too. "Yes...?" she asked through the screen door.

"Mrs. Moreno?"

"No...?" She sort of sings it at me, dragging the word along and up.

I lean back a little and double-check the number running down the stucco wall. "This is four ten South Pinos, isn't it?"

"Yes ... ?"

"Does *Mr.* Moreno live here?"

"No...?"

At this point, her singing me nos and yeses is getting a little annoying; but I try to bite my tongue as I say, "Does *any*body with the last name Moreno live here?"

"No...?"

"Anyone anywhere *around* here named Moreno?"

She hesitates, then manages to spare me a whole sentence. "Try in B."

"In ... B?"

"In the rear." She points around the right side of the house. "Through that gate."

It was a six-foot wooden gate with a pull wire sticking through a plank. And when I tugged on the wire, the latch swung up just fine. But as I pushed the gate forward, the gate sagged onto the ground and stuck. I collapsed Grams' umbrella and squeezed through, then muscled the gate closed, put the umbrella back up, and headed down the muddy path in front of me.

There were tall fences on both sides, and I felt like a little rat nosing along in a maze. The fence on my right kept going, clear to an intersecting alley. But the fence on my left stopped a few feet before a rickety garage and took a sharp left, separating the garage from the house.

I walked past some bushes growing wild along the side of the garage and stopped when I came to the alley.

Now, I'm not big on alleys. I've had some really *slimy* experiences in alleys. And this one wasn't looking any friendlier than the ones I'd been down before. There were overturned garbage cans and beer bottles, and the ground was grimy. It seems strange when you think about it, dirt being dirty, but that's what every alley I've ever been down is paved with—dirty dirt.

I peeked to my left and took a look at B. The garage had been converted into an apartment, a regular door cut right into the garage door, a fiberglass awning bolted overhead. There were no steps, just a small pad of cement poured in front of the door and a glaring bare bulb to the side.

People lived here? I couldn't quite believe it. But the alley stretched for blocks in both directions, and there were bare bulbs at other Bs, speckling the darkness, and even a couple of cars pulled way off to the side, telling me it was true.

I looked again at the front door of this B. Was this Lena's home? Had she had her baby here? Maybe she wasn't missing after all. Maybe she'd just given me Pepe because she didn't want him to grow up this way.

My mind was spinning, trying to weave together some sort of picture from what few threads I had. And I wanted to find out more, wanted to know who was inside. But the truth is, I was afraid to knock. Afraid of this place. Afraid of being alone at night in an alley.

So there I am, sort of shivering under the tent of Grams' umbrella, trying to convince myself to go up and knock, when a car turns down the alley. The headlights bob up and down as it swings around and begins to inch forward.

I back out of view and peek around the fence to keep an eye on the car. The headlights cut to parking lights, and now I can see that it's a lowered sedan with a dark blue finish, a big gold hood ornament, and shining mag wheels.

The whole car seems to glow in the alley light as it creeps over potholes, and the closer it gets, the more I want to find someplace to hide. Trouble is, there *is* noplace. I can't go forward into the alley, and I can't go back along the path. All I've really got to work with are some scraggly overgrown bushes along the side of the garage. But as the car gets closer, I decide that scraggly overgrown bushes are better than nothing.

So I collapse Grams' umbrella and back into a gap between two bushes, then crouch down, keeping my eye on the alley.

The front of the car comes into view, then passes along. And I'm thinking I'll give it a couple minutes before I stand up when I realize that the car has stopped. Right there, where the path intersects the alley—it's stopped.

Now, the back end of the car is blocking the alley, so I'm sort of trapped. I hold my breath and shrink back deeper into the bushes, trying to decide what to do. Should I make a break for it? I could climb over the trunk of the car and charge down the alley, but I know from experience that it's hard to run with shoes caked in mud and alley dogs at your heels. But going back the way I'd come felt dangerous, too. I'd be easy to spot, and I'd be trapped in the corridor of fences, blocked by a heavy broken gate.

So I'm busy thinking I should stay put for a little while—that a little rain never hurt anyone, and that really, in a few minutes whoever drove up would drive off—when I hear "Who you hiding from?"

The voice is soft, but it shoots through me like a jab in the rear. I leap forward a few feet and choke on a yelp, and when I turn around and look, what I see is someone crouched *inside* the bush next to me.

"Man, you're jumpy. Must be somebody bad," came the voice. It was young. Female.

I inched toward her. "What are you *doing* in there?" I asked.

"Waiting," came the voice.

"For what?" I scooted in a little more.

"You're getting pretty wet. Why don't you use that umbrella?"

I could see her now, crouched inside a little cave in the bush.

"Put it *up*," she says.

The rain was coming down harder, but I didn't want to risk putting the umbrella up. I didn't know where the driver of the car was, but they couldn't have gone far. I could hear the car idling, and puffs of exhaust were coming from behind the wheel. There was something about the wheel, too, that was creepy. It was smooth and deep, with only lug nuts, no hubcaps. With a shiver I realized that it looked like the chamber of a gun.

"They won't see you. Put it *up*."

"Whose car is that, do you know?"

"Put it up and I'll look."

Who am I to argue with a girl hiding in a bush? It was like having an argument with myself—I was bound to lose. I pushed the umbrella up and it rested across the bushes like a little tent.

"Wow," she says, crawling out and crouching next to me. "This is great." Her hair's pulled back into a long braid and she's clutching a one-legged Barbie. She smiles at me. "Much better." Then she leans forward and looks at the car. "Dunno," she says.

"You think they're visiting you?"

She shrugs. "Dunno." Then she adds, "But probably not."

So I'm trapped in the bushes with a little girl and a one-legged Barbie, and before I can figure out what in the world to do or say, she looks me in the eye and asks, "Your old man drink, too?"

"What?" I ask her, not believing my ears.

"Is that why you're hiding?"

"Is that why *you're* hiding?"

She nods and strokes Barbie's hair back. "It's probably okay now, though. Been quiet a little while." She looks up at me again. "Does yours throw things? I hate when he throws things."

I was staring. "How old are you?"

"Seven," she says.

To me she looked five or six. Max. "But...do you have a mom?"

She nods. "She don't come out here with me, though."

"But she knows you're here?"

She shrugs. "Dunno. She's passed out."

"Passed...out?"

"Your mom don't do that?"

I just shake my head.

She shrugs again. "Mine says it's the only way."

I felt like saying, You've got to be kidding! but I could tell she wasn't.

"He starts coming at me when she's passed out, so I hide until he's out, too. Then everything's okay."

Rain's streaming off the edge of the umbrella into little puddles in front of us, and she's stroking the hair on her

Barbie like the doll's a kitten nestled in her lap. She looks up at me and smiles. "This is *way* better."

Now really, I don't know how to ask her any of the questions running through my brain. Like, Why doesn't your mother stop him? and, How can she let him hurt you? I mean, she's talking about her parents passing out and beating her up like most kids talk about the weather. Is it like that for her? Some days stormy, other days calm? Or does she have to batten the hatches every night?

So finally I just ask, "What's your name?"

She smiles at me. "Tippy."

"Tippy?" I tried to think what that could be short for—Tipper? Tippanita? I couldn't think of a thing. So I just asked, "Tippy...Moreno?"

"Yeah!" she says, lighting up like a hundred-watt bulb. "How'd you know that?"

"I, uh...I've met your...sister."

She starts stroking Barbie's hair like mad. "I miss her so bad. I wish I could've talked to her tonight, but—"

All of a sudden my heart was racing. "She called? Tonight?"

"Uh-huh."

"When tonight?"

"Before."

"Like an hour ago? *Two* hours ago?"

"Uh-huh."

"Did she say anything? Anything at all? Like where she was, or *how* she was?"

She shrugged. "Mama say she barely told her hi, then the phone went dead."

"Well, do you have Caller ID or Star Sixty-nine?"

She gives me a puzzled look. "What's that?"

"Well, does she call home a lot? Do you think she'll call back?"

"Nuh-uh. She don't never call. She did at Christmas, but Papa got the phone and he yelled at her."

Christmas. That was only about two months ago. "Did you get to talk to her that time?"

"A little. She tol' me she was sorry she didn't get me nothing, and promised me a surprise for my birthday."

"When's your birthday?"

"February twenty-first."

"Yesterday?"

She blinked at me, and in that instant I knew—everyone had missed her birthday, even Tippy.

I wished with all my heart I could take it back, but it was too late. She burst into tears, burying her face in my chest. "I'm sorry," I whispered, thinking that Tippy's parents made mine look like positive saints.

Finally she sniffs and says, "Lena always made me a party." Then she wipes her face with the sleeve of her shirt and smiles at me. "You're really nice, you know?"

"So are you. And I'm sorry about your birthday."

She strokes her Barbie's hair, then looks at me and says, "What's your name?"

"Sammy."

"That's a boy's name!" She's smiling at me, tears all gone.

I almost said, And what kind of name is *Tippy*? but I

laughed with her instead. "Yeah, it is. But mine's short for Samantha."

"Oh," she says; then we're both quiet, just listening to the rain pattering on the umbrella. Finally she looks at me and says, "Are you going to wait for him to pass out?"

"Who?"

She cocks her head at me like I'm a boulder brain. "Your old man! Where do you live, anyway?"

"Uh . . . up the street." I nod over my shoulder. "How long are you planning to stay out here?"

"I could probably go back inside. I'm pretty cold."

I was, too. And I did want to get going, but how could I just grill her and disappear? She wasn't *just* someone who maybe had some information I wanted. She was also a wet barely-eight-year-old with a one-legged Barbie, hiding from her parents in the bushes in the rain. I smiled at her, and of all the questions I could have or *should* have asked, what came out of my mouth was "So how'd you lose the leg?"

Her eyebrows wrinkled together and her eyes got stormy. "It's the only part I couldn't find back. He tore her all apart—even the head!"

"Who? Your dad?"

She nodded. "I tried to catch them, but he threw them so hard and they came so fast! Her head hit me right here," she said, pointing to her temple. "Felt like a rock." She stroked Barbie's hair. "At least I got it back, though. Don't know what I'd do without the head."

Head-butted by Barbie. Normally, the thought would have just busted me up, but now it made me cringe.

"Have you ever told anybody about...you know... your parents?"

"What do you mean?"

"Like your teacher or someone like that?"

She shook her head.

"You do go to school, don't you?"

"Used to." She looked up at me. "Do you?"

" 'Course!"

"Did you tell *your* teacher?"

"Uh...no, but my dad doesn't throw stuff at me."

"He don't? Then why you hiding? From your mom?"

"Actually, I'm hiding from...well, *actually*, I'm here because I'm trying to find Lena. Do you think your mom knows where she is?"

"Nuh-uh. No one seen her since Joey died."

"Joey? Who's that?"

"The guy she married."

"Married?"

"Uh-huh."

"What was his last name?"

"Dunno. But he was really nice. He let me visit at the muffler shop and called me Tippy-toes. Funny, huh? He had the funniest freckles and used to buy me pretzels. Those big soft ones they sell at the mall? And he'd always get me double cheese." She stroked Barbie and sighed. "The cheese is so good. I wish I could have some right now."

"Well, how did he die?"

She shrugged. Like it didn't really matter.

I sat there for a minute, trying to make sense of everything she'd told me. Finally I asked her, "Do you know a guy named Raymond Ra—?"

Before I could finish, her eyes got really stormy. "I hated him! He was so mean! One time Lena brung me with her and I accidentally spilt some paint. He hit me! Right across the face!"

"You're kidding!"

"I didn't spill it on nothin' important, either. Just the floor."

"In his house?"

"No! His garage. Where he was fixin' up a car."

"Do you know what street it was on?"

She shrugged. "But my eye swole clear up. It looked real bad."

"So what did your sister do?"

"She made me promise not to tell."

"Why?"

"I wasn't suppose to be there." Suddenly she breaks into a smile. "She tol' me I could get a donut if I didn't say nothing, and brung me to a shop where I got the best donut ever. Puffed clear up with strawberry creme and tons of sugar dust. Made my eye feel lots better."

The car was still idling in the alley. "You sure you've never seen that car before?"

She shrugs and shakes her head.

There was no doubt that I needed to get going. The rain had let up, and I'd found out enough from little Tippy to know that I wasn't going to find Lena here. But still, I didn't like the thought of leaving Tippy shivering in the bushes. So I said, "I've got to get home. What are you going to do?"

"Can you leave the umbrella?" she asks me.

"Uh . . . no. It's not mine."

"Whose is it?"

I collapsed it. "My grandmother's."

She considers this a minute, then nods. "My nana would make me give it back, too."

All of a sudden I had an idea. "Where does your nana live?"

She shrugs. "In a different city."

"Which one?"

"Santa Luisa."

"Santa Luisa? Well, why don't you go live with her? She'd probably love to have you!"

She cocks her head, blinks, then goes back to petting Barbie's head. "She don't want me."

"What? I don't believe it."

"She's not legal."

"You mean not a citizen?"

She nods.

"When's the last time you saw her?"

"Dunno."

"Last week? Last year?"

"Long time. Papa threw a can at her and she won't come back no more."

What a champ. I shook my head and said, "Tippy, I hate to leave you here, but I have to go. . . ."

"That's okay. It's not raining no more."

"I'm not worried about the rain." I stand up and say, "Do you want to go to the police? Tell them about your mom and dad?"

She looks at me, horrified. "No!"

I crouch down again. "Why not? They're not taking very good care of you. I'm afraid they're gonna really hurt you someday. Is there anyone else you can stay with? An aunt? Someone like that?"

She shakes her head. "Besides, I gotta make them breakfast."

"Who? Your *parents?*"

She nods. "It helps them feel better."

My heart completely bottomed out. I could picture her scrambling eggs and buttering toast, serving breakfast to a couple of monsters who'd turn around and throw things at her. I wanted to grab her hand and take her home with me. I couldn't just *leave* her here.

But then she takes *my* hand and says, "If you give me a boost, I can get in easier."

"Get in where?"

"The window."

I looked back and forth along the side of the building. "Where?"

"Back here." She pulls me along behind the garage and sure enough, there's a window. "It falls down, so it's hard gettin' back in," she says.

"Are you sure there's no one else you can stay with?"

She raises her foot for a boost. "You gotta go home,"

she says, like of course she's willing to climb in and out of windows and dodge bottles and Barbie heads to be at home.

She wiggles her foot at me and says, "Hurry. I'm cold!" so I weave my fingers together and let her plant a fat wad of mud in my hands as I lift her and her one-legged Barbie up to the window.

The window's an old heavy wooden one, and as Tippy scrunches through, it rubs against her backside and legs, then clunks closed as her feet disappear inside. A second later the window rasps up and there's Tippy, smiling down at me. "See?" she whispers. Then she waves and says, "Bye, Sammy!"

She ducks out of view, but I just stand there for a minute, looking at the window. Finally, I rub the mud off my hands the best I can, pick up Grams' umbrella, and head for the walkway. Car or no car, it was time to get home.

Now, in the back of my mind I heard water splashing, but I wasn't paying any attention. I was thinking about Tippy and how you shouldn't have to grow up with a one-legged Barbie. I mean, if you're going to have a Barbie at all, it should have all its parts.

So the sound of splashing water didn't alarm me because, hey, it had been raining, right? It could have been water splashing out a downspout or something.

But when I come out from behind the garage, I stop short, because right by where Tippy and I had been hiding, there's a man, relieving himself in the bushes.

And it's bad enough that there's someone, *any*one

there, but when this guy faces me across the bushes, my blood freezes stiff in my veins.

He's got hatred for eyes.

Steel for a mouth.

And there's no doubt about it—he recognizes me, too.

TWELVE

I didn't waste time while Snake Eyes got himself assembled. I hauled down the pathway toward the gate, and I must have been flying with fear, because I shot over six feet of pine like a bottle rocket.

Then I ran. And I ran so hard I thought my lungs would burst from the pain. The truth is, I'd never been so scared in my whole life. Not when I was trapped behind a Dumpster by a desperate thief, not when I was driving the wrong way down Cook Street in a hijacked motor home, not even when I was face to face with a dangerous drug dealer. No one, *nothing*, had ever scared me as much as seeing Snake Eyes.

I can't explain his eyes. They're dead. Cold, black, and dead. But when he saw me, they instantly came to life.

I started kicking myself for telling Tippy my name. If he asked her, it would be a snap—or a slap—to get her to tell. And I kicked myself even harder for not checking out the car better. I could have had a license-plate number right now if I'd just gone snooping a little! Instead, I'd hidden in a bush with a girl named Tippy and a legless Barbie. I could've been peed on!

But okay. Now I knew what he was driving. At least I'd be able to be on the lookout for him.

I dove behind some bushes at the mall and checked up and down Broadway, then Cook Street. Was he after me? In his car? On foot? I hadn't even looked over my shoulder to see if he was chasing me — I'd just bolted.

Then I remembered how he'd been tracking Pepe's mom at the mall.

Slowly.

Methodically.

With his *nose*.

Was he out there sniffing me down? Was I leaving some funny muddy odor everywhere I went?

I checked the soles of my high-tops — they'd been washed squeaky clean. And I was relieved that the rain was starting to fall again. If there was a trail, it would be washed away.

Wouldn't it?

I didn't put up the umbrella. It would slow me down, and I had to get *home*. Grams was probably having a fit!

I charged up the street as fast as my legs would take me, snagging Mrs. Wedgewood's bag out of the bushes without even slowing down. And before I started up the fire escape, I checked around, this way and that, making triple sure Snake Eyes wasn't on my trail.

By the time I reached the fifth-floor landing, I was drenched. Your basic drowned, breathless rat, sneaking into a building. Though Mrs. Wedgewood seemed more concerned about what had taken me so long than how I looked.

I completely lucked out, too, because Grams was taking a bath and didn't even hear me come in. So I was home, I was safe, but boy! was I shaking. For one thing, I'd run harder than I'd ever run in my life, and that right there will make you shake. But I was also scared. Scared of Snake Eyes, scared for Tippy, scared to think what had happened to Pepe's mom. I was scared of everything, even Grams. I could just hear her: What had I been *thinking*? How many times did I have to do something like this before I *learned*? Did I want to get myself *killed*? What was she going to *do* with me?

And I knew she'd be right. Completely right. I'd been an *idiot*.

I stripped out of all my clothes, put my shoes by the heater, and hid everything else under the sink, thinking I'd slip them in the hamper when Grams was out of the bathroom. Then I pulled on my pajamas, and in my panic I decided I had to wash my hair to cover up the fact that it was drenched.

I checked around the kitchen sink. My choice was dish soap, dishwasher soap, or bar soap. I chose the dish soap.

I didn't even use that much, but when I was done, my hair felt like straw. But as I wrapped it up in an old cotton dish towel, I wasn't worrying about my hair, I was worrying about what I should *do*. I wanted to talk to Officer Borsch *bad*, but he was off duty.

I told myself that at least Lena was still alive. Or she had been a few hours before, when she'd tried to call home. And Tippy seemed to have everything under control—for tonight, anyway. And if Snake Eyes had Lena, then why was he stopping by her parents'? Maybe he *didn't* have Lena. Maybe he was still looking for her!

My brain wouldn't stop echoing with questions. But in the end, I decided that what I'd do was write everything down for Officer Borsch, seal it up, and leave it for him in the morning on my way to school.

School! Oh, no! I looked at the stack of books on the kitchen table. How was I ever going to do all of last night's *and* all of tonight's homework? I slid into a kitchen chair and started organizing my assignments. I was going to be up all night!

Just then Grams comes out of the bathroom. "Samantha!" she says. "Why didn't you tell me you were home? I was in there worrying about you!"

"Oh, sorry," I tell her.

"You washed up in the sink?"

"Mm-hm."

"How did it go? Did Mrs. Wedgewood reimburse you?"

"She's got the receipt. Says she will tomorrow."

Grams says, "Hrumph!" and then I remember the change, crammed in my jeans pocket under the sink. "There was some change—I'll...uh...I'll get it to you as soon as I'm done with this."

"You think I don't trust you?" she says with a smile, then goes off to read on the couch.

Well let me tell you, that shot a pang of guilt straight through me. But at that point I couldn't get sidetracked with confessions—I had to get busy on my homework!

I had trouble concentrating, though. Tippy and Snake

Eyes kept running through my brain, and I couldn't help feeling like I'd done things wrong. *All* wrong. Like nobody who needed help was actually *getting* any help.

I also had trouble concentrating because I was sort of overwhelmed by all my homework. It had only been two days, but I was so behind! And I started thinking about Pepe's mom and how she'd probably never factor another polynomial or study the structure and function of cells or the thees and thous of Shakespeare. How could you keep up when you had diapers to change and spit-up to clean and formula to mix *every* day? After one day and night with Pepe, I was already miles behind.

I got back to work, making myself concentrate. And when Grams finally headed off to bed, she asked me, "Still not done?"

"A lot to make up from yesterday." I looked up at her and asked, "Grams?"

"Yes, dear?"

Then I blurted out something that had been haunting the back of my mind. "Did . . . did Mom drop out of high school?"

"Drop out?"

"Because of . . . you know . . . me."

She studied me a minute, then said, "No. You came the following year."

"But . . . so did she drop out of college?"

Grams hesitated, then nodded. "But you need to ask your mother these questions."

"But she won't talk to me!"

She kissed me on the forehead. "Give her time. She will." And with that she headed off to bed.

I woke up the next morning with my head and arms sprawled across the table and drool all over Officer Borsch's letter. "Samantha!" Grams cried. "Oh, lord! We both overslept. Come on, come on!" she said, gathering my papers. "You'll be late to school!"

My hair was still wrapped in the towel. Sort of. And while my grams deluded herself into thinking she could whip me up some oatmeal, I tried raking a brush through the outrageous tangle on my head. Finally I gave up and hosed it down in the sink to start over. But it was still like straw, and really, I didn't have time to fix it. I just pulled it back into a scrunchie, threw on some clothes, whipped together a peanut butter sandwich for lunch, grabbed an envelope, and flew out the door.

Some mornings oatmeal is just not in the cards.

And I didn't have *time* to go by the police station, but I did anyway. Just flew in the door, picked up the courtesy phone, told them about the envelope I'd slid under the door, and hightailed it over to William Rose Junior High.

My legs were like jelly by the time I got to school. And normally, I would've just served my lunchtime detention for being tardy, but after Ms. Rothhammer's phone call, I was paranoid about doing *any*thing that might make me lose my spot on the team.

But as I raced up the steps to the school, I realized that

something was wrong. Half the school was still out front, huddled around the lawn, and Vice Principal Caan was talking to them through a megaphone. "All students should be heading to class at this time. The tardy bell will be ringing in two minutes, so if you don't want to have lunch with me, get to your classes!"

Could I make myself go directly to class? No way. I raced over to the lawn to see what everyone else had already seen: PB RULZ branded in four-foot letters across our lawn.

Mr. Caan came over to shoo me and a group I was standing near to class. "Go on, guys. This is really not worth spending lunch with me."

I followed Mr. Caan as he made for the administration building. "How'd they *do* that?"

"Gasoline," he says, then stops short. "Don't you get any funny ideas, Sammy. This sort of thing will not be tolerated, whether it's done by Paul Bruster students or ours."

"I wouldn't do something like that! It's ... *stupid*."

He eyes me skeptically and says, "Well, then we have stupid people on our campus as well."

"What do you mean?"

"Bruster got egged yesterday."

"So?"

"*So?*"

"Well, egg washes off, doesn't it?"

He frowns. "It's a pain in the neck once it dries!"

Uh-oh. "Don't look at me like that.... *I* didn't do it!"

He hurries toward the admin building and I race to

136

homeroom and manage to slide into my seat just as the bell finishes ringing. Heather sees me and sneers. "Up all night messing with your hair?"

"Pretty much, yeah," I tell her, trying to act cool about it. But I did feel self-conscious. It had been *days* of looking like I slept in the gutter.

But school itself actually went better than normal. I turned in the assignments from the day before plus that day's, and I think I caught some of my teachers off guard, because they were really nice about it. Especially Mr. Tiller, when I turned in my math. "Well, Sammy! *This* is what I like to see in a student. Responsibility. Conscientiousness. Follow-through." He was dying to ask what had gotten into me, I could tell, but he stopped himself. "Keep this up and you'll ace this course."

I went to my desk and Henry Regulski whispered, "Kiss-up," but I was feeling good enough that it didn't bother me.

Then in history, I was trying to feed Marissa bits and pieces of what had happened the night before when Billy Pratt comes waltzing into class with a message in his hand. He acts all cool, nodding and slapping five on a few of his friends as he makes his way to Mr. Holgartner at the front of the classroom.

Mr. Holgartner stops writing on the board and scowls at Billy. "Are you here to entertain us or deliver a message, Mr. Pratt?"

Billy struts up to him and says, "I try to do it all, sir."

The class laughs while Mr. Holgartner's frown digs in deeper. But Billy just grins as he slaps the slip in

Mr. Holgartner's hand, then spins around, *whoooooosh*, a full 540, and struts to the door, nodding and slapping five on his friends again on his way out.

Mr. Holgartner takes a deep breath and shakes his head, then opens up the note and says, "Sammy, you're wanted in the office."

Like a dork, I point to myself and say, "Me?"

He sighs and says, "The only Sammy here," like he can't believe how much of his thimbleful of patience I'm making him use up.

So I grab my backpack and head off to the office, wondering what in the world I've done wrong *now*.

THIRTEEN

On my way to the office, I couldn't come up with any-thing I'd done that could qualify as an expellable offense. Or even something that would land me in the Box for detention. I hadn't bitten at anyone's bait—not even Heather's! I'd been as good as I know how to be the whole entire day.

Mrs. Tweeter gave me a soft smile over the top of her glasses as I opened the door to the administration build-ing, and then I saw him, looking like an overstuffed doughboy in one of the waiting chairs. "Officer Borsch!" I said. "Are you here to see...," I point to myself, "...me?"

Mrs. Tweeter and Officer Borsch exchange looks, and then he says, "Who else?"

I can see my envelope sticking out of his back pocket. And I'm thinking that maybe he's here to tell me what an absolute moron I was for going out to South Pinos last night, but hey, he didn't have to pull me out of class to tell me that! I already knew it, and I'd *told* him so in my note.

He wasn't looking mad, though. He was looking... *quiet*. Serious. He turns to Mrs. Tweeter and says, "Is there a conference room or office we can use?"

I knew there was a conference room. I'd been in it once before. With Heather. And her mother. And Grams. And Vice Principal Caan. I've actually got fond memories of the place. Red fur went *flying*.

Anyway, Mrs. Tweeter leads us there and closes the door behind us. Then very quietly, Officer Borsch says, "Have a seat."

I'd never heard him sound this way before. Normally he's gruff as a billy goat, but now he sounded tired. Weak.

"Officer Borsch, what's *wrong*?"

He slaps my letter on the table as he takes a seat, then sucks in a deep breath and holds it. Finally, he lets it out and says, "Sammy, you worry me."

"I know it was stupid! I *told* you it was stupid. Believe me, I'm not going to do something like that again, okay?"

He sucks on a tooth, then says, "I also know you're concerned about that little girl, so I wanted to tell you what's going on."

I sat down, saying, "What is going on?"

"Well, presently Tito Moreno is cooling his heels downtown."

"Meaning?"

"He's been arrested."

"For...child abuse?"

"No, for assaulting a police officer with a deadly weapon."

"Holy smokes!" I say, jumping out of my chair. "What did he do? Try to knife you?"

"Sit down, Sammy. I'm fine."

"Well what? What did he do?"

"He attacked me with some refried beans."

I blinked at him. "With some . . . *beans?*"

He pulls a face. "A *can* of them, Sammy."

I sat back down. "Oh. Right. A can."

He's still frowning at me. "He's got a wicked arm, Sammy."

"I believe you!" I tell him, then add, "So what did you do to set him off?"

"Well, I went there with a woman from Social Services." He eyes me. "Just to check things out." His top lip pulls tight, practically disappearing for a minute before he says, "No kid should have to live like that. The location's bad enough, but the place is a pigsty! Broken doors, trash everywhere. Unbelievable."

"So when did he start throwing beans at you?"

He squints at me.

"I'm serious!"

"When I started 'harassing' him about his older daughter."

"Lena? Did he say anything?"

"Yeah. That he's not hiding her."

"*Hiding* her? Why would he be hiding her?"

"Because," he says, taking another deep breath, "I found out this morning that your friend Lena Moreno is wanted for murder."

My jaw dropped, my eyes popped, and I'm sure I looked like some sort of pine-faced puppet when I clacked, "What?"

"You heard me."

"Are you *sure?*"

"Oh yeah."

"Well who'd she kill?"

"One Joey Martinez."

"Joey? *Joey?* She killed her own husband?"

"Husband? Where'd you get that?"

"From Tippy! She said Lena married a guy named Joey."

"Well. I don't know about that. All I know is she's wanted for his murder."

"How did she..."

"A drive-by on the north end. There were several witnesses, including Martinez's brother."

"I... I don't believe it."

"Well, it makes certain things make sense."

I nodded and whispered, "Like why she was so afraid of me going to the police."

"Look, Sammy, I'm sorry to interrupt your school day, but I thought you should know." He eyes me. "I also am asking you *once again* to stay away from the situation."

"I will," I mumbled.

"I know you've got a soft spot for that little girl, and I can just see you running over there, trying to see how she is. Don't. Do you hear me? *Don't.*"

I nodded. "But what's going to happen to her?"

"That's in the hands of Social Services now and something will be done. I don't like to see that sort of thing either, you know."

"Did you ask them what Snake Eyes was doing there last night?"

"Oh, sure. I got nowhere with that, either. He knows nothing about nothing, if you know what I mean. The mother, too."

"But Officer Borsch, we have to do *some*thing. Lena called home. She's looking for help!"

"*We* don't have to do anything. *You* need to stay out of it completely, you hear? And maybe she's looking for help, and maybe she's not. The mother says she never got a call."

"But Tippy said—"

"She's a little kid, Sammy."

"But—"

"Look. I'm going to try and get a log from the phone company. We'll see what it turns up."

All of a sudden my heart starts racing. If they had a log showing who called the Morenos, Grams' number would be on it. *I'd* called the Morenos. From the *Senior Highrise.*

What kind of idiot was I?

Officer Borsch was saying, "Outside of that, there's really not much I can do at this point. No one's reported her missing—"

"*I* have! And Pepe would if he could!" I was trying hard not to panic about the phone log. Trying to stay focused on finding Lena.

"But those aren't, well, they're not—"

"We don't count? Is that what you're saying?"

He shrugs. "Not legally, anyway."

"But Officer Borsch—"

"Keep in mind, Sammy, we've been looking for her for about a year already." He sighs, then stands and says, "I know this is going to be hard for you to do, but try to just put it out of your mind, okay? At this point, there's nothing more you can do." He gives me a halfhearted grin. "Now get to class before people around here start thinking you're tangling with trouble again."

"Me?" I grumble. "It wouldn't even cross their minds."

I went back to class, all right, but all I could think about was Pepe's mom. Wanted for murder? *Murder?* How could that be? I tried to picture her, driving up Broadway, looking for Joey, and then *blam!* blowing him away. And the more I thought about it, the more I thought that there had to be more to this than the police knew. I mean, a year ago, Lena wasn't even old enough to drive a car. How could she do a drive-by? Did someone else drive? And if so, who? Something about all of this didn't make sense.

Didn't *feel* right.

And I couldn't push the whole phone-log mess out of my mind, either. What was going to happen with that?

Then at lunch, I did find myself tangling with trouble. Not murderers or gangbangers. A sneakier kind of trouble.

The junior high kind.

All the Sluggers' Cup players had to meet in the locker room to paint banners for the tournament. And when we broke into groups, our snotty new shortstop came over to our alcove to work with Marissa, Dot, and me.

This made me nervous. Very nervous. But I couldn't figure out what Heather was up to, and since it would've looked real bad for me to tell her we didn't want her helping us, I just tried to work as far away from her as I could.

But she was acting so weird. She kept *crowding* me. When I'd move away, she'd move right beside me. When I'd paint with yellow, she would, too. When I switched to green, she did, too.

Then Ms. Rothhammer comes out of her office, announcing, "I've got permission! We'll be practicing out at the high school today. Anyone whose parents might have a problem with that, see me ASAP." She ducks into our alcove and says, "Did you hear that back here?"

Marissa says, "Yeah! That's *great*, Coach!" while Ms. Rothhammer does a double-take. And instead of jetting off to check on the other girls, Ms. Rothhammer stands there a minute, giving us a great big smile. "Say!" she says. "Looking good, girls." But what she's thinking is, Wow, Sammy and Heather working together? Now *this* is a miracle!

Heather smiles real big and says, "This is, like, the best thing that could have happened to us, Coach." Then she turns to me and says, "Huh, Sammy?"

Well, no kidding she's putting on a show for Ms. Rothhammer. But I can't exactly say, "No, you sneaky faker!" so I just stare like my head is full of dust.

Then, the minute Ms. Rothhammer's back is turned,

Heather dips her sponge in the pot of green paint, and with it fully loaded, she squishes it all *over* my right hand.

Her eyes get real big and she gasps, "Oh, Sammy! I'm so sorry!" Then she flutters around, pretending to look for a rag.

Paint is running down my hand, dripping on our poster, getting everywhere. And I'm plenty mad to begin with, but when Heather's sponge drips on my *high-top,* well I just about splat her across her nasty red head to even the score.

In a flash, though, I see her plan. She's baiting me. She *wants* me to whale on her because if I do, there's a good chance I'll get suspended.

And if I'm suspended, I can't play.

It's the rules, and everyone knows it.

So I take a deep breath, take some paper towels that Marissa's snagged for me, and force myself to swallow the whole incident without splatting her back.

It's the most self-control I think I've ever shown.

And while Heather's fussing all over me, making the spot on my shoe into a big nasty smudge, I'm saying, "I've got it, okay? Just leave me alone, would you?"

Then I saw it—that evil, sneaky light in her eyes. "Sure," she says, and all of a sudden she's gone. Over to work in a different alcove with some eighth graders.

My hand's a complete mess. Even after ten minutes at the sink, it's still green, especially around and under my fingernails.

When I come back from the bathroom, Marissa and Dot have trashed the old poster and started on a new one. Dot sees me and whispers, "She *so* did that on purpose."

"I think she was baiting me—trying to get me suspended."

Marissa puts her hand out for me to slap. "You stayed so cool—I can hardly believe it. Did you tell Ms. Rothhammer?"

"No. I mean, why? Heather'd just say it was an accident and I'd look like a tattletale." I picked up my sponge and dipped it in paint. "I am *not* going to let her trick me out of playing. It's just not going to happen."

And that's what I focused on for the rest of the day. I turned in my make-up work to Mr. Pence, had my regular homework ready with the rest of my table, and in the middle of the lecture, when Heather whispered, "Soakin' it all up, loser?" I ignored her. Just ignored her.

And all through practice at the high school, I kept my focus on the game. She tried to cut me down by hissing "Twitty Turtle" and "Grid-Faced Gorilla" because of all my catcher's gear, but I took a deep breath and ignored her some more. She was not going to make me lose my cool.

She was not.

Even Mr. Vince and Babs hovering around at practice didn't get to me.

Too much, anyway.

I just told myself I wouldn't give them a reason, *any* reason, to horn in on my spot. All I had to do was stay in control. I could handle Babs being there. I could handle Mr. Vince. And yeah, I could handle Heather Acosta, too. If I just bit my tongue when she baited me and checked my fist at the dugout, I could get past her. She was a pest. A miserable mosquito. All I needed was the right repellent, right? She wouldn't be able to touch me. She'd buzz and whine in my ear, but she wouldn't light.

It wasn't until the next morning that I found out exactly what the Miserable Mosquito would go through to suck my blood.

And just how badly it would hurt.

FOURTEEN

I didn't notice them until after practice, when we were climbing up the hill behind the dugout. And at first I thought it might just be my imagination. But when they saw me do a double take, they turned away too quick, they started walking too fast, and *then* they kicked into cool 'n' casual.

Definitely suspicious.

Dot asked me, "What are you looking at?"

I reached right over her and tugged on Marissa, because Marissa's got the eyes of a hawk. "Look! By the trees. Is that the Gangster Girls?"

Marissa's also got the nerves of a chicken. She went from an ace-pitcher strut to a squawk and a flutter in two seconds flat. "Oh, no! Sammy, do not, do you hear me, do *not* follow them!"

"Who, you guys? Who are they?"

Poor Dot. I flew right past her question, saying, "I don't want to follow them, Marissa! But what do you think they're doing here?"

Marissa goes white. "Ohmygod. They're following *us*?"

"I'd say watching. Definitely."

"But why?"

"Good question."

Dot tries again, pointing across the field. "Are you guys talking about those girls way over there?"

Marissa slaps down her hand. "Don't *point*."

"Well, who *are* they? And why are you guys acting so scared of them?"

"They're *gangsters,* that's who they are!"

Dot squints at the three of them in the distance, saying, "*Gangsters?* How do you know they're gangsters? They look pretty normal from here."

"Yeah? Well that's 'cause they're a long way off. You can't see their *scars*. Or their faces."

"They've got scars on their faces?"

"No! They've got gang scars on their arms, but their faces are, you know, *hard*. Like they could kick your tush from here to Sisquane!"

"Oh," she says, then, "Hmm." Like she doesn't quite believe her. "Well, how do you know them?"

Marissa rolls her eyes and says, "How *else*?" and throws me a dirty look.

So on our way over to where Dot's father is waiting in his truck, I give her a lightning-fast outline of what's been going on. And through the whole story Dot blinks a lot, but she doesn't say a word. Not until we're at the truck. Then she rests her hand on the passenger-door handle, looks straight at me, and says, "Sammy, I'm with Marissa on this one. The whole thing sounds crazy and dangerous."

"I know! I agree, all right? Why does everyone think I don't agree with this?"

Marissa and Dot look at each other and shrug, then Dot yanks the door open and asks me, "So why do you think they were here?"

"I don't know! It's not like I invited them! They go to *school* here. Maybe that's all it was. You know, hanging around after school."

She shakes her head and climbs in, whispering, "I doubt it. And I'd be nervous if I were you. Very nervous."

"Oh, thanks. Thanks a lot!"

Mr. DeVries calls, "Hi, girls!" across the bench seat. "Will you be taking a ride today?"

I call, "No thanks," but Marissa totally bails on me, saying, "You know, I think I will." She leans in the door. "Is there room for my bike in back?"

"*Ja,* sure!" he says, and as he gets out, Marissa rolls her bike to the back of the truck, saying, "No offense, Sammy. I'm just beat." Then she adds, "And I have a ton to do tonight."

I almost said, Yeah? Like what? But I bit my tongue. Then before you know it, off they go, leaving me to clomp my way up Broadway alone.

At first I was just sort of irritated. I mean, Marissa and I always walk as far as we can together. Lots of times I go way out of my way just so I can walk with her a little farther. I even go to the arcade with her. Not to play—just so I can hang with her a little longer.

Which, now that I think about it, is how I got myself involved with gangsters to begin with. I mean, if I hadn't been hanging with Marissa at the arcade, Pepe's mom

151

would never have given me her little to-go bag. And if Marissa hadn't wanted to come to the high school fields, we never would have even *met* the Gangster Girls.

But really what I was, was hurt. I mean, if Marissa was just tired and wanted to go home, that was fine. But it felt like more than that. It felt like she didn't want to be around *me*. Like I was a jinx or something.

Now, I don't believe in jinxes. And I'm sure Marissa would tell you *she* doesn't believe in them, either. But since we had the tournament coming, well, it seemed almost logical.

See, softball players are superstitious. For example, Marissa won't wash her winning-game socks. Seriously. She'll let them petrify before she'll wash them. She'll wear them game after game after game until we lose, and *then* she'll wash them.

And okay. I have little rituals, too. Like I check the knots on my mitt and I pull and tug and, you know, adjust it. I also have little imaginary conversations with my dad, but the mitt was originally his, so that makes sense, right?

Besides, these are things I got in the habit of doing because I was nervous. And now I do them because they make me feel centered and happy. What I do is nothing like not washing your socks because you think they're lucky. That's just gross.

Anyway, I was clomping along Broadway, feeling like a leper, when I decided to switch out of my cleats and back into my high-tops. You can't exactly *sneak* anywhere in cleats, and I was getting near the Senior Highrise, so I finally decided to stop and change.

I was on the mall side of the street, where they have nice little grassy knolls and benches to rest on after you've worn yourself out shopping. And I was plenty worn out from thinking jinxing thoughts about my friend Marissa McKenze, but as I sat down on a bench I sensed a quick movement to my left.

My instinct was to whip around and look, but I caught myself in the nick of time. Instead, I reached down to untie a cleat and tried to act casual as I scooted my eyes over. I'm talking, I cranked them *way* over in my head. And what did I see?

Nothing.

There was no one there.

But the chills running down my spine told me that I hadn't imagined someone there. The chills told me I was being watched. I was being *followed*.

Then I saw something move again. A quick out-and-back behind some bushes.

I switched my shoes, my mind racing. I couldn't let them know where I lived. I had to lead them *miles* away from the Senior Highrise, and I had to do it without letting on that I knew I was being followed.

Which ruled out going to the police. I'd give myself away if I backtracked to the station. I couldn't go west, either. Why had I crossed Broadway if I lived on the west side? So I stuffed my cleats next to my mitt in my backpack, threw it over my shoulder, then took off across the mall grass, through a small plaza, and around a parking lot to Main Street.

Now I'm trying to calm down, but adrenaline's pumping through me like crazy. How could I have come so close to leading them straight to the Senior Highrise?

I forced myself not to look back, not even once. Then, when I got clear over to the intersection of Main and College, I pushed the Walk button and scooted my eyes around in my head again. And there they were, half a block down Main—the Gangster Girls.

Believe it or not, I was relieved. As Hudson says, there's nothing like knowing your enemy.

I crossed Main and headed north. Just trucked along like I didn't have a care in the world, but the whole time I'm wondering: *Why* are they following me? If they wanted to powder my bones, they could have done that ages ago. I mean, the three of them against me? I wouldn't have a chance.

But if they didn't want to beat me up, then what? Did they want to know where I lived so they could beat me up *later*? What had I done to them, anyhow, except ask a few questions? It's not like I'd been rude or anything.

I kept walking, pulling them away from the Highrise. And I'd nearly made it to Donovan Street when I decided to hang a left into a residential area. And the minute I was around the corner, I *ran*.

At the first intersection I took another left, then the first right. I ran a few more blocks, jogging left and right, and finally I ducked beside a tree, watching to see if the Gangster Girls had been able to trail me.

After a few minutes, there was still no sign of them, so I headed for Broadway.

The north end of Broadway is always busy. People, traffic, road construction—the place is always honking and smelling of tar. And that section of Broadway is like a mecca for mechanics. It's got tire stores and tranny shops, Spiffy Lubes and body shops. There are at least three parts stores, and every block's got a used-car lot. You may *think* your car's gone off to the great junkyard in the sky, but chances are good it's been resurrected and put up for sale somewhere on North Broadway.

And even though the air was clashing with revving motors and whining wrenches and clanging metal, my mind was still preoccupied with the Gangster Girls and Snake Eyes and Pepe's mom because I *still* couldn't figure it out. Why were the Gangster Girls following me? Why had Snake Eyes been following Lena? Why was Lena so afraid of Snake Eyes? How could Lena have killed her own husband, or boyfriend, or whatever? Tippy had made Joey sound like a nice guy. Why kill him?

Then all of a sudden I remembered that Tippy had said something about Joey working up at a muffler shop. I slowed down and scoured Broadway for a muffler-shop sign. Both sides, both directions. And what did I see? Nothing.

A mechanic's mecca with no muffler shop? I didn't believe it. So I found a phone booth, hit the yellow pages, and started digging.

There were two muffler shops on North Broadway, all right. And according to the phone book, Manny's

Mufflers was in the same block I was standing on. Speedy Muffler was about six blocks down.

So off I went, checking addresses, looking for Manny's. And pretty soon I see a yellow and black MANNY'S MUFFLERS sign, stretching above the BOOM-BOOM BABY STEREO and WATSON TIRE signs, trying to claim its own little piece of the sky.

I head straight for the garage, where three guys in dirty blue overalls are working. Two are across the garage, measuring a length of pipe, and the one closest to me is standing under a car on a lift, a welding mask flipped up on his head. "Excuse me!" I call to the guy with the mask.

He doesn't budge.

I take a few steps past the AUTHORIZED PERSONNEL ONLY sign and call, "Excuse me!" again, this time louder.

He does a double take, then comes over. "Yeah?"

"I was wondering...did a guy named Joey Martinez used to work here? It would have been about a year ago."

He doesn't answer me. Instead, he calls, "Hey, Luis!" across the garage and waves another guy over.

The Luis guy comes over, wiping his hands on a rag. "What's up?"

"I'm wondering if you knew a guy named Joey who maybe used to work here."

The guy just stares at me.

"Joey...Martinez? Ever heard of him?"

He keeps staring at me, and let me tell you, he's not looking too nice.

"He had freckles, used to go out with Lena Moreno...?"

At that the guy spits. Right on the asphalt, *splat*. "That witch'll burn some day."

My heart starts skipping around. "You really think she killed him?"

"I know it! I saw the whole thing with my own two eyes. First she calls his name, then the gun comes up and *blam!* Joey's gone."

"But *why?* Her sister said they were married."

He snorts. "Once a banger, always a banger. I warned him, Mama warned him, but he knew better. One thing about Joey—he wouldn't never listen."

I could feel the click in my brain. And I tried not to sound too stupid as I said, "He...he was your... brother?"

He squints at me. "Why you here? You some friend of hers or something?"

"No, I—" I stopped suddenly. "When's the last time you saw her?"

"The day she gunned my brother down, that's when."

"Then you don't know."

"Know what?"

I took a deep breath and decided that it was a chance I ought to take. "That you're an uncle."

"What?"

"Lena had a baby."

"No way."

"According to my grandmother, he's about three months old."

I could see him doing the math in his head. "Then it's not Joey's."

"Oh yeah?" I took another deep breath. "Well, she says it is."

His face clouds over. "So you know where she is?"

I shook my head. "She's disappeared. A couple days ago she asked me to take care of her baby—I haven't seen her since."

He stands there for a minute, not saying anything, then shakes his head, muttering, "No way it's his. Probably belongs to that creep she went with before."

"Ray Ramirez?"

"I don't know his name. Some hot-shot banger who came up from Vegas and likes to roll the dice. That's all I know about him." He stands there wiping grease around his hands with the rag. "So where's this baby?"

"I turned him over to the police."

"So they know about all this?"

I nod. "All about it."

A man with an oily face and a clip-on tie comes out of the office, saying, "Hey, what are you doing back here?"

Luis says to me, "If you see that witch, you tell her I ain't never gonna forget what she did to my brother. You got that?" Then he says, "Sorry, Mr. Thorton," and gets back to work.

By the time I hit the sidewalk, I had more questions than ever. What in the world had happened? Here I'd just spoken to an eyewitness, and still I didn't believe it. But maybe I was just all wet. Maybe Lena was a coldhearted banger. Maybe Pepe's father didn't have freckles at all. Maybe he had hatred for eyes. Steel for a mouth.

Was Pepe a baby Snake Eyes?

Would he grow up and get scars and tattoos?

In my mind I could see little Pepe on his back on the roof of the mall, cooing and kicking and spraying the world with pee. What would he be like in ten years? In twenty years?

The more I thought about it, the more helpless I felt.

FIFTEEN

It was late. And I knew Grams would be worried, but still, I thought I should make triple sure the Gangster Girls hadn't followed me back to the Senior Highrise. So I wound up crouching behind a bush near the fire escape, waiting and watching until I was positive the coast was clear.

When I finally made it to the apartment, I closed the door without a sound and whispered, "Hi, Grams!" as I unloaded my backpack.

Grams was all preoccupied with some book she was reading at the kitchen table. She smiled at me, then glanced at the clock. "Practice run late?"

I couldn't believe it. Normally she'd be wringing her hands, fretting about where I'd been, and here it was way past dinner and there *she* was, back with her nose in a book.

And what was I supposed to say to her question? Uh, gee, no. Actually, I'm late because there was this group of South West gangsters hunting me down and I had to ditch them?

I don't think so.

So I just said, "Uh-huh," and peeked under her book at the cover. "What'cha reading?"

"It's absolutely fascinating."

"*Online Marketing?* Grams, we don't even have a computer!"

She nods. Like I'm somewhere in the distance of her consciousness. "Hudson does."

"*Hudson?*"

She snaps to. "Don't jump ahead of yourself, young lady. I'm just reading."

"Does, uh, Hudson know you're reading?"

"Not yet."

"But what are you planning to market?" I ask her, then mutter, "Online. With a computer you don't own."

She snaps the book closed, shoves away from the table, and says, "I thought we'd heat up leftovers tonight."

"Don't change the subject! I really want to know."

She just scowls at me.

"Okay, I'm sorry. It just seems so out of the blue and, you know, not you."

"Oh, really? Well, I don't make fun of your ideas, and I happen to think this one's a pretty good one." She starts passing cold food to me from the refrigerator.

"Grams, really. I'm sorry. What's the idea? What are you planning to market?"

She hesitates, then says, "Handkerchiefs. Mono-grammed handkerchiefs."

I didn't want to put my foot in my mouth again, but I had the hardest time not saying, *Handkerchiefs?* Who's gonna want those?

I guess it was written all over my face, though, because she says, "Brides. Babies. Sweet-sixteens. Victorian

161

*tea*rooms—which are becoming very popular again, in case you didn't know."

"Tearooms? Why would they want handkerchiefs?"

She tisked at me and closed the refrigerator. "Or cloth napkins, Samantha. You have to think broadly if we're going to go into business."

"We? You mean, you, me, and . . . Hudson?"

"Well, I don't know about Hudson. We'll see."

"But Grams—"

"We'll see!"

One thing about my grams. When she's excited, you can always tell because she moves fast. And right now she was *flying* around the kitchen, whipping those leftovers in and out of the microwave, shoving me plates and utensils to put on the table. And I thought, Okay. If she's excited about it, well fine. Who was I to break it to her that there was a *reason* Kleenexes were popular.

"Scraps, Samantha. Do you understand? I can make them out of scraps. Remnants from the fabric store. The embroidery's nothing—it's just a monogram. Or a name. Say, I could charge by the letter! Yes! That makes more sense. And imagine, Samantha, pennies to make, and I could easily charge eight or ten dollars apiece, don't you think? Plus shipping and handling. That's why handkerchiefs and napkins and not blankets and towels or some such bulky product. The book says you should charge just under ten dollars for shipping and handling, but postage would be next to nothing!"

"Ten-dollar shipping for an eight-dollar handkerchief?"

"Well, you would prorate it, of course, but think! Just think! There's real money in this!"

I felt like saying, That's only if someone *buys* them, but I didn't. And then the next thing she said made me really glad I hadn't. "Samantha, I am bound and determined to find us a way out of here. We can't wait forever for your mother, and with Mrs. Wedgewood next door, why, it seems that any moment we might be thrown out on our ear."

I felt awful. She'd probably been racking her brains for a way she could earn some money, and why? Because my living with her was putting her at serious risk. So rather than send me off to live with my mother—which she knew would *kill* me—she'd come up with the master plan. A way to save us from despair and desolation. A scheme so big, so broad, so bold, we would dominate the world! And it all revolved around...

Snot.

But I'd never seen Grams so excited. So I didn't say one snide word to her about marketing nose-nugget napkins. I just let her talk.

After dinner she invited me to do my homework next to her at the table. So while she took notes from her book, I scribbled answers out of mine. And you know what? It was really nice. It made me feel, I don't know, *safe*. Like if I was with Grams, nobody could hurt me. She wouldn't let them. She didn't think of me as a jinx that brought her bad luck. Everything *else* was the jinx, and she'd be doggoned if she was going to let it ruin our life. No, my grams would find a way to save us.

Hankies to the rescue!

The minute I hit the fire escape the next morning, I was back to feeling stressed. Three nights had gone by since Pepe had been handed off to me, gangsters had tried to follow me home, and Snake Eyes was out there sniffing around. By now he probably knew my name, where I went to school...stuff you sure don't want gangsters to know about you.

So I took a new way to school, trying to mix things up a little, but I still kept looking over my shoulders.

And instead of just walking past graffiti like I used to, I started trying to make out what it said. It was scary, too. Well, not scary like *boo*, more unnerving. *It* had been there all along, I just hadn't stopped to analyze it. Like the day you realize where hamburger comes from. You feel squeamish and sort of unsure. Like everyone around you has been playing some sort of gross joke on you.

Everyone except the cow, of course.

Anyway, even though a lot of the graffiti still looked like scribbles, I was beginning to be able to make out bits and pieces.

The graffiti at school, though, anyone could read. Still. They'd tried to clean the red BRUSTER'S #1 off the steps, but it was still legible. The lawn was looking worse than ever, too. It had gotten browner overnight.

I ran past it all and slid into homeroom while the bell

was ringing, then waved to Marissa and Holly and ignored Heather's sneer from across the room. All in all, it was a pretty typical start to my school day.

But then in the middle of the Pledge, Vice Principal Caan appears. He stands looming in the doorway fidgeting with his scuba watch, and it's easy to see something has him pretty agitated.

The second we're done pledging, he goes up and whispers with Mrs. Ambler. Then it happens. Mr. Caan crooks his finger, right at me.

I jump up and I'm about to say, What did *I* do? when Mr. Caan does something that makes my heart stop.

He crooks his finger again.

Right at Marissa.

Marissa looks at me like, What is going on? and I shrug at her and shake my head, but as she looks from me to Mr. Caan and back again, I can tell what she's thinking.

Jinx.

Holly gives us worried looks on our way out, so I shrug and smile. But then I see Heather, and my smile disappears. There's a twinkle in her eyes. A *twinkle*.

Mr. Caan wouldn't talk about it on the march back to the administration building. And I kept telling Marissa, "I don't know! I swear, I didn't do anything!" but she was worried, too. Worried big-time.

Then we entered the conference room and relief swept over me. Officer Borsch was there!

"What's going on?" I asked him as I slid into a chair.

"Hrmph," he says, his arms folded across his chest. "As if you don't know."

Marissa sits down next to me. "I swear," she says to the whole room, "we didn't do a thing!"

"Officer Borsch, why are we here?"

He sits down across from me and produces two cans of green spray paint from beneath the table. He clanks them down right in front of me. "This is the thanks I get for teaching you how to read walls?" He shakes his head. "I was trying to educate you, not turn you into taggers!"

"But...we didn't tag any walls!" I tell him.

"Look, there's no sense playing dumb. We have eyewitnesses. You signed your *names*."

"We signed our *names*?"

Mr. Caan clears his throat and says, "Samantha, I warned you not to retaliate. And even though I understand it's a temptation and you feel a strong sense of school spirit, that was not the way to show it."

I threw my hands up in the air and said, "I can't believe this! Whatever 'that' is, I didn't do it. And neither did Marissa!"

"Is that so?" Officer Borsch says. "Well, there's graffiti all over Paul Bruster Junior High, and these were in the garbage can waiting for pickup in front of sixty-three seventy-five East Jasmine." He looks from Marissa to me and back again. "That *is* where you live, isn't it?"

I was in a pickle. An enormous pickle. See, a long time ago I told Officer Borsch that I lived with Marissa. That I'm her foster sister or something like that. And he's seemed suspicious but he's never really pressed it. Vice Principal *Caan*, though, thinks I live with my mother. Where, I'm not sure, but with my mother. Grams' phone number is in my school file as my *mother's* number, and so far, that little lie has held up pretty well.

But now both lies were in the same room. And I could tell that any minute Mr. Caan was going to say, Wait a minute—you're saying Samantha lives with *Marissa*? Or worse, Officer Borsch would say, Uh-huh, I knew it. You're really living with your grandmother, aren't you?

I was stuck in a squeeze play, and I didn't see any way of sliding to either base without being tagged out.

Then Marissa sits straight up and says, "You went digging through our *trash*?"

"That's right," Officer Borsch tells her. "Hoping the trash collector would haul away the evidence this morning, huh?"

"No!" she says.

"And Samantha, you're carrying around some pretty strong evidence against you right there," he says, looking straight at my hand. "And there," he adds, pointing under the table at my shoe.

Mr. Caan nods. "I noticed that."

"But—" I jump up. "Heather did this to me yesterday when we were painting posters for the tournament. She did it to me on purpose!"

Mr. Caan shakes his head and says, "Don't. Samantha, just don't."

"Don't what? Tell the truth? Ask Marissa!"

He looks at me like I've got fog for brains.

"Okay, well, Dot saw the whole thing! Ask her."

Officer Borsch tisks and produces a notebook, saying, "We've got neighbors who describe 'two young teens,

167

female, both wearing green ball caps. One in white high-tops, jeans, and a navy blue sweatshirt. One in a number-nine green-and-gold jersey.' " He looks at Marissa. "I understand you're quite a pitcher. And that your number's nine."

Marissa gulps and nods, then whispers, "But it wasn't me . . . !" and I add, "Officer Borsch, we didn't do it!"

Mr. Caan shakes his head and says, "Look, I made a deal with the principal at Paul Bruster. We—meaning *you*—will paint over the graffiti. In return, they'll send a crew over to clean up their graffiti and fix our lawn. If you want to escalate this into parent conferences and citations and possible criminal proceedings, just keep this up and that's exactly what will happen."

It wasn't the criminal proceedings that was striking terror in my heart. It was the parent conference. Officer Borsch looks at me and adds, "Can your parents verify your whereabouts yesterday evening?"

"What *time*? 'Cause I was at Manny's Muffler up on North Broadway yesterday trying to get some information about Pepe's mom and—"

"You *what*?" Officer Borsch snaps, and let me tell you, he's turning red in a hurry. "I told you to stay out of it! And this is *not* helping your cause. Now, is there some-one—some responsible *adult*—who can corroborate your professed innocence?"

"What time?" I ask him again, but suddenly my throat feels like it's tied in a knot.

"Five-fifteen."

I just blinked. At five-fifteen I was somewhere north of Main, ditching gangsters.

He snorts at me. "What about you?" he growls at Marissa.

An eight on the Richter scale would've had me on steadier ground. I held my breath and braced myself for the worst. But then Marissa did something only a true friend would do. She looked down and shook her head.

There was a moment of complete silence, and then Mr. Caan said, "Well, then. Let's go."

"Go?" I asked.

Officer Borsch hiked up his gun belt. "Over to Paul Bruster."

"*Now?*"

Mr. Caan headed out of the room. "I'll inform your parents—I'm sure they won't object, considering the alternative." He hesitated in the doorway. "Now go clean up your mess."

So off we shuffled behind Officer Borsch, whispering frantically to each other on our way to the squad car.

"How did those spray cans get in my trash?"

"Can you spell *framed*?"

"Yeah," she grumbled. "H-e-a-t-h-e-r."

"But Marissa, why didn't you stand up for yourself?"

She eyed me. "You know why."

"I'm sorry. I'm really, really sorry," I said, and at that moment I felt like the world's biggest jinx.

But then she mumbled, "Plus, my parents *can't* verify my whereabouts."

This was no big surprise because Marissa's parents are always at work, even when they're at home, it seems. But Mrs. McKenze had hired a nanny to watch after Marissa's little brother, who likes to sneak out of the house and buy up the candy store. Which meant that if Marissa's parents weren't around, well, Simone had to be. So I asked, "What about Simone?"

"She can't, either." She looked away. "Actually, I'm grounded."

"You're *what?*" I asked, because Marissa McKenze has never been grounded in her entire life.

"Grounded," she grumbles. Then she whips around and says, "I got in a big fight with Mikey, all right? He stole the toilet paper out of my bathroom *again,* if you can believe that. I was totally stuck in there with nothing to use and . . . and I just got mad."

"So . . . ?"

"So I left."

"To get toilet paper?"

"No, I snagged that from my parents' bathroom."

"So . . . ?"

She blurted, "So I went to the mall and played video games."

I eyed her but didn't say a word. And she knew what I was thinking—too tired to walk home with me, but plenty energetic enough to ride clear back to the mall? But I bit back what I wanted to say and shrugged. "So? They always let you go to the mall."

"Except I wasn't home when they got home, and I

hadn't told Simone where I was going. So there," she says. "I'm grounded."

"For how long?"

"I have no idea. They were so mad at me and brought up about Hollywood again."

I cringed, remembering the little unauthorized trip we'd taken to Hollywood. It had been my idea. All my idea. And I'd been in the McKenze doghouse ever since. "I'm sorry!"

"I know. I just hope they don't believe Mr. Caan."

As we slid into the backseat of the patrol car, she held my arm and whispered, "I'm sorry I bailed on you yesterday, Sammy," and I could tell she meant it.

What neither of us knew was that by the end of school, we'd both be a whole lot sorrier.

SIXTEEN

Officer Borsch didn't say a word to us on our way over to Paul Bruster Junior High. And yeah, I felt pretty miserable. Here I'd finally gotten him to trust me, but the reality was he *couldn't* trust me. Not because I wasn't trustworthy. No, he couldn't trust me because I couldn't risk trusting *him*.

It was, I was starting to see, a two-way street.

Now, six months ago I wouldn't have cared that Officer Borsch didn't believe me. Six months ago it didn't matter, because I *hated* the guy.

But I don't hate him anymore. I don't exactly *like* him, but I understand him better than I used to.

I know him better.

Which is the whole problem. It's hard to keep up a lie with someone you talk to a lot. Especially a cop. But he *is* a cop, and that's exactly why I can't tell him the truth about living with Grams.

So, sitting in the back of the squad car, I decided—I had to back away from Officer Borsch. Knowing him had gotten too complicated.

Too dangerous.

Besides, I could tell from the way he was acting that he

wanted nothing more to do with me. He was sick of my snooping, and now he thought I'd defaced public property.

Like the juvenile delinquent he'd always suspected me to be.

When we got to Bruster Junior High, Officer Borsch delivered us to the vice principal—a grouchy-looking woman named Ms. Toalz. She was Bruster's version of Mr. Caan, only instead of thinning blond hair and a scuba watch, she had stiff brown curls and a gulch of a wrinkle between her eyebrows. Even when she thanked Officer Borsch and smiled, that wrinkle didn't ease up.

Officer Borsch wished Ms. Toalz good luck and waddled off without a word to us. And right away I told Ms. Toalz that we weren't the ones who'd sprayed the school—that we'd been framed. And do you know what she said?

She said, "Yeah, you and O.J."

Can you believe that? Then she starts laying into us about defacing public property and civic responsibility and all of that. And I did try to be respectful and listen, but pretty soon my eyes are wandering up to that wrinkle between *her* eyes and those super-stiff ringlets wound tight to her skull. Then my *mind* starts wandering, too. I'm imagining tiny gnomes living on her head, using her curls for caves. And I can just see them, grabbing hairs from the middle of her forehead, using them as ropes to rappel down the great gorge between her eyes, when all of a sudden she yells, "Wipe that stupid grin off your face!" grabs my elbow, and marches us over to the gym.

The outside wall of Paul Bruster's gymnasium has a nice glass-covered marquee with a great big picture of a rooster painted above it. In the marquee it says BRUSTER'S ROOSTERS HAVE A LOT TO CROW ABOUT! and under that there's a list of upcoming events.

Now, you've got to wonder about how a school picks its mascot. Maybe they decide it should be something strong or heroic or just plain fierce. Or maybe it's their way of saying Whoops, sorry! to an endangered species that lived there before they plowed the land and put up the school. In the case of Bruster, I'm sure a bunch of adults sat around and came up with cute little slogans for the school. Like having a lot to crow about. And I guess being a rooster would be better than being a whippoor-will or a hummingbird or a *chicken,* but what you can do to make fun of a mascot should be a factor, too. I mean, the brains at Bruster definitely would have changed their choice if they'd considered the *field* day the teenage mind can have with roosters.

Still, any kid who attends William Rose Junior High would trade mascots with Paul Bruster in a heartbeat. Our mascot isn't fierce. It's not smart. It's not quick. It's not endangered or even cute. We are—get this—the William Rose Junior High...

Bullfrogs.

Go! *Ribbit-ribbit.* Fight! *Ribbit-ribbit.* Win! *Ribbit-ribbit.*

I guess William Rose—the man who gave all the money for the school—had a thing for amphibians. Frogs in particular. So we're stuck being slimy little wart-inducing, lily-lodging bug snaggers.

Anyway, the Bruster marquee was mounted up high enough not to get tagged with spray paint, but starting about three feet under the marquee, the wall was slashed with green. Just covered in green. BULLFROGS RULE, GREEN POWER, WRJH ROCKS—stuff like that. There were also rooster-related slams written on the wall. The kind of thing you've probably heard a million times but wouldn't actually say yourself unless you didn't care about getting suspended.

So there's all this stupid stuff written all over the place, and there, right under BULLFROGS RULE, are the signatures.

They don't exactly say Sammy Keyes and Marissa McKenze—they're more clever than that. One of them's the letter S with two skeleton keys drawn hanging from the bottom curve, the other is two M's—one stacked on top of the other. But anyone who knew the Bullfrog lineup would know who the symbols stood for.

Grouchy Gulch sets us up with paint and rollers, and snaps, "You're here for as long as it takes. And don't get funny with that paint. It'll cost you."

I call after her, "We didn't do it!" but she just throws us a scowl and keeps on trucking.

The minute she's gone, Marissa says, "God, I'm so embarrassed. Look at this!"

I nod. "We've got to prove we didn't do this."

"But how?"

"I have no idea." I slap the roller onto the wall and push the paint out hard and fast. "What ticks me off most of all is that nobody ever believes me!"

Marissa paints over her initials and says real matter-of-factly, "That's because you lie about everything, Sammy."

I stop painting. "I don't lie about everything!"

"Sure you do."

"Marissa! I'm a really *honest* person!"

"I know. But you still lie about things. A lot."

"I tell the truth whenever I can."

"I'm not saying it's your fault, I'm just saying you do. Which is why people don't believe you."

"Well, why didn't they believe *you?*"

She looks my way and says, "Because I'm your best friend."

I start rolling really really fast. "You think I'm a jinx, don't you?"

"A *jinx?*" She thinks about this a minute, then says, "No, but I do get in a lot more trouble being your friend than I would *not* being your friend."

"Are you saying . . . are you saying you don't want to be my friend?"

She laughs. " 'Course not! I just wish you hadn't told Officer Borsch that we live together. It makes *me* have to lie."

"I know," I tell her. "And I'm sorry."

"Well, it wouldn't be a problem if you would just stay out of trouble."

"But I *try* to stay out of trouble."

"Uh-huh."

176

"Marissa!"

"Okay...let's take this whole Snake Eyes thing. If you hadn't gone snooping that night, you wouldn't have seen him outside that shack, and he probably wouldn't be trying to track you down, and—"

"But Marissa, Pepe's mother is missing. Don't you feel any kind of responsibility about that?"

"Me? No! Why would I? I didn't tell her to ditch her baby."

"But Marissa, I think she's in *trouble*. And Pepe's going to grow up without his mother!"

"Have you thought that maybe that's a good thing if she's a murderer?"

"But I don't think she is."

"Sammy, you don't even know her!"

"There's just something wrong with the whole story."

"Whatever." She quits midstroke and looks my way. "Look, I just want to get this done and get back to school, okay? The tournament's tomorrow and there's no way I'm going to miss practice."

So we put our shoulders into it. And as I pushed and shoved the roller back and forth, sweating over repainting Bruster's wall, I could see why people got really mad about this kind of thing. Maybe it took only minutes to tag, maybe it seemed like an innocent little prank, but it was going to take us hours to fix it.

We finished a little before noon. Ol' Grouchy Gulch took us back to school and delivered us to the office without a word. We were told to wait in the admin-building foyer while she was let into Mr. Caan's office. And after she left, we *still* had to wait. "He'll be done with his meeting in just a few minutes," Mrs. Tweeter said. "Just sit tight."

"Can we please go get our lunches?" I asked. "We're starving!"

"I'm sorry, dear. He shouldn't be much longer." She went back to some papers she was sorting through.

"Mrs. Tweeter?"

"Yes, dear?" She looked at me over her reading glasses.

"We didn't do it."

She whispered, "Now, now," then glanced over her shoulder before leaning across the counter. "We used to T.P. our rival's campus. Try that next time. It's much less offensive, if you ask me."

I wanted to say, *What?* because I couldn't quite believe my ears, only just then Mr. Caan stepped out of his office, followed by Dr. Morlock, the *principal*—whom I've seen like three times the entire year. And then behind them came Ms. Rothhammer and Mr. Vince.

Mr. Vince?

My blood stopped moving the minute I saw him. Something had just gone down. Something big. And from the looks on their faces, I could see that no one was too happy about it.

No one, that is, except Mr. Vince.

SEVENTEEN

It's not that Mr. Vince was grinning from ear to ear or anything. He more looked like Sylvester with Tweety trapped in his mouth.

Marissa spins my way and whispers, "Oh, no!" because we can both tell—we're off the team. And while Dr. Morlock, Ms. Rothhammer, and Mr. Vince file away from the door, Mr. Caan says, "Sammy, Marissa, in my office please."

As we pass by Ms. Rothhammer, we look at her like, Please, *please* help us.

At first she just shakes her head like she can't. But then she stops, looks over her shoulder at Mr. Caan, and follows us right back into his office.

Mr. Vince tries to come in, too, but Mr. Caan tells him quietly that he thinks it would be best if he stayed out. He starts to argue, but Mr. Caan closes the door on him. Right in his face.

Mr. Caan tucks himself into the roll-around chair behind his desk and tells us to have a seat in the chairs facing him. Ms. Rothhammer doesn't bother sitting. She stands against a bookcase with her arms folded and says, "I'm very disappointed in the two of you."

Marissa bursts into tears while I jump up, saying, "But Coach, we didn't *do* it!"

Mr. Caan shakes his head and sighs.

"Well, we didn't!" I tell him.

Ms. Rothhammer has still got her arms crossed. "There's a lot of evidence against you, Sammy."

"And you know who put it there, don't you?"

Mr. Caan's still shaking his head. "Sammy, please."

"I'm serious! I told you, I'm all green because Heather splatted me with paint yesterday. She set this whole thing up!"

Ms. Rothhammer says, "Sammy? What I saw yesterday was the two of you working nicely together. At least *she* was trying to work nicely with *you*."

"Yeah! And the minute you had your back turned that faker squished my hand full of paint and got it all over my shoe."

"So why didn't you do something about it? Why didn't you tell me?"

"I didn't *do* something about it because I was trying to have some self-control for once! I thought she was trying to get me to splat her back so I'd get suspended and not be able to play in the tournament, that's why! And I didn't tell you because all I need is to have her add Tattle-tale to the monster list of names she already calls me!"

Ms. Rothhammer looks at Marissa, sobbing in her chair. "Marissa?"

"It's true, Coach." Marissa flings tears off her cheeks. "Ask Dot!"

"What about the cans of spray paint in your trash?"

180

"She must've put them there!"

"That's pretty extreme, don't you think?"

"No!" I tell her. "Obviously you don't know Heather like we do!"

"But your names are on the wall, and people *saw* you."

"Do you really think we're dumb enough to sign our names? And wear our jerseys?"

"But," she says very quietly, "neither of you has an alibi."

I plop back into my chair and mutter, "Don't we know."

"Which puts you in a very bad predicament." She looks from me to Marissa and back again. "Where were you? Isn't there anybody who can vouch for you?"

We're both just quiet, staring at the floor, so Ms. Rothhammer says to Mr. Caan, "Could we have a minute?"

Mr. Caan hesitates, then gets up and leaves the office. When he's gone, Ms. Rothhammer drops her arms and says, "Girls, I want to believe you, but you're not giving me much to work with."

Marissa sits up a little and says, "Coach, there's some personal stuff that we can't discuss. You understand that, right?"

Ms. Rothhammer chews the inside of her cheek a minute, then says, "Sure."

"But just because we can't tell you everything, and just because we don't have alibis, that doesn't mean we did it." She leans toward Ms. Rothhammer and squints, saying, "I would never write some of the stuff that was on that wall. Never!"

181

Ms. Rothhammer sighs. "Which, by the way, turns out to be the sticking point. According to the handbook, that sort of language is suspendable."

"Let me guess," I grumble. "Mr. Vince pointed that out."

Ms. Rothhammer didn't comment, but it was written all over her frown.

"So now what?" Marissa asks. "Are we really not going to be allowed to play tomorrow?"

"Why don't the two of you wait outside. I'll discuss it with Mr. Caan, okay?"

We both give her a real grateful, "Okay," and swap places with Mr. Caan. And while we're waiting, I whisper, "Look, Officer Borsch isn't here anymore, so why don't you just tell them the truth about you? No sense in us both getting kicked off the team."

"But Sammy, I don't *have* an alibi!"

"Maybe somebody who works at the arcade could—"

"Are you kidding? We all look alike to them."

"But you go in there so much. . . . It's worth a try, isn't it?"

She sighs and says, "Maybe," then adds, "But I don't want to play without you. How am I supposed to play with Babs catching? I hate Babs!"

So we're just sitting there, racking our brains about what to do, when Mr. Caan's door flings open and Ms. Rothhammer comes steaming out with our illustrious vice principal chasing behind her. "Sarah, please. You're being unreasonable—"

"No, Joseph!" she snaps. "*You* are! Have you heard of

innocent until proven guilty? Have you heard of reason-able doubt?"

"They don't have a collective leg to stand on!"

"It wouldn't be the first time Heather's pulled a prank like this. Have you even questioned her?"

"Okay! I'll do that." He drops his voice. "But please, Sarah. Don't blow this out of proportion. There's no need for you to resign."

Resign? Marissa and I look at each other, eyes bulging like *real* bullfrogs.

She points at us, sitting there with our jaws dangling. "Reinstate them and I won't."

"I can't just—"

"Then don't expect me to coach. I will not be a party to this." She spins on her heel, then turns back and looks Mr. Caan square in the eye. "I believe them, Joseph. And I think it's unconscionable that you're not giving them some benefit of doubt. Especially in light of who's pro-pelling this."

His head bobs; then he looks down and says, "I'll call Heather in. Right now."

Heather, it turns out, had an alibi. Her mother. In no time Mrs. Acosta comes cracking through the office like a bolt of angry lightning, wearing spiky gold shoes, a highly ratted red flip, and a low-cut green minidress. She spits some nasty comments in my direction, pushes past Mrs. Tweeter, barges into Mr. Caan's office, and slams the door.

It's not long before we can see Mr. Caan's sweat vaporizing through the cracks around his door. And when Heather and her mother finally emerged, we knew the score.

We'd been skunked by a couple of redheads.

The Acostas dispersed, but their vile fumes seemed to hang in the air. And then Mr. Caan decided to send us back to class, which was weird, if you ask me. I mean, if we're bad enough to kick off the team, we ought to be kicked out of school, too, right? But he made us finish off the day with some lame comment about not falling behind in our studies. Studies. Like either of us was going to be able to concentrate on anything after what we'd been through.

The news had spread through the school like a bad case of lice. Everyone was itching to pass along the gossip, and of course they all tried to look real inconspicuous as they pointed Marissa and me out. I finally took a Magic Marker, went into the bathroom, and wrote WE DIDN'T DO IT across the back of my shirt. It didn't do any good, but at least I could quit saying it every two seconds.

The minute Dot heard what had happened, she cornered Ms. Rothhammer and said, "Coach, I hope you don't mind, but I quit."

I hope you don't mind. That is *so* Dot.

Anyway, then she adds, "If Sammy and Marissa can't play, I *won't* play."

"Tell it to Mr. Vince," Ms. Rothhammer grumbles. "He has, of course, agreed to take my place."

Marissa says, "You're not really resigning, are you?"

"From the tournament? Yes." She studies us. "Look at me and tell me you didn't do it."

"We didn't do it, Coach."

She holds our gazes for a minute, then nods. "Good enough."

By the end of the day, rumor was that not only had Ms. Rothhammer been replaced by Mr. Vince, but Emiko Lee would be pitching, Gisa Kranz would be taking over for Dot on third, and Big-Mouth Filarski would be squatting behind home plate.

They'd gotten exactly what they wanted.

And maybe I should've told Ms. Rothhammer not to quit. Maybe I should've told Dot to stick it out. I mean, the Junior Sluggers' Cup is a big, *big* deal. But what had happened to Marissa and me was so *wrong*, and it seemed that the only people doing the right thing were Dot and Coach Rothhammer. I just felt lucky to have them on my side.

That doesn't mean I wasn't ticked off, let me tell you! And Marissa, boy, she was beyond ticked. She was falling apart. At the bike racks after school, she was going on and on about how she should never have gotten so mad at Mikey over toilet paper and how if only this or if only that when this voice behind me says, "You didn't do it, huh?"

My head whips around, and there's Casey, grinning at my shirt. I turn completely around and take a step back. "No, as a matter of fact, we didn't!"

"Well the dirt's flying fast and furious out there, so I thought I should get it straight from you." He's still grinning. "Rumor is my *mom* made an appearance today."

"Yeah. To provide that backstabbing snake-in-the-grass sister of yours with an alibi!"

He laughs. "Could you be a little more direct? All these niceties are going to make me miss the bus." I just glare at him, so he gets serious. "You really think it was her?"

I tell him, "Du-uh!" and then right away I feel bad, so I give him a lightning-fast rundown of everything that happened and why I'm sure his sister's behind it all.

And when I'm done, he checks over his shoulder at the buses, then says, "But I heard that some neighbors around Bruster reported a girl in high-tops and another in a number-nine jersey."

"Just how dumb do people think we are? You think we'd do this in broad daylight, with our *numbers* on our backs?"

"You *swear* you didn't do it?"

I just turn my back on him so he can read my shirt.

"Swear, Sammy."

I whip back around and shout, "I swear, okay? I didn't do it!"

"Okay, okay!" he says, backing off toward the buses. "I believe you!"

I grumble, "Yeah, sure you do," but then Marissa yells after him, "Hey! When are you going to give back her skateboard, anyway?"

"Marissa!" I hiss at her, because what in the world's she doing, bringing up my skateboard *now?*

"You want it?" he calls to me, still backing his way to the buses. "I thought you didn't want it anymore."

"It's *mine*, isn't it?" I yell after him, because now I'm mad. I'm just mad.

"You gotta ask nice!" he yells back, then turns around and races to catch his bus.

I kick the rack with my high-top. "It's genetic—it's gotta be genetic."

Marissa's actually taking time out from her misery to grin at me. "He's cute."

"Shut up."

"I especially like his freckles."

"Shut *up*, Marissa! He's Heather's *brother*."

"Uh-huh," she says as she pulls her bike from the rack. "And unlike his sister, he *likes* you."

I punched her in the arm.

Hard.

EIGHTEEN

I have real trouble sitting around the apartment when my head's zooming with questions. And let me tell you, with everything that was going on, it felt like my skull was hosting the Indy 500.

So instead of doing like Marissa did and heading straight home after school, I headed straight over to Hudson's. Hudson has a way of steering me in the right direction. Of getting me back on track.

He wasn't hanging on his front porch watching the world go by, like I was hoping he'd be. And for a minute I was afraid he *still* wasn't home. But as I knocked on his door, I spotted him through the window, sitting in front of his new computer.

"Sammy!" he says as he throws the door open. "What a nice surprise! Feels like ages since I've had a visit from you."

"Yeah, sorry. I tried the other night but you weren't here. Plus, I've been tied up getting ready for the Sluggers' Cup tournament."

He leads me inside. "Say, that's right. It's tomorrow, isn't it?"

"Yup. Only as of today, I'm not playing."

He stops in his tracks and studies me for all of two seconds before saying, "Cocoa or iced tea?"

"I don't know," I tell him, looking down. "Got any juice?"

"Sure." He heads for the kitchen. "Apple or cranberry?"

"Apple."

"Sounds good."

So he pours us both a glass of apple juice and says, "Shall we?" and leads me out to the front porch. And after we're settled there and his feet are propped up on the railing, he says, "So. What happened."

There's something about Hudson that makes me want to tell the truth. The whole truth. And even though I started out intending not to tell him everything, well, before you know it I'd spilled the whole enchilada. In fact, I'd spilled the whole plate, refried beans and all.

And when I was done, I turned to him and whispered, "Hudson, they scare me. Everywhere I go I feel like I've got to be looking over my shoulder. It used to be I only had to do that around the apartment. That was bad enough! Now I'm watching my back all the time. And it makes me feel so, you know, all *alone*. Marissa's sick to death of me getting involved with stuff, Officer Borsch is back to thinking I'm a juvenile delinquent, Grams would have a total fit if I told her a tenth of what was going on..." I threw my hands into the air. "I wish I could just forget about Lena, but I can't! I mean, Hudson, I cannot believe she killed her husband. I just can't. And maybe it's because I don't know her or understand any of that gang-life stuff, but I just don't believe it. She was so scared of Snake Eyes. *So* scared. You should've seen her shaking. It doesn't make any sense!"

He was quiet for the longest time, just clicking the toes of his boots together, looking across the rooftops on the other side of the street. Finally he says, "You need to avoid this situation. At all costs." He sits up and says, "Sammy, it's dangerous."

"I know," I grumble. "I *know*."

"And I do understand that you feel responsible, and I know that you're having trouble letting it go because of your own situation, but—"

"My own situation? What do you mean?"

He studies me a minute. "You haven't thought that maybe the reason you want Pepe to have his mother back is because you'd like to have your own back?"

I blink at him, then look down. "I'm past that, Hudson."

He smiles at me. Kindly. "We never get past that, Sammy. And what you're feeling's okay. You've just got to stop putting yourself in jeopardy trying to rectify Pepe's situation."

"But Hudson, what if they don't find her?"

"Sammy, listen," he says, trying to sound cheerful. "Maybe the mother's fine. Maybe she's decided Pepe will be better off away from gang life."

I scowl at him. "I don't believe that for a second."

"Well, regardless of where she is, Pepe will be fine. He'll be well taken care of."

"How can you say that? Remember Holly? Remember her nightmare life bouncing around from foster home to foster home?"

"There are lots of good foster homes. And there's a good chance he'll be adopted."

"Hudson! He should be with his mother!"

He eyes me but doesn't say a word about *my* mother. Instead, he swings his boots back on the rail and says, "So Heather's at it again, huh? Now *she's* someone worth taking on." He smiles at me. "How are you planning to expose her this time?"

I sigh and tell him, "I'm not."

He looks at me, shocked.

"Hudson, the tournament's tomorrow! I've got no alibi and no proof."

"You're not going to just let it go, are you?"

I throw my hands up in the air again. "What am I supposed to do? I almost don't care. If they want to be so dense as to think I would write that stuff and sign my *name* to it, well, it's hopeless."

He thinks about this a minute, then says, "A person's true colors tend to emerge in these types of situations, don't they? That Ms. Rothhammer sounds like a fine woman. And you've got a real friend in Dot. It's not always painless to do the right thing, but those two are certainly making a stand for you."

"I know. And if the rest of the school wants to be peabrained about Heather Acosta, I'm tired of trying to change their minds."

"There must be some way to expose her."

"Well, if there is, I'm clueless. I just feel bad for Marissa. I wish I'd never said I lived with her."

He nods. "The majority of your problems would vanish if you didn't have to be a fugitive from the authorities yourself."

"I know. But that's just the way it is, okay? I am *not* going to move to Hollywood to be with my mother."

"What do you think about staying here?"

"Wow," I said, blinking at him. Then I realized—it wouldn't change a thing. "There'd still be that whole mess about who's my legal guardian."

"True," he said, clicking his boots again. "I already tried to sway your grandmother, but she didn't seem to think it was doable, either."

"You . . . you *did?*"

"Sure." His eyes twinkled. "Invited you both, but I got turned down cold."

I sat up straight. "Seriously?"

"Thought it would be a fine way for us all to get to know each other better." He swirled the last bit of juice around in his glass. "Very strong-willed woman, that grandmother of yours. Says she'll find her own solution."

I slumped back into the chair and grumbled, "Yeah. Hankies."

"Pardon?"

"I take it she hasn't told you about her master plan yet?"

"Noooo."

"Well, she'll kill me if I tell you first. Just be warned

that it involves your computer and some fancy booger catchers."

His head crept up and down in a nod. "I see."

"You will, anyway. Eventually."

The phone rang. Hudson said, "Let me get that," as he swung his legs off the rail. "I won't be but a minute."

Twenty seconds later he was back, his head poking through the door. "You haven't spoken with her all day?" he whispered. He had the phone to his ear, the mouthpiece covered by a hand.

"Who?"

"Your grandmother!"

"Uh-oh."

"Run, child!" he said. "I'll try to calm her down."

Whatever he tried didn't work. She was steamy as a sauna when I walked in the door. "Samantha Jo, I thought I could trust you!" she said, then gave me the longest tongue-lashing I've ever gotten. Even from my mother. And believe me, I tried to tell her that I hadn't tagged the walls of Bruster, but I couldn't get half a syllable in edgewise, let alone a whole word.

So I just sat there taking my verbal licks, getting more and more upset. And when she finally sputtered to a stop, I said, "I can't believe you believe them, Grams. Why do you and everybody else automatically believe everybody but me?"

"I didn't! I stuck up for you! I told Mr. Caan that you would never pull such a prank and that you would certainly not be stupid enough to advertise yourself as a vandal by signing your name! And I was actually feeling sorry for you when I found *this*." Then she does something that makes my heart bottom out. She whips out the clothes I'd hidden under the sink the night I'd been caught in the rain with Tippy. She shakes them at me, saying, "*This* made me realize that I don't know you, Samantha. I delude myself into thinking I do, but apparently I don't. And at first I couldn't figure out what in the world these rancid clothes were doing in the cupboard. But then I remembered that this is what you were wearing the night you went down to Maynard's for Mrs. Wedgewood." She pulls a rumpled wad of bills off the kitchen counter. "*This* was still in the pocket. Soaked!" She slaps the money back on the counter and says, "You may take me for an idiot, but I assure you, young lady, I am not. One does not get one's clothes soaked while under the shelter of my umbrella. One remains virtually rain free. And yet these"—she flings my clothes at me—"are still soaked two days later!"

"Grams, I—"

"You told me you'd washed up in the sink—it was all just a cover-up, wasn't it? I don't care so much *what* you're hiding from me, it's the fact that you're hiding things from me at all!"

"But Grams, I—"

"You need to make a decision, young lady. From now on, either you tell me the truth, the whole truth, and nothing but the truth, or you go live with your mother. I will not be deceived any longer, is that clear?"

194

"But Grams—"

"Is that clear?"

"Yes, Grams, but—"

"No buts! Is that clear or isn't it?"

There was a boulder in my throat. "Yes, Grams," I whispered. And I was really hoping she would calm down and say, So, Samantha—explain yourself. Because I would have. No matter how much it scared her or worried her, I would have. Nothing was worth her being this mad at me.

But the minute I whispered Yes, Grams, she spun around, marched to her bedroom, and slammed the door.

She came out twice all night. And I tried to talk to her, but she refused to even acknowledge that I was there. I could tell that she'd been crying, and she could tell that I'd been crying, but still, she wouldn't talk to me. Not one word.

So I wrote her a letter. An eight-page letter, explaining everything. Apologizing for everything. And a little after midnight, when I was finally done, I signed it Love, Samantha, then blotted off the tears, folded it up, and slid it under her door.

I knew she was sleeping. I could hear her snoring through the door. But I was real quiet anyway as I made myself a peanut butter sandwich and stuffed it and a banana in my backpack. Then I grabbed my afghan off the couch, kissed Dorito between the eyes, and slipped out the door, down the fire escape, and into the night.

NINETEEN

The chairs on Hudson's porch didn't push together to make a very comfortable bed, and the afghan wasn't exactly a down comforter, but I fell asleep anyway. Well, sort of. It was one of those sleeps where it feels like you never quite go out all the way, but you're not awake, either. Where you could easily believe that the fog is a blanket, and the breeze is a current of words whispering in your ear.

"Samantha Jo...I thought I could trust you...trust you, trust you, trust you..."

"It's not always painless to do the right thing...do the right thing...do the right thing..."

"It's the fact that you're hiding things from me at all... hiding things...hiding things...hiding things..."

And suddenly Officer Borsch was there, too; I could hear him. But it wasn't words coming out of him. No, it was more just a long, low hum. The kind of sound you make when you plug your ears and try to stop someone's voice from coming into your brain.

And then Mr. Caan appeared, doing a plug-and-hum. And then Marissa. And Dot. And Ms. Rothhammer, too. All with their fingers in their ears, humming! Then all of a sudden Grams wasn't talking anymore, either.

Now she had her fingers in her ears and was humming louder than anybody!

I woke up with my heart pounding and Hudson, real live Hudson, standing over me, saying, "Sammy! Child, you must be freezing! Come in, come in!"

I dragged in behind him, shivering. The clock in the kitchen said it was five forty-five, but it felt like two in the morning to me.

Hudson clanked around, pulling down a mug, filling it with milk, and slapping it in the microwave. "What on earth happened, Samantha? And why didn't you wake me?"

"It was way after midnight."

"Does Rita know you're here?"

I nodded. "It's in a letter I left her."

"A letter? But why? What happened?"

So I told him. And when I was all through, I said, "I just couldn't stand being there anymore, knowing she was in the other room hating me."

He put a few drops of vanilla in the milk and added a couple spoonfuls of sugar. "She does not hate you, Sammy. She was just distraught." He handed the mug to me, saying, "This'll warm you right up."

"Hudson," I said, but then stopped.

"What is it, Sammy?"

My chin wouldn't stop quivering, but I managed to say, "I . . . I'm really glad I know you."

He sat down beside me. "Your grandmother loves you dearly. That's what this is all about! You must tell her the things you told me yesterday."

"I tried to, but she wouldn't listen. So I wrote her a big

letter and put it under her bedroom door." I shook my head and sighed, "She's going to be mad at me all over again."

"But at least it'll be honest anger. That's the kind that blows over."

I nodded. "I still feel like I've let her down. Again."

"We all make mistakes, Sammy. The key is learning from them."

"I know," I said quietly.

"Do you want me to call her?"

I shook my head. "Can I go lie down, Hudson? My head hurts."

"Sure. Let me get you set up in the study."

I crashed the minute my head hit the pillow. And two seconds later the phone woke me up and the clock said it was 9:30.

Grams! I thought, my heart jumping like a puppy. She wants to talk to me!

The call *was* for me, but it wasn't Grams. It was Marissa. "Did Grams tell you where I was?"

"Yeah, and guess what? My mom says I can go."

"Go?" My mouth felt like I'd been chomping sawdust. "Go where?"

"To the tournament!"

"The *tournament*? Why do you want to go there?"

"Don't you want to see them lose?"

"No! I just want them to leave me alone."

"Sammy! What if something happens and they let us play?"

"Don't you think we would've heard by now? Besides," I grumbled, "I don't even think I'd want to play."

"Sure you would. Now come on. I'm getting ready to leave the house. Dot's going to go. So's Holly."

"Really?"

"Yes! I'll pick you up in about ten minutes, okay?"

"I can't believe you really want to go."

"I'm bringing my cleats and glove, just in case."

"You're deluded."

"Do you have yours?"

Unfortunately, my mitt was still in my backpack. That's where I kept it. "Seriously, Marissa. You're deluded."

"Bring them! Just in case." Then she said, "See you in ten," and hung up.

Hudson handed me a plate of scrambled eggs and steaming tortillas, saying, "I think you should go. Show them you have nothing to feel remorseful over." He sat down at the kitchen table and started rolling up an eggorito. "A guilty person would avoid the event. You, on the other hand, should go there with your head held high."

I rolled my own, saying, "Marissa's hoping that by some miracle she'll get to play."

"Stranger things have happened. But I think you should go regardless."

I scarfed down some eggorito, thinking. Finally, I said, "I was hoping that was Grams calling. I really want to stay here until she does."

"If she calls, I'll handle it. Besides, I was thinking of paying her a visit this morning."

"You're going over to the apartment?"

"Why not?"

"Well...you've never been. It's going to make her pretty nervous, I think."

"Hmm. Maybe I'll invite her to meet me someplace, then. Either way, I'll handle your grandmother. You go with Marissa to the tournament."

We finished breakfast, and then all of a sudden there's Marissa, banging on the door. She comes in all out of breath, saying, "Come on, let's go! It's already started, can you hear?"

With the door open, I could. It was like an ocean of sound, rising and falling, crashing and rolling—the roar of Santa Martina softball off in the distance.

"Oh, man!" Marissa cried, stomping her foot. And at that moment I knew I had to go. I had to go for Marissa.

"I'm sorry," I told her.

"It's not your fault," she said, but there were tears welling in her eyes. And when she added, "I mean it, it's not," well, suddenly there were tears stinging mine, too.

Marissa McKenze is my idea of a real friend.

"Thanks," I told her. "C'mon, let's go."

I must've been feeling really warm and fuzzy about Marissa because I actually agreed to take a ride on her handlebars. I knew I was risking life and limb, but she was dying to get to the high school and there was no way I could run as fast as she could ride—especially not saddled with a backpack.

She pedaled hard and fast, too, and for once she didn't catapult me or skid me across asphalt. Don't get me wrong—my nerves were shot by the time we got there, but other than that, I was completely intact.

"Oh, look!" she cried, pointing to the lower field. "Bruster's got runners on second and third!" She pumped her arm. "Yes!"

It was a perfect day for softball, too. The sun was hot, the fields were dry, and the place was packed with people. I'm talking the bleachers and every inch of grass where you were allowed to sit. Covered. People had huge ice chests and lawn chairs, blankets and beach umbrellas. Some people were already drinking beer and scarfing hot dogs. It was take-me-out-to-the-ballgame, Santa Martina style.

I weaved in and out of the crowd behind Marissa, saying, "I don't get it, Marissa. If you're hoping to play, why are you wanting us to lose?"

"It's not 'us' unless we play, get it?"

"Well, if we're losing—"

"Then maybe they'll sub us in! Do you think they're going to do that if we're winning?"

I muttered, "I don't think they're going to do it at all."

"Well, then we deserve to lose," she said with a huff. "We deserve to go down in flames! What a sorry excuse for a school we go to, anyway."

"Ribbit-ribbit."

She busted up. "Our school is the lamest."

"Unless we're playing," I laughed.

"Yeah. And then we're the best!"

She put her hand up, so I slapped it and followed behind her, saying, "We're not really Bullfrogs like the rest of them, you know. We're just caught in an evil spell."

"Ooo," she called over her shoulder. "Waiting for love's first kiss?"

"No! Don't be stupid. The spell breaks itself automatically after two years."

"And then what? You turn into a Saint?" She eyes me over her shoulder. *"You?"*

It was true. In a year and a half we'd be attending Santa Martina High School—home of the Saints. I shook my head and said, "You're right. I make a better bullfrog."

"Ribbit-ribbit."

The lower field didn't have much in the way of bleachers, but what there was, was packed. I scoured the Bullfrog side for Dot and Holly, but Marissa spotted them first. "Over there!" she cried. "And Ms. Rothhammer's with them! See her? She's wearing dark glasses and a Yankees hat."

We wedged in around them as Ms. Rothhammer filled us in on the game. "Top of the third, no outs, full count, Bruster's winning three to nothing."

Marissa sat beside her, whispering, "Do you think they'll sub us in?"

"Because we're losing?" She pulls her sunglasses down her nose and gives Marissa a pitiful look. "Oh, McKenze, you've got a lot to learn."

"What do you mean?"

She shakes her head. "He'd rather die than give in now."

"Who? Mr. Vince?"

"*Coach* Vince."

Marissa says, "Right," because that's the way Mr. Vince is—always making you call him Coach or Coach Vince. It's a major ego thing with him.

Anyway, we settle in and watch the game. Emiko Lee's on the mound working a toehold before she delivers the batter's last pitch. Babs is behind the plate, and I know what she's busy doing because she's done it to me a hundred times—she's harassing the batter into swinging when she shouldn't.

Heather's out at shortstop, looking completely intense, and Gisa Kranz is at third, where Dot ought to be.

We all hold our breath as Emiko winds up and delivers the pitch. It slams into Babs' hand, a puff of dust rising from her glove. The ump calls, "Striiike three!" and yanks his thumb in the air.

The batter goes down and everyone around us cheers, but Marissa looks at me and mutters, "Rats."

"She's a good pitcher," Ms. Rothhammer tells her. "And *she's* not your problem."

"I know," Marissa says. "I actually like her."

The next batter looked way more like a bullfrog than a rooster. She was short and at least two hundred pounds, with a huge double chin. She started out saying something back to Babs, and just when I thought the pitch was going to buzz past her, she cracked it wide open, sending it by Cindy in right field. Cindy caught up to it and hurled it in, but the toady rooster managed to hop-a-doodle all the way to third, driving in the other two runners.

Shooting ahead to a 5–0 lead, the Roosters went wild, crowing and flapping like you've never seen. And Marissa had the hardest time not cheering, too. Things were not looking good for the Unenchanted.

Mr. Vince was up to his usual gross ways, spitting and yelling and spraying his verbal sewage everywhere—at the umps, at the team, at the Roosters' coach—everywhere.

I saw Ms. Rothhammer catch Mr. Caan's eye, and let me tell you, he looked pretty miserable. Ms. Rothhammer didn't let him off the hook, though. She just shook her head and basically gave him a visual tisk. Like, You poor fool.

Later, during the fifth inning, I was in the middle of choking down part of my peanut butter sandwich when Marissa grabbed my arm and pointed across the diamond. "Look!" she said. "Is that Casey?"

It was him all right, wearing a ball cap and carrying a black sports bag over his shoulder. "Knock it off, Marissa," I tell her. "Watch the game."

And that's exactly what I get back to doing. There are two outs, Kris Zilli's made it to first, and Mr. Vince is spraying her with instructions from the coach's box.

But then all of a sudden, Casey's over there, trying to get Mr. Vince's attention. Mr. Vince waves him off, but Casey's not backing away—instead, he moves in closer.

This time Casey gets the full spray of Mr. Vince's fountain of foulness, which does make him back off a few steps, but the minute Babs Filarski strikes out, he moves back in, talking a hundred miles an hour as he follows Mr. Vince back to the dugout.

Heather comes flying out of the dugout, and two seconds into a huddle with her brother and Mr. Vince, she attacks Casey. Just *pounds* on him with both fists.

"Hopping herring!" Dot says. "Will you look at that!"

"Yeah," Holly says to me. "I've only ever seen her that mad at *you*."

Mr. Vince pulls Heather off of Casey and points at her like, Stay! Then he puts his arm around Casey's shoulders and nods and talks to him like they're the best of chums as he takes the sports bag from him and heads over to the dugout. And Heather's trying hard to get in on the conversation, but basically, Mr. Vince just holds her back.

The four of us and Ms. Rothhammer had craned around the Bullfrog fans to see as much as we could, but when Heather and Mr. Vince disappear into the dugout and Casey takes off through the crowd, Ms. Rothhammer sits back down and mutters, "I wonder what the devil that was about."

"You want to go snoop?" Holly asks me. "We could hang behind the dugout. Maybe we'll hear something."

I look at Marissa and Dot, and then at Ms. Rothhammer. Ms. Rothhammer shrugs and says, "Don't see what it could hurt. Just the two of you, though." Then she asks, "Did you bring a cap?"

"No."

She takes off her Yankees cap and hands it to me. "Here. Wear this. And Holly, pull yours down."

I grin at her. "Yes, ma'am," and tuck my hair up in her cap.

"Even better," she says, then hands over her sunglasses. "Cool!"

Marissa kind of eyes her and says, "You scare me sometimes, Coach."

Ms. Rothhammer smiles at her. "Me? I'm harmless."

We reached the dugout in time to watch the team pile out. Through the chain-link, we could see Mr. Vince pull Heather aside so she was the last one to leave. He still had the sports bag and sort of shook it at her. And even though we couldn't make out what he was saying, it was obvious he was talking about something more intense than fielding grounders. Finally, he let her go. And when she was gone, he looked around, over both shoulders.

For a second there, I thought he'd seen me. We ducked out of view, and when I finally dared to look again, well, Mr. Vince was on his way out of the dugout, and the sports bag was nowhere to be seen.

"Darn! Where'd he put it?"

Holly whispers, "Maybe he stuffed it in one of the bat bags."

"Only one way to find out," I said.

"But Mr. Vince is right there!"

We could see him pacing back and forth in front of the dugout.

"As soon as he leaves, I'll go in the back way—through the warm-up cage."

"It connects?"

"Jogs around."

But Mr. Vince stayed right there in front of the dugout, pacing back and forth the whole time. And since Emiko pitched a dynamite inning, striking out three Roosters in a row, the team was charging the dugout before I had the chance to do a thing.

Babs flips her mask up and starts to come in with everyone else, but at the last minute she turns and calls, "I'm gonna take a potty break, Coach!" and shuffles off in all her gear.

So Holly and I hang back and watch the game the best we can. Heather's at bat first and winds up making a good, solid hit, which is bad enough. But then she manages to stretch it into a double. I would have held at first, but Heather charges second and dives for the bag. It was, you know, a real crowd-pleaser.

Boy, did it tick me off.

Then Emiko gets on first, and next in line is Becky Bork. Or Becky-bot, as we've started calling her. When she's up to bat, she's stiff like a robot, and either she'll just stand frozen while strikes fly across the plate, or once in a blue moon she'll send the ball sailing out of the park. There's no in between with her.

Well, somewhere in the sky the moon was blue, because on the third pitch, there went the ball—out of the park.

"Man," Holly grumbled as Bullfrogs everywhere hopped up and down, slapping five all around. *"Man."*

After that, you could feel the momentum build. You could feel the roar of the crowd begin to power right through you. And by the end of the inning, our side was back in the game. I couldn't believe it. They'd scored four runs in one inning and were feeding on the unstoppable power that only a comeback can give you. And as they piled out of the dugout to start the last inning, I could feel it.

They were going to win.

TWENTY

I had nothing left to lose. Heather and her cronies would be heroes; Marissa and I would be branded losers for the eternity of junior high.

Maybe beyond.

And I didn't know what was in that sports bag, but I did know that Heather was in some kind of hot water with Mr. Vince about it.

And it had come from Casey.

Casey.

I had to find out what was in it. So the minute the team was out of the dugout, I looked at Holly and said, "I'm going in."

She hung back, and in I went, through the pitching cage and around the barrier like a hamster to pellets. Trouble is, I'd barely gotten inside when the home-plate ump calls, "Coach, where's your catcher?"

All of a sudden there's Mr. Vince, looking in the dugout, right at me.

Well, forget it. I was going to find that sports bag if it killed me. I started scrambling through the gear like crazy, but in a flash it was all over. Mr. Vince's hand clamped around my arm, and the next thing you know he's yanking on me, growling, "Where's Babs?" like he's going to kill me.

"How should I know?"

Then all of a sudden the ump calls, "Well, hey, we got her mask—where's the rest of her?"

Mr. Vince drags me out of the dugout by the arm. "Let me see that," he says, hauling me over to home plate.

The ump gives it to him, saying, "Someone said they found it by the bathrooms. Says Bullfrogs right here."

Over my shoulder I can see Heather having a fit out at shortstop because she recognizes me. And pretty soon the other players start saying stuff like "Hey, is that Sammy?" and "Where's Babs?" and "What's going on?"

Mr. Vince checks out the mask, and I tell the ump, "That's ours, all right."

"Who are you?" he asks, kind of looking at the way Mr. Vince is playing tourniquet with my arm.

"The real catcher," I tell him.

The ump gets this puzzled look on his face, and Mr. Vince yanks me away from him, yelling, "Filarski! Filarski, you get your butt over here right now!" into the air.

I eye the ump and call, "A fine role model, isn't he?"

Mr. Vince gets back in my face, shaking my arm. "You shut up, you hear me?" Then he calls again, "Filarski, get over here! Now!"

Well, Babs doesn't show, but Ms. Rothhammer does. So does Mr. Caan. And the principal. Ms. Rothhammer goes right up to Mr. Vince and says, "You unhand her. Now!"

Mr. Caan whispers, "You trying to get us sued, Coach? Calm down and tell me what is going on."

The ump calls, "We haven't got all day, people. If she's the catcher, suit her up and let's get a move on!"

"Where's Babs?" Mr. Caan asks Mr. Vince.

"I have no idea."

"Then let's play Sammy."

"That's right," says the principal. "Just play Sammy."

What can Mr. Vince do? His boss is telling him to play me. His boss's *boss* is telling him to play me. His team can't exactly play without a catcher. . . .

And that's when it hits me. There's no way I'm going to play. No way.

By now everyone from the team has moved in, and I can see Dot and Marissa charging across the diamond. And I know Marissa's going to kill me, but getting put in like this is not what I wanted.

I try to sound calm, but I can't keep my voice from shaking. "Mr. Caan, if it was against the rules for me to play before, then it's against the rules for me to play now."

"What?" Mr. Vince says to me. Like now all of a sudden he *wants* me to play.

"What's going on?" all the kids on the team are asking as they crowd in. "What happened to Babs? Is Sammy playing?"

I clear my throat and try to firm up my voice. "I said, if it was against the rules for me to play before, then it's still against the rules for me to play."

"She's right," Ms. Rothhammer says. "Unless you're willing to admit she should have been playing all along."

Well, let me tell you, Mr. Caan and the principal are

looking about as comfortable as skewered squirrels. They exchange looks, and finally Mr. Caan says, "I'm willing to admit that there was an element of doubt...."

I stretch out a little taller and say, "Then why didn't you give us the benefit of that doubt? Like Ms. Rothhammer asked you to?"

Now really, I couldn't believe I'd just said that to the vice principal in front of the *principal,* but I guess there's something about being right that makes you sort of gutsy.

"Okaaay...," Mr. Caan says, "maybe I didn't make the best call. But at this point we'd like you to fill in for Babs."

"You'd like me to take my rightful spot at catcher, you mean. And if I can catch, then Marissa can pitch, right? And of course Dot belongs on third, *and,*" I say, looking right at Mr. Vince, "you'll let Ms. Rothhammer coach, not him."

All of a sudden there's chaos. Mr. Vince is blowing a nasty gasket, Gisa's going, "I vill not give up my spot! I play the whole game!" Emiko's saying, "Wait a minute...," and everyone else is talking a hundred miles an hour while the adults and umps all start to argue. And then people on the Bruster side start chanting, "Bullfrogs croak! Bullfrogs croak!" and our side retaliates with, "Bash those birdbrains, bash 'em!" *Clap-clap.* "Bash those birdbrains, bash 'em!" In no time things got nasty.

Then Holly comes charging out of the dugout with the sports bag. And from the look on her face, I can tell there's something really important in it, but before she reaches us, out of *nowhere,* Babs Filarski tackles me. I'm talking my hat and glasses go flying, I hit three people on my way down, and all of a sudden I'm lying in the dirt, on my back, with the wind knocked out of me.

Babs gets up. Her gear's all crooked and her face is so red it looks like it's been dipped in a bucket of blood. She comes flying through the air at me *again,* screaming, "You little *sneak!*"

I didn't have time to catch my breath or scramble to the side. Instead, I threw my legs up and pushed, flipping her up and over me so that she was on her back, too, head to head with me.

We both rolled over and got up, facing each other. And right off, Mr. Caan pulls her away from me. But Babs is big, and Babs is strong, and it was like trying to hold back an angry alligator. "You had me *kidnapped,*" she cries. "I had to *run* all the way back here from the mall!"

"The mall? Like I'd have you kidnapped to the *mall?*"

"Calm down, Babs!" Mr. Caan says. "I don't think Samantha had you kidnapped."

"Oh yeah? Then why'd they keep saying her name?"

"Babs," I tell her. "I did not have you kidnapped!"

"Oh, shut up. You'd do anything to play!"

Then Heather chimes in with, "Yeah, and isn't kidnapping a federal offense or something?"

Babs says, "It *should* be a federal offense. That guy was scary, man! I thought he was going to kill me!"

"What guy?" I ask her, and in the back of my brain I can feel an icicle forming.

"The guy who kidnapped me, you moron!"

"Girls, girls!" Mr. Caan cries.

"What did he *look* like?" I ask her.

"Like you don't know!" She turns to Mr. Caan. "There were these girls with him and they pinned me facedown on the floor of his car until—"

"Babs! Did he have a snake tattoo on his arm? Black hair, slicked forward. Hatred for eyes, steel for a mouth?"

"See!" she cries. "She does know him!"

Heather snorts, " 'Hatred for eyes'? 'Steel for a mouth'?" and everyone sort of snickers.

"He did!" Babs cries. "Majorly! And it proves she knows him!"

"He was after *me*, Babs. He knows I play catcher."

She's about to yell at me some more, but stops herself. "What?"

"I was supposed to be playing catcher? He got you by mistake."

"But—"

"What did they say to you?"

"They were mostly talking in Spanish, but they said your name, all right? And something about someone dying. I thought you were having me killed!"

"Babs...!"

"Then when we got to the mall, they let me up and kicked me out. Way in the back corner of the parking garage."

"What did the car look like? Was it a—"

"It was a blue low-rider with a big gold chariot thing on the hood."

"A chariot?"

"Yeah, like a gladiator or something."

The ump says to Mr. Vince, "Look, I don't know what this is all about, but obviously she's fine. And I'm gonna call this thing for Bruster if you don't get her in position. *Now.*"

"One minute more," Ms. Rothhammer says, and that's when I notice Holly's beside her and the sports bag is wide open. Ms. Rothhammer pulls out a brown wig, a number-nine jersey, and some high-tops. "Heather," she says, "I'm going to push for an expulsion."

"They're not mine!" she screams. "My brother's trying to frame me 'cause he's all in love with that...that... *kidnapper.*"

I tell her, "You're sick, Heather," and then the ump cuts us short with, "I'm giving you thirty seconds!"

Mr. Caan says, "Wait a minute. Where'd those things come from?"

"Why don't you ask Mr. Vince?" Ms. Rothhammer says. "He's had them since the top of the fifth."

Mr. Vince starts babbling about not understanding what was going on and how he told Casey to find me so we could clear things up, only all of a sudden I'm not hearing his lame excuses anymore. I'm not hearing the crowd jeering or the team whispering. It all just sounds like words in a giant blender whirring off in the distance. And the reason I'm not hearing anything is because all of a sudden I'm *seeing* something. Something out on Morrison Street.

It's sleek.

Midnight blue.

With wheels like the chamber of a gun.

"Where are you going?" Mr. Caan calls as I take off running.

"Let Babs play," I yell back.

"But I thought this was important to you!"

"It's a *game*, Mr. Caan!" I call over my shoulder.

I was way more worried about a matter of life and death.

TWENTY-ONE

That's the way I saw it, too—as life and death. Not mine—I wasn't actually too worried about that. I was worried about Lena. Now, believe me, I wasn't planning to be stupid. I was just planning to shadow that shady low-rider as far as I could, hoping that maybe, just maybe, he'd lead me to her.

By the time I got up to Morrison, he was almost out of view. Almost. Low-riders can't take bumps and dips very fast, and lucky for me, Morrison's full of speed bumps because it runs along the high school.

And I was already out of breath from charging up the hill from the fields, but I couldn't even *think* about slowing down now. If I did, I'd lose him. I took off down Morrison, running past the park and the back side of the fairgrounds, trying hard to keep the car in view.

Snake Eyes slowed *way* down when he got to the railroad tracks, then bumped over them and turned into a 7-Eleven parking lot. I moved in as close as I dared, then tucked myself behind an old pickup truck.

And I'd been trying to catch my breath for all of ten seconds when a bike skids to a stop beside me. My head snaps around and I can't believe my eyes. "Marissa!"

She yanks her bike between the truck and the car behind me, panting, "God...you run...fast."

"What are you doing here? Aren't they going to let you play?"

"Mr. Caan forfeited the game."

"What?"

"I refused to play, and Dot said she wouldn't if I wouldn't, and Ms. Rothhammer said she wanted nothing to do with the mess they'd created." She shrugs. "Mr. Caan didn't think Heather or the other subs should play, so he forfeited."

"Wow."

"Yeah," she says with a grin. "Heather and Mr. Vince are in some real trouble, too."

"It's about time."

"Speaking of hot water...what are *you* up to?"

"See that lowered car in the 7-Eleven parking lot?"

"The blue one?"

"Uh-huh. That's the carriage that whisked Babs to the mall."

"Really?"

"Yeah. And that," I say as the front door swings open and the driver steps out, "is Snake Eyes."

She watches him a minute. "He's...he's kind of *little*. I was expecting some sort of, you know, monster, or something."

"You haven't seen him up close."

The Gangster Girls pile out behind him, and as we watch them all head for the 7-Eleven door, Marissa says, "So what's the plan?"

I blink at her. "I can't believe you're up for this."

She wraps her hair and stuffs it into her ball cap. "As long as we're not going to be *stupid* or anything..."

How in the world did I deserve a friend like Marissa McKenze? I smiled and said, "Cross my heart," then looked around. "Can you leave your bike somewhere? I think we'll be able to move around better without it."

She nods at a railroad-crossing sign behind us. "I'll lock it to the pole. And here," she says, peeling my backpack off from over hers, "you can carry your own now."

I strapped it on. "Thanks."

Snake Eyes came out while Marissa was locking up her bike. "Duck!" I whispered, and she scurried back to where I was.

We watched the Gangster Girls pile in through the passenger door while Snake Eyes slowly scanned the area, from his left shoulder clear around to his right. Like he was an alien taking in information. Processing it.

Then suddenly he holds real still and sniffs the air. Slowly. Like he's smelling something suspicious.

He squints around from side to side again, then finally slides in through the driver's-side door.

I whisper, "He is the single creepiest person I have ever met," and Marissa nods, saying, "I'm beginning to get the picture."

Snake Eyes pulls out of the parking lot and starts back in our direction, but then turns before the railroad tracks and heads north.

"You ready?"

Marissa gives a small nod.

"Let's go."

We stalked the stalker for about five blocks, and even though he was just cruising along, it was really hard to keep up—especially since we were trying not to be seen. And pretty soon we found ourselves in an area where a lot of houses had boarded-up windows or burglar bars. Plus, there was graffiti everywhere—on garbage cans, on old cars, on telephone poles and stop signs; in some places it even covered whole sides of buildings and fences. No paint-over patches like you see downtown. No, there was no ignoring it—we were in occupied territory.

"Okay," Marissa pants as Snake Eyes disappears around another corner. "I think we've taken this far enough."

"He can't be going much farther—he's making too many turns. Come on, just one more block?"

Marissa grumbles something about me needing a new definition for stupid, but she runs with me to the next intersection anyway. And the minute we turn the corner, I skid to a stop and yank Marissa down behind a chalky orange Mazda. Snake Eyes has pulled up in front of a dilapidated house across the street, his car facing the wrong direction.

Marissa tries to bolt, but I hold her down while she yanks on my arm, saying, "What if he saw us?"

"He *will* see you if you run now. Just sit still a minute!"

Snake Eyes doesn't get out of the car, but the Camo-butt Queen does. She folds the passenger seat forward and lets the Quiet One out. They exchange nods, then Camo Butt gets back in and the car pulls away.

"Now what?" Marissa whispers.

The truth is, I didn't know what. We couldn't go forward *or* back until Snake Eyes' little homegirl went inside the house. But she *didn't* go inside. She watched the car go down the block, then just sat down on the stoop with her head in her hands.

"Darn!" I said as Snake Eyes' car disappeared around a corner. "He's getting away...!"

Then a screen door slams closed behind us, and when we whip around, we see two boys coming toward us, looking at us like we're stealing the flat tires off their Mazda. The smaller one's not wearing shoes, and the bigger one's not wearing a shirt.

I put my hands out like, See? No tools. Only they keep coming.

"Wha's up?" the smaller one says.

Now, these kids are maybe eight and ten—young. And I'm about to shoo them off with, Oh, we're just waiting for a friend, when I see something I can almost not believe—they're flashing South West signs.

Then I look in their eyes and see it—a flicker of the ice that's on fire in Snake Eyes' eyes. And I want to ask them, Why? Why are you *doing* this?

Shirtless says, "You down or what?" and from the palm of his hand a switchblade flicks open.

I look at Marissa and she's all bug-eyed, so I turn back to them and smile. "Hey, chill. We just playin' with our homegirl, is all."

"Who. Who you playin' with."

"Sssh!" I tell him, trying to act like I'm cool with

what's going on. "Ain't you never played hide-'n'-seek before?"

"Dang," says the little one. "You dumb."

"Yeah," says his brother. Then he calls, "Yo!" across the street.

Marissa cringes and looks at me like she's going to cry. I signal for her to stay calm, but there's the Quiet One across the street, standing up saying, "Hey, Jon-Jon. Wassup?"

"They over here!" Jon-Jon tells her, pointing at us behind the car.

"Who?" she asks, coming forward.

I'm racking my brains, trying to remember what her real name is—trying to picture what I'd written down for Officer Borsch. Then it clicks—Sonja. Sonja Ibarra. So I stand up and say, "You're no fun," to the boys, then wave across the street. "Hey, Sonja. How's it goin'?"

At first she doesn't recognize us. But as we move at her across the street, her eyes widen and her mouth drops. And I almost don't know what to do next because she doesn't look mad or like she's going to kick my tush.

She looks scared.

"Go on, go *on*," I say over my shoulder to the baby bangers. "We're cool, go on home."

The bigger one folds up his switchblade and slips it in his baggies, then takes off, his little brother tagging along behind him.

Sonja's eyes are huge, and she's looking down the street the way Snake Eyes' car had gone, then back at us like *we've* got switchblades. "Why you here?" she whispers.

"Turnabout's fair play, right?"

"What?"

"You followed me...." I shrugged. "I followed you."

"But..." She looks around frantically. "No way you want to be here!"

Now it's weird. This gangbanger's acting like a skittery little mouse. She whispers, "He's looking everywhere for you! I was hoping you'd left town or something!"

"Left town? I'm thirteen! I can't just leave town."

She waves us through a patch of thorny weeds, right to the stoop of a patched-up back door. And at first it looks like she's going to want us to follow her inside, and there's no *way* I'm doing that, but then she slumps down on the stoop, crying. "I just want out! Out of this place, out of this life!"

I squat beside her and whisper, "Then get out! You're old enough, right?"

"You don't get it! Once you're in, you can't get out! Look at Lena! *That's* what happens when you try to break out!"

Ice trickled down my spine. "What happened to Lena?"

She flicks tears off her cheeks. "He's gonna kill her. I swear to God, he's gonna kill her."

"But he...he hasn't yet?"

She shrugs. "He don't tell me that stuff, and I don't want to know. He just told me to find *you*."

"But why?"

"You got the baby!"

"But I don't! Not anymore."

It's like she didn't hear me. She hugs her knees again. "He'll track you down until he's got Lena *and* the baby."

"But why?"

"Because she humiliated him! She was *his,* you get it? You can't just take up with someone else!"

"Sonja," I whisper, "where is she? Where's he got her?"

She just shakes her head.

"Well, if you don't want to tell me, then call the police. You don't have to give your name, just tell them what you know!"

"You don't get it, girl, 'cause you don't live this life." She starts sobbing. "The way it is, is, either you die or I die. There's no in between!"

That makes me back up. But then I take a deep breath and squat down again, saying, "It doesn't have to be that way! We'll help you."

She looks at me like I'm crazy. "You can't help me!"

"Really, we will. Why don't you come with us? We don't have to tell anyone where we're going."

"I didn't want this! None of it! I just wanted family. Friends I could count on. I thought it'd be like the team, only with protection twenty-four-seven, you know?"

The team? Then I remembered—her softball picture in the high school yearbook.

"God, every time I see a game I just want to die. I miss it so bad."

That must have hit home with Marissa, because she squats next to me and says, "Come on. We'll help you, I promise!"

She stands up. "You don't know what you're askin' me to do!"

"You'll be saving her life!" I whisper, "Sonja, please! Put yourself in Lena's shoes!"

She yanks the back door open. "If I turn on Caesar, that's *just* where I'll be!"

"Caesar? I thought his name was Raymond."

She freezes for a second, then whispers, "Oh, Jesus," and shuts the door in my face.

TWENTY-TWO

"Let's go," Marissa says, tugging on my shirt.

I practically stomped my foot. "Why won't she *do* something?"

"She's scared, Sammy, and badgering her isn't going to change anything." She pulls on me harder. "Get away from there, would you?"

"But—"

"Get *away* from there!" She yanks me off the stoop. "What if she's calling that creep right now?"

That got me moving. "She did say Caesar, didn't she?"

"Yeah."

"Do you think that's his street name?"

"Maybe. Sure. Fine. Now could you move a little faster?"

"Maybe he thinks he's king or something. You know, like Julius Caesar?"

"Sounds good, now come *on*."

"Hey! Remember how Babs said that hood ornament was a gladiator in a chariot or something?"

"You're right, Sammy, that all makes sense, now step it up!"

I followed her, trying to sort through everything I

knew about Snake Eyes. And every now and then Marissa would say, "Is this where we turned?" or, "Are we going the right way?" and I'd say, "Yeah, I think so," or, "Uh-huh," but I wasn't really paying attention. Then all of a sudden Marissa stops, spins completely around, and whimpers, "Where *are* we?"

That snaps me out of my head and back to reality. And one look around, I know where we are. "Tigertown," I tell her. "We're still in Tigertown."

"But how do we get *out* of here?"

"Do you know which way's east? West?"

She just stares at me.

"North?"

"No! Every way feels like the wrong way! There are so many dead ends and curves—I'm twisted all around!"

"Okay...well...what street are we on?"

"I don't know...!"

So we went to the end of the block and looked at the street sign. "Cutter?" I said. "Never heard of it." I looked down the cross street. It went a block and T-ed into another street that was bordered on the far side by a graffitied block wall. "Well, that goes nowhere," I said, but then I noticed that the building on the corner down that street was a market. "Marissa, look! Let's go ask at that market."

So we hurried along, and even though we were obviously in a poor part of town, it didn't seem *dangerous.* Sure, there was graffiti, and a lot of the houses had boards instead of windows, but there were also kids' toys in some of the yards.

We got to the T in the road and went around the corner to the front of the store. The sign said MARIA'S MARKET, and out front there were open crates of bananas and potatoes and onions, and wire stands holding free papers and firewood—it was a whole lot friendlier-looking than Maynard's. Maynard and T.J. are so paranoid about people stealing stuff, you think they'd leave open bins of food out front?

Please.

Anyway, before we went inside, I looked around. To the right, the street curved. To the left, it seemed to go on forever. And the block wall across the street just seemed to divide the road we were on from a newer residential area on the other side. Some of the graffiti on the wall was pretty elaborate. Actually, very artistic. And I could read some of the words, but it was still a struggle to make things out.

Marissa notices me studying the graffiti and moans, "Oh, not the walls again!"

"Marissa, calm down. It's high noon. No one's going to shoot us, okay?"

"High noon? High *noon*? That's exactly when showdowns happen!"

"That was the Wild West, Marissa. This is Tigertown. I wouldn't want to be here at night, but there's nothing going on now." A man shuffled out of the market carrying a six-pack of beer and got into his car. We could have been light posts for all the attention he paid us, but Marissa started doing the McKenze dance anyway. "See?" she says. "He had a six-pack!"

I eyed her. "You need to hang around Maynard's more." Then I pointed across the street and read, "*Can't Stop, Won't Stop*—see it? It's in blue."

"And that's helping us get out of here how?"

"Sorry. It just felt like, you know, a breakthrough. Like it's starting to make sense. Some of it's even easy to read now. I recognize some names from that roll call by the park. Like right there—that says Buzzface and Crawler. And that purple on a diagonal? That's CZR, just like Officer Borsch showed us before, and that big black R swirling around it means that CZR rules."

"That's just ducky, Sammy. I'm so glad you've had a breakthrough. Now can we please get out of here before *I* have a break*down*?"

My shoulders scrunched way up. "Okay, okay! Sorry!" I broke my eyes away from the wall and hurried into the market.

It was definitely not high noon inside Maria's Market. It was dark and cool and bacon was cooking somewhere in back. "Hello?" I called across the counter. *"Hola?"*

"Un momento," came a voice from the darkness, and then a woman with graying black hair came from behind the maze of cigarette dispensers and coffee thermoses to the register. She smiled at us and said, "Yes?"

"We're, uh, sorta lost," I started, but Marissa interrupts me with, "What's the fastest way back to Morrison?" and then starts jabbering away, saying, "I parked my bike there and I have to get back to it. Right away. It's near the railroad tracks? We had to leave it there because—"

I stepped on her foot and smiled at her while I crossed my eyes a little.

"Oh, sorry," she says, then asks the lady, "Maybe you can just tell us how to get to Morrison?"

She smiles at both of us and nods. Then she points behind her, saying, "Take theeese street theeeese way. Turn right at the donut shop. Will take you to Morrison."

"Thank you!" Marissa said. "Thank you *very* much."

Now, Marissa's already halfway out the door, but there's a little tingle running down my spine that's making me stay put. "A *donut* shop?"

She nods.

"Uh, it wouldn't happen to be *Peg's* donut shop, would it?"

"See?" she says, smiling at me. "You know your way now."

Marissa drags me out of there, and as we're doing the get-out-of-Tigertown power walk, I'm trying my best to remember what Officer Borsch said about Peg's. Because I'm *also* remembering that Tippy said something about her sister taking her out for a donut after Snake Eyes hit her. And from the way she talked about it, it seemed that it was close to where they had visited him.

So I only half hear Marissa grumbling, "CZR Rules. Just like Bullfrogs Rule and all that other stupid stuff they put up on Bruster's wall. Well, obviously, we do not. And you know, the more I think about it, the madder I get. That stupid Heather blew the Sluggers' Cup for all of us. We worked really *hard* to get a shot at it, and what did she do? She totally *stole* it from us. I hope she gets expelled. She's the sneakiest, lyingest—"

Then something snaps in my brain. "Say that again."

"They should tie her up and hang her by her earrings and—"

"No, before that."

By now I've stopped, and I'm looking over my shoulder, back at the graffiti. Marissa turns around and pulls on my arm. "This is no time to turn into the Sammy Zombie. Let's go!"

It was too late. The Sammy Zombie had taken over. "You said 'CZR rules.'"

"I said Heather stinks!"

I blinked at her. "Say it fast."

"Heather stinks!"

"No! CZR rules. Say it fast."

"CZR rules."

I leaned in. "Faster."

"Ceezer rules." All of a sudden her face turns pale.

I nod and whisper, "Caesar rules. It's his street name. Those CZRs we've seen? They were put up by one Snake Eyes Ramirez."

She just stands there blinking at me for a minute, then yanks on my arm. "Great. Wonderful. All the more reason to get *out* of here."

"But Marissa, don't you get it? His name is all over the walls *here*. So he must live around here, not with his mother out on Las Flores."

"Maybe he works somewhere around here. Either way, Sammy, unless when you said 'Cross your heart' you meant 'Cross your heart and hope to *die*,' can we please get going?"

I followed her, but I couldn't stop trying to piece it together. Where would he work around here? It was all residential. And if Caesar the Snake-Eyed Kidnapper did live in this neighborhood, then maybe this was where he was keeping Pepe's mom.

"Sammy! Stop dragging!" Marissa doubled back and started pulling me along.

"Paint. She said something about spilling paint."

"Who?"

"Tippy. She spilled the paint. In the garage. He got mad and hit her."

"Okay...?"

"It was in a *garage*."

"So what! There are a million garages in this town!"

We walked along without talking, but when we got to the donut shop, I grabbed Marissa by the sleeve and pulled her inside.

"Why do I know we're not here for donuts?" she says between her teeth.

Nobody's inside except a big man sweeping up behind a long glass case that has about ten donuts left in it. But I go right up to the counter and ask, "Do you make some with strawberry creme filling?"

His head's big and bald, and with the stubble on his chin and one cauliflowered ear, he looks pretty burly. Like a chewed-up Mr. Clean. But he nods at me and smiles, showing off his capped front teeth. "Yes, miss. But they're seasonal."

"Oh," I say. Then I just stand there like a moron, not knowing what to ask next.

"You come in for one?" he asks me with one eyebrow up.

"No. I mean, yes! I mean, actually, is Peg here anywhere? I was hoping I could talk to her."

His mouth scrunches from one side to the other, and finally he says, "You new around these parts?"

"Well, we live in Santa Martina, but this is kind of new, um, territory for us, yeah."

He nods. Slowly. Then comes around from behind the case and just stands there. And I can't help staring, because popping out of the left side of his army shorts is a wooden leg.

A *peg* leg.

"So," he says. "What do you want to see ol' Peg about?"

My mouth moves up and down like a fish filtering water until finally I sputter, "I'm...I'm sorry. I didn't know."

"Hey. That's aaaaall right. But give me a little peephole into your brain, would you? What're you here about?"

"Well, um...you got held up about a year ago, right?"

His eyes sharpen on me and his cauliflowered ear looks like it's wadding up for a fight. "Uh-huh. Punk thought I couldn't chase him down with this thing." He thumps his leg on the floor. "Didn't expect me to be packin' one of these, either." He lifts his shirt and there, poking out of the side of his pants, is the black grip of a handgun.

Marissa starts doing the McKenze dance, so he drops his shirt and says to her, "Don't worry, hon'. Don't expect I'll have to draw down on you."

She gives him a wavery smile while I ask, "So do you know anything about the guy who robbed you?"

"Ramirez? Sure. Good-for-nothing punk. I don't know what he was thinking. Like his bandanna was gonna cover his identity? Ain't had trouble since, though." He chuckles, "I may *make* a fluffy cream puff, but I ain't no fluffy cream puff."

"Do you know if he lived around here? Or worked around here?"

He shrugs. "Before he got sent up the river, he *hung* around here."

"So you haven't seen him, um, lately?"

He studies me a second. "You're tellin' me he's out already?"

I nod.

"Figures." He hobbles back behind the cases. "He won't dare set foot in here again, though." He looks at me and says, "Flip that sign over, would you? I've had it for today."

So I turn the OPEN sign over and say, "But he used to come in a lot?"

"Nah. You know those bangers. They *hang*. On their cars, on the corner. They spend the whole day waitin' for night." He eyes me. "Which is why I close up early. Part of my survival tactic."

"But did you ever hear him talk about what he did or where he lived or anything like that?"

233

"I don't exactly keep an ear to the ground, miss. As long as they leave me alone, I leave them alone. It's when that understanding breaks down that things get ugly."

He opens the donut case, then stops and looks at me. "The cops'll have a rap sheet on him. It'll show his address if that's what you're after."

I just shook my head. "That shows that he lives with his mother, and his mother says he's a perfect angel."

He grins. "God bless mothers." Then he pulls a couple of donuts out of the case and hands them to us. "Don't have the strawberry cremes, but try these—they'll tickle your tummies."

Powdered sugar dusted my hand as I took a donut. "Thank you," we both said to him. "And thanks for trying to help us," I added.

Marissa chomps into her donut and says, "Wow!" which makes Peg grin and say, "Mango. You like?"

"Mmmm-hmm!"

I'd never tasted a donut so delicious. And as I downed it right there in the shop, I realized I was starving. Starving! "Wow," I said. "That was great."

He grins at us and hands us napkins. "Thanks. Being stuck in Tigertown with the world's most delectable donuts can get a tad discouragin'."

We'd said our good-byes and were on our way out the door when Peg says, "It probably won't do you no good, but they're all the time talking about meetin' at the Palace. Don't know where that is or what that means—and it sure as shootin' wouldn't be in *this* neighborhood."

"The *Palace*?"

"Yeah. They say stuff like, He's chillin' at the Palace, or, He'll hook ya up at the Palace—you know the way those bangers talk."

Marissa tugs me along, saying, "We should really get *going*...?"

Peg starts bagging the leftover donuts, saying, "Come back in June. I'll have some strawberry cremes. You think mango's good? You ain't tasted nothin'."

So off we go, up the street. And I'm thinking, the Palace...the *Palace*...where have I heard that before? And then it clicks. Camo Butt had muttered something about checking at the Palace the first day I met her.

Now, I was following Marissa toward Morrison all right, but I felt like I was hiking in the wrong direction. Like I'd climbed switchback after switchback just to give up and go home.

So I lagged behind, looking at everything, wishing for *something* that would make the whole thing make sense. And Marissa's nearly half a block ahead of me, calling, "Sammy, come *on*," when I notice a yellow-and-black DEAD END sign with graffiti on it. Thin, silver graffiti, with long messy runs. Even with the runs, though, I recognize it.

CZR.

I look down the cul-de-sac. It's short, only about four houses deep. And the houses look like the ones we'd been seeing—run-down, boarded up, sprayed with graffiti. But at the end of the dead end is a garage door that's *completely* covered in spray paint. Some of it's bright and artistic, some of it's just a mess. But in the middle of it is something I can read. Something that makes my heart start pounding and my hands start sweating.

And I know I can't leave Tigertown.

Not yet.

TWENTY-THREE

"Marissa!" I called as quietly as I could. "Come here!"

She turned around, looked around, then shook her head.

"Please!" I called and waved her over like crazy. "Please!"

She rolled her eyes and shook her head, but came my way as I snuck along the cul-de-sac and tucked behind a van parked at the curb. "You're never going to let me out of here, are you?" she asked as she scooted in beside me.

"Look!" I said, pointing to the garage door at the end of the street.

She sighed. "What *are* you seeing in that mess?"

"In the middle. In royal blue." I waited. "Don't you recognize it?"

She cocked her head. "CZR?"

"Yes! Caesar. And next to it? Same color, on the diagonal? The PLZ?"

She read the letters slowly. "Puh-luh-z?"

"Right! Palace!"

Her mouth dropped and she whispered, "Caesar's Palace! Like the place in Las Vegas!"

"What place in Las Vegas?"

"Haven't you ever heard of Caesar's Palace?"

I shook my head.

"It's this big gambling place—people from all over the world go there. It's really gaudy, with this huge statue of Caesar on a horse and..." She eyes the house down the street. "It looks *nothing* like that."

My heart was beating like a jungle drum. "But that makes sense! That makes a *lot* of sense. His hood ornament, the dice on his tattoo, his street name, what Joey's brother said about him coming from Las Vegas...it all fits together!"

"But he can't *live* there. The windows are all boarded up, the *door's* nailed over...that place has got to be condemned."

"Uh-huh."

"We are *not* going over there, Sammy."

"I agree."

"Then let's get out of here, okay?"

I nodded and was just getting up to race to the police station when something scary happened.

The door to Caesar's Palace swung open.

I yanked Marissa back behind the van.

"Ohmygod!" she gasped as Snake Eyes' car inched out of the garage. "Do you think he saw us?"

"No. But come this way a little farther, would you? I want to keep it that way."

We became one with the van's back fender and sneaked peeks as Snake Eyes lowered the garage door. He was moving faster than he had at the 7-Eleven, but even so, he took time to sniff the air before getting back in his car.

We scooted around the van to stay out of sight as he bumped down the driveway and zoomed up the road. And when he hung a right at the top of the cul-de-sac, Marissa whispered, "Wow...if we'd kept on walking..."

"He'd have seen us," I finished for her.

"Sammy, aren't you scared? If that creep's really looking for you...what's going to happen when he finds you?"

And that was the moment I realized this was a race. If I could find Pepe's mom before Snake Eyes could find me, I'd make it out of Tigertown in one piece. But if he found me first—well, I'd probably do like a real bullfrog and croak.

I stood up and headed for the Palace.

"Where are you *going?*"

"I have to check it out."

"Oh, Sammy, no! Please, *please* don't do this."

I stopped and faced her. "Marissa, he's not here. It's not going to get any safer than this."

"But what if someone *else* is inside?"

"That's exactly what I'm hoping."

"You think she's here?"

I nodded. "I think there's a real good chance."

"So let's go to the police!"

"*He* just went down that way."

"But Sammy..."

"Look, why don't you go to the police station and get somebody over here? He doesn't really know what you look like—especially with your hair in your hat like that. You'll be all right."

"Sammy, I'm not going to do that!"

"Okay, then wait right here on the curb. Whistle or something if he shows up. I just want to take a quick look inside. If I'm not back in five minutes, go to the police."

She covered her face with her hands, then plopped down on the curb. "Five minutes. That's all I'm waiting. Five minutes."

I made a beeline to the Palace. There was a dirt path between the garage and the house, and I went right down it without looking over my shoulder. I passed by two small windows on the side of the house. They weren't boarded over, but still, I couldn't see inside. They were up too high.

I hurried around the house and looked in a back window. There was a table with a pile of fast-food wrappers and some edible-looking French fries. Okay, I told myself. *Some*one's been using the house.

The next window was up higher, but there was a wide wooden ramp built onto the house that made it easy to peek into the kitchen. The faucet was dripping, and one of the handles was broken and lying sideways on the counter. I could see empty beer bottles and cans, a couple of big potato-chip sacks, empty salsa tubs, super-size soda cups, a couple of cookie packages—junk-food wrappers were everywhere.

Through the kitchen I could see into the room up front. It was pretty dark because the windows were boarded up, but I could make out a television and the arm of a ripped-up couch.

The TV was off, and I hadn't seen a soul, so I came off the ramp and tried the back door.

Locked.

So I *banged* on the back door, then hid along the far side of the house, spying around the corner to see if someone would answer. No one did.

There was one last window, right above me. It was up too high to see inside, but I used the rickety fence running along the property line and a sorry-looking tree growing against it to get some height. Then I leaned against the house, cleaned off the window, and looked inside.

And what did I see?

A dresser with clothes hanging out of it.

An open bathroom door with the light on.

A mattress on the floor, and on the mattress was...

Nobody.

"Darn!" But if she wasn't here, where *was* she?

I knew I was about out of time, and the last thing I wanted was to freak Marissa out by not coming back. So I hopped off the fence, only on my way down these two scrawny cats come shooting across from the neighbor's yard, flying right in front of me.

I about had a heart attack. And in one totally klutzy move, I landed off balance, sort of twisted my ankle, and choked on a cry.

The cats never slowed down. They dashed along the wall, then dived through a small vent under the house.

I caught my breath, rubbed my ankle, and started back toward the street. And I was on the path between the house and the garage when I heard *clank-thump-rowwwwwr!*

Clank-thump-rowwwwwr? The *rowwwwwr* was a mad cat—I knew that from the times I'd accidentally stepped on Dorito. But the clank and thump? It sounded like something *falling*.

Then all of a sudden here come those cats again, pushing through another vent right in front of me, the screen pivoting on diagonal corners as they squeeze out and zoom off.

It didn't make sense. Where's there to fall in a nine-inch subfloor? I got on my hands and knees and pivoted the vent. And at first I couldn't see anything but light from the other vents around the house. But then I started making out pipes. Pipes going *down*. Down to a water heater. Which was next to a wheelbarrow.

A wheelbarrow? How'd a wheelbarrow get down there? Or a water heater, for that matter? The more my eyes got used to the darkness, the more I could see that I was looking into a basement.

Then I saw the cement steps leading up to my right. I backtracked and realized that the ramp I'd walked all over wasn't just a ramp—it was the basement door!

There was a latch that folded over an eyebolt on the side of the door, and through it was a stick. No lock, just a stick.

I yanked the stick out, flipped the latch back, and pulled the door open.

It was heavy and it creaked, but when daylight flooded

down the steps, it seemed to flood my heart, too. There she was! Lying on her side on a skinny old mattress, her arms and legs tied with wide bands of something gray. It had to be her!

"Lena?" I whispered.

No answer.

"Lena?" I said louder.

She didn't budge.

"Oh, no!" I whimpered. And really, I didn't know what to do. I wanted to race down the steps and see if she was alive, but I also wanted to run to Marissa and tell her to go get the police.

I decided to do the smart thing. I let the door down, then ran to where I'd left Marissa.

Trouble is, she was gone.

Okay, I told myself, trying to calm down. She's gone for the police. She'll have them here in no time. Get back and help Lena.

So that's what I did. I hurried back to the house, propped open the basement door, and worked my way around some super-sized black widow spiders as I went down.

"Lena?" I whispered as I knelt beside her. It smelled awful all around her. "Lena?"

I reached out and touched her skin. It was warm!

"Lena!" I shook her, and this time she moaned. "Yes!" I whispered. "You're alive!"

The bands around her hands and feet were duct tape. She also had a strip of it from cheek to cheek across her mouth.

"Lena!" I shook her again. "Can you hear me?"

I pulled at the tape on her mouth and she whimpered.

"I'm sorry!" I whispered. "Here. Let me get your hands free and then you can do it."

The tape around her wrists made an awful ripping noise as I worked the layers off. He'd wrapped it around five or six times, and it seemed to take forever to get it off. And when I finally had her hands free, she just lay there. Like she wasn't even conscious.

"Lena!" I said, shaking her.

One hand moved up to her mouth, but a second later it flopped back down.

"Do you want me to do it?"

She nodded. Barely, but she nodded.

So I worked the tape off, cringing the whole time, trying to sound convincing as I told her that everything was going to be all right.

Her cheek was red and raw where the tape had been, and she kept moaning something I couldn't understand. Not until I got a corner of her mouth free—then I knew what she was saying.

"Water..."

I looked around madly. There was a water heater, but even if I could get water out of it, it would be hot. I was out of the basement in a flash, and I thought about busting open a window and filling one of those Big Glug cups from the leaky kitchen faucet, but then I saw a hose by the garage. It was kinked and looked brittle, but it was connected to a spigot, and when I turned it on, water came gushing out.

244

Trouble is, it didn't reach around to the basement door, let alone down the steps. So I ran the hose through the basement vent. It would reach. It had to reach! Then I charged back down the steps, kinked off the flow, and worked it over to Lena.

"Lena, here. Can you sit up? I've got some water."

She didn't budge.

I unkinked the hose a little and trickled some water on the corner of her mouth. "Lena! You've got to try. Come on!"

I propped her head up on my lap, then tried again, letting the water run across the opening in the tape. Her tongue came out the side of her mouth. And slowly she started lapping in water. "That's it," I whispered.

"Can you pull the tape off?" I asked after a minute. "You've got to get the tape off."

Her eyes fluttered opened for the first time, and I whispered, "Remember me? Don't worry—we'll get you out of here."

She said something, but I couldn't understand it. "What?"

She blinked at me, then pulled on the tape. Just pulled like she didn't care if her whole mouth came off with it. And when it was dangling from her other cheek she gasped, "Joey."

I just stared at her. Then it hit me that she might be hallucinating from dehydration. "Here," I whispered, holding the hose up to her mouth. "Drink."

"Is he...dead?" Her words came out sounding thick. Like her tongue was swollen.

"Lena, please just drink. We've got to get you *out* of here."

Her face crinkled up and she collapsed in my lap.

"Please! Just a few swallows."

She shook her head and moaned, "I don't want to live."

I held her head up and tried to unkink the hose so it didn't blast her right in the face. But she clamped her mouth shut and shook her head. I pinched the hose off again and said, "Lena, that was a long time ago. I don't know what happened, but there's nothing you can do about it now. You've got to get better for Pepe. He needs you!"

"Pepe?" Her lips stuck together as she said his name. Like they were tacky with glue.

Then all of a sudden it hits me—Pepe's not his name! Not his real name, anyway. "Your baby, Lena. Your baby needs you!"

She sits up, gasping for air, teetering from side to side. "He's okay? Joey's okay?"

"His name's *Joey*? He's fine!"

She takes the hose, leans over, and starts guzzling. And I'm smiling, thinking, Yes! She's going to be just fine! when I hear footsteps crunching along the side of the house.

My heart starts slamming around as I stand up. Marissa, I'm thinking, Please be Marissa!

And looking out the vent, I can see that it *is* Marissa, and she's not alone.

Only those baggy pants behind her definitely do not belong to Officer Borsch.

TWENTY-FOUR

Snake Eyes threw Marissa in the basement and closed the door. And he was acting madder than a rabid rattler, but he didn't say a word.

He turned the water off and tried to pull the hose back up, but I held on with all my might, so he just hacked through it with his switchblade, spilling water inside the basement as our piece of it tumbled down. I grabbed the cut end and held it up with the other end, trapping what water I could inside it.

As soon as he's gone, Marissa starts whimpering, "Ohmygod, Sammy. He came out of *no*where!"

Lena's sitting up with her head in her hands. "That's his way."

"He kept asking about the baby—I thought he was going to slit my throat!"

"Did you tell him we don't have him?"

"Yes! But he wouldn't let me go! That Sonja girl must've called him because he knew you were with me. I'm sorry, Sammy! I'm so, so sorry!"

"I'm the one who's sorry, Marissa." I put my arm around her because she's shaking so bad her teeth are chattering.

"You were taking forever, Sammy! I thought, you know, that someone had caught you."

"I'm sorry," I whisper again, kicking myself for putting her through all this. "I came back, but you were already gone."

"He is so...so...*evil*. He oozes evilness! You should have seen the way he tore apart my backpack! I don't know *what* he was looking for."

I turn to Lena and hand her the hose. "Drink this. All of it. We've got to get out of here."

She shakes her head. "It's no use—he'll be back." She eyes me. "With a gun."

Marissa starts shaking even harder. "A gun?"

"There are three of us and one of him, Marissa. We'll figure something out."

But then Lena says, "You don't know Caesar. He'll do you quick. Probably have a baby bust a cap in you. But me?" She collapses on the mattress. "He'll make me suffer."

"What do you mean, a baby?"

"Some kid who's dying to jump in," she says.

"You mean he'll let them into the gang if they *kill* us?"

"Yeah." She nods like it happens all the time. "That's the way."

"Great," Marissa says, still chattering. "Just great."

"Look, we're not tied up. There's got to be some way we can get out of here! Why don't we all just scream for help? What's stopping us?"

"You think I didn't try that?" Lena says. "I screamed my stupid heart out for hours and no one came. No one but him, to tape me up." She shakes her head. "They close up their windows, they roll up their hearts...they just want to stay out of it."

"But—"

"Try it. Go on. He'll just come down here and wrap you up with that." She nods at a fat roll of duct tape lying near the mattress. "Believe me, it ain't worth it."

"Well, I'm not giving up. I still say it's three to one, and I haven't spent the last week of my life trying to find you just to let him kill you. Or us." I force the hose on her. "Now drink this."

She studies me a minute, then drinks. Seriously drinks. And when she hands the hose back, she starts pulling the duct tape off of her ankles, saying, "Where's my baby?"

"He's in some kind of temporary care home until you show up."

She nods.

I hand the hose ends to Marissa, who's calmed down quite a lot, then I dig through my backpack for my squished banana. "Here," I tell Lena. "It looks gross, but eat it. I've got part of a peanut butter sandwich when you're done with that."

Then I start looking through the stuff in the basement, hoping to find a length of pipe or a two-by-four or something I can use to pulverize snake brains. There's the wheelbarrow, but no hoe or shovel or *rake* to go with it. Just a good-for-nothing old stirring stick for non-existent paint.

But the wheelbarrow does have handles. I wrestle it around to see how they're attached. Six big rusty bolts.

"Okay! I need a wrench. A screwdriver. Something hard. Flat. Wedge-like!"

Lena's chewing on the banana like her jaw's rusted. "Before he tied me up, I dug everywhere for tools. You ain't gonna find a thing. There's a couple sacks of cement in the corner, but that's about it."

"Cement?"

She points. "Back there."

I read the sack: "EZ-CRETE. Sets in thirty minutes."

Marissa wails, "What good's *that* going to do us?" and she's right. They're too heavy to throw, and besides, he'd come in from above. Gravity was working against us. So I started looking around again, saying, "Maybe we can ram the door. *Pry* the door."

"With what? A *hose?*" Marissa says.

"There's got to be something down here! Help me search."

So Marissa starts looking around, and that's when she sees them, nesting in the rafters in their sticky, messy webs about a foot above her head. She shrieks and the hose flies out of her hands as she freaks. "Black widows!"

"Uh-huh," Lena says, nodding. "They're everywhere."

I snatch the hose off the ground, rescuing whatever water I can keep from running out. Then I give it to Lena and say, "Drink this. Every bit of it."

She nods and takes both ends in one hand and I can tell—she's feeling a little better already.

Then I go over to Marissa and hold her by the shoulders. "Marissa, look at me. Look at *me*."

She pulls a horrible face and whimpers.

"They're bugs, Marissa. Squash, splat, smear—they're dead."

She's practically hyperventilating. "They're exoskeletons and they crunch. They're the grossest, ugliest, poisonest—"

"Poisonest?"

"Yes! They—"

"They leave you alone," Lena says, taking a sip from the hose.

"See?" I said to Marissa. "She's been down here for *days* and she hasn't gotten bitten."

"I'd take them over Caesar any day," Lena mutters. "Once you're in his web, you ain't never gonna get out."

"I don't get it," I tell her. "Everyone says you killed Joey—that you were back in the gang after marrying him."

She shakes some water out of the hose and onto her palm; then she rubs her hand all over her face, saying, "All my life I've got to live with this."

"You *did* kill him?"

She shakes her head. "Caesar set me up. Said he wanted to give Joey and me a wedding present. He had Buzzface driving, which right there shoulda told me something. But I was so wantin' to just put it all to rest and get on with my life that I fooled myself into believin'." She eyes me and says, "Caesar can ooze smooth when he wants to." She shrugs. "So we're drivin' up to meet Joey and when I see him waitin' outside, I wave and call, and the next thing you know, shots is blastin' from through my window. Caesar shoved the gun right under my arm and out the window. Set me up good."

"Why didn't you just tell the police that?"

" 'Cause everyone, *everyone*, who was eyewitness or in the car was claimin' it was me. So I hid. And then I split. Joey was dead and I didn't care about nothin' no more. Then I found out I was pregnant and I just had to shift my head. Get over myself, you know? Ain't nothin' like a baby to make you see what a chump you've been."

She shook her head. "Caesar's all about power, but it's power over *nothin'*. He wants to do me in, do my baby in, 'cause I dissed him? Like that's gonna make him king? Of what? This dump? This neighborhood? His little kingdom's nothin' but a big heap of trash."

She'd finished the banana, so I dug up what was left of my peanut butter sandwich. "Here," I said. "Work on this."

She pulled a face. "I'm feeling really weird from that banana. . . ."

"Well, just nibble." I looked at Marissa, still petrified by all the spiders.

"We're looking for tools, Marissa. Any kind of tool. Or weapon. Those spiders aren't going to hurt you nearly as much as that snake will."

"Snake?" Marissa jumps back, crying, "What snake! Where? Where?"

"The snake slithering around up there," I said, pointing to the creaking floorboards above. "What's he *doing* up there?"

"Talkin' on his cell," Lena says. "Makin' plans." She nibbles on the crust. "He paces when he's uptight."

"Help me, you guys! Help me find something we can use!"

Lena stands up, wobbles for a few seconds, then crumples back onto the mattress.

Marissa grimaces at Lena's pants and whispers, "You're a mess."

Lena nods. "I don't even smell it no more, but it burns pretty good."

"So Marissa, help me!"

"Okay, okay!" she says, then walks around muttering, "A tool. A tool."

I checked all around the water heater. Behind it, under it, on top of it. No pipe wrench, no loose pipe, nothing.

"That thing kept me from freezing at night," Lena said. "It makes god-awful popping noises, but at least it's warm."

It was more than warm, it was *hot*. No insulation around it, just a giant radiator flaming on in the corner. Then I had an idea. I got on my hands and knees and nearly burned my fingers trying to open a small door near the bottom of the water heater. Inside was a big orange-and-blue pilot light. "Marissa! Check it out, Cavegirl. We've got fire!"

She comes over, looks inside the door, and scowls at me. "Pack any miniature marshmallows?"

"Maybe we can start something else on fire!"

"Like what?"

"Like...like..." I look around. "The stirring stick!"

"And pretend it's what? A torch?"

"No! We can take the stick and light . . . the mattress!"

Marissa crosses her arms. "You're going to kill us before he does, aren't you."

"Okay, maybe we can catch the *door* on fire!"

"And then the door'll catch the house on fire and the whole house'll come collapsing down on us! They won't even have to buy us plots at the cemetery!"

Lena snickers. "You two are somethin'."

I look at Marissa and smile, because she's not shaking anymore—she's up for a fight! "Come on, you guys! Let's figure *some*thing out!"

So we all look around, thinking, the creaking of Snake Eyes' footsteps above like a scar on the silence. Then Marissa actually finds a brick, which we decide will be just great for knocking Snake Eyes out. If we can get that close to him.

It wasn't enough, though, and even though I searched all around, I kept coming back to the water heater. There had to be *some*thing we could do with it. We didn't *have* anything else. Just a stupid wheelbarrow I couldn't get the handles off of, a mattress rank with pee, a good-for-nothing stirring stick, a roll of duct tape, and some cement. And oh yeah—a boatload of icky, crunchy exoskeletons.

Lena held the hose to her mouth to wash down some peanut butter, and pretty soon, she'd worked the full length of it.

"It's empty?"

"Yeah," she says.

"You need more?"

She smiles at me and puts the hose down. "You're sweet, you know that? You planning to run out and get some, or what?"

"Well, we could maybe drain some from the water heater...let it cool down? I mean, if you're thirsty, we should try it."

"I'm fine," she says. "Fine."

"Try standing up, then. See what it feels like."

She does, and her legs hold her up like Jell-O.

"See? You're all dehydrated and weak. You've got to keep eating that sandwich, okay? And I'll try to drain some water for you."

Now, water heaters and I haven't spent much time together. I don't even know where the one in the Senior Highrise is. But inspecting this water heater, I notice it's got a kind of spigot—with a handle and a place to attach a hose. So I figure that's what we'll do—attach the hose and turn the handle. Trouble is, when I go to do it, I realize I've got the wrong end of the hose.

"Darn!"

"What's wrong?" Marissa says, her eyes back to bugging out at the rafters.

"I need the other end!"

She made herself come over. "What if you hold the hose up to it and I turn it on? We'll spill, but who cares?"

So I held the hose to the spigot and waited. And waited. And waited. And finally Marissa grunts and says, "It's stuck, Sammy! I can't get it to budge. Plus, it's hot. Man!" She flicks her hand up and down. "It's *really* hot!"

So I tried it myself. And yeah, it was stuck. And hot. "Sorry," I told Lena. "No water."

She stood up and wobbled at the knees, but didn't fall down. "See? I'm gonna be fine."

I tried the valve one last time and nearly burned my hand on the pipe.

Then all of a sudden I had an idea. And at first I'm telling myself, Nah—that'll never work—I've got the wrong end of the hose. But then I started thinking, Hey, I could use the rubber end, not the metal end, because right there next to me is a roll of the world's thickest, stickiest tape. It could work! It could! I cried, "My high-tops for a wrench!" which made Marissa eye Lena and say, "She seriously wants some tools, can you tell?"

"Let me have that brick!" I said, and tried tapping the spigot handle to loosen it. But right away, the brick broke in two. Our only weapon, split right in two.

So I go over to the wheelbarrow and say, "Okay, Marissa. Grab that end."

"What are we doing with it?"

"We're going to tap the handle."

"With a *wheelbarrow*? That's like tiptoeing with an elephant."

I stop and look at her.

"I'm serious. You cannot *tap* with a wheelbarrow."

I lift up my end and say, "Watch me."

She helps me aim the front brace over the crank and I say, "Not too hard—we don't want to break it. Ready? Set? Tap!"

We did about ten *tap-tap-tap*s all over the top of

the crank, then put the wheelbarrow down. I tried the valve, really *leaned* on the valve, but it was stuck, same as before.

I grabbed my end of the wheelbarrow. "Try again!"

"Sammy, why?"

"Just help me!"

She lifted her end. "This isn't about drinking water, is it?"

"No. It's about getting *out* of here."

"But how?"

"Tap! If we can get this valve open, I'll show you!"

So *tap-tap-tap* we went, only this time harder. Lots harder. And when we put the wheelbarrow down, I took a deep breath and cranked that valve with all my might.

And in less time than it takes to say, Holy shipwreck! I was on my rear end on the ground with hot water blasting out.

"Man, that is *hot!*" Marissa cries, jumping to the side.

I hurried to shut the valve, then turned the heater setting dial from medium to high.

The burner kicked on.

The water heater rumbled.

I grinned at Marissa. It wouldn't be long before *we'd* be ready to rumble!

TWENTY-FIVE

"What are you *doing*?" Marissa asked as I crammed the cut end of the hose over the spigot.

"We are going to hydroblast our way out of here!" I said, then pointed behind me. "Duct tape!"

She hands it over, saying, "I don't get it," but Lena does. She nods and says, "Oh, hurt him, girl. Hurt him bad."

I ripped off a section of duct tape and wrapped the hose onto the spigot, saying, "If he's got a gun, that's exactly what we're going to do."

The water heater rumbled and shook, then seemed to jump. Marissa backed away a little. "That thing's acting like it's going to explode!"

I stretched the hose toward the steps, wishing for about four more feet. "Let's test it, okay?"

"Are you serious?"

"Yes! You turn the valve, I'll see how far it'll blast." I pinched off the hose with my left hand, held the end with my right, and waited.

Marissa opened the valve, and right away the hose got hot. Very hot. I let the pressure out and nearly roasted my hand. And although the first spurt of water shot up the steps, the rest of it just sort of rolled out, doing its best to burn me. "Turn it off!"

Marissa shut the valve and said, "Uh-oh."

Uh-oh was right. I could barely hold the hose, let alone put my thumb across it for pressure. I needed a pressure nozzle. Or a way to flatten the end into a pressure nozzle. I needed vice grips. A hammer! I needed tools!

I settled on half a brick. But after two whacks the darn thing crumbled. Just fell into a million pieces right there in my hand.

So we tried using the wheelbarrow again, but that didn't work, either. We wound up splitting the hose *away* from the metal end. And I was just thinking that the whole idea was bust when it hit me—there was still a way to make a nozzle on the end of the hose.

I tore and twisted the metal end until it was completely out of the hose. Then I grabbed the duct tape, ripped off a strip, and ripped that strip in half lengthwise. Lena came over and said, "You want me to pinch the hose while you wrap?"

I smiled. "Exactly."

So we pinched and wrapped and made our own power nozzle. And when we were done, I kinked the hose off and said to Marissa, "Try again!"

This time, the water shot out hard and fast. But I couldn't hold the hose for very long—it was blazing hot.

Marissa cut the flow and cried, "I know! Use your mitt!"

I smiled at her. "That's a great idea!" I said, and dug my catcher's mitt out of my backpack.

Lena frowned. "You know, if you hit him on the way down, he'll just turn around and lock us in again. We gotta wait 'til we're face to face."

She had a point.

"And you can't hide around the corner like that. He'll get suspicious."

"So . . . so what do we do? Sit here out in the open?"

She frowns, then looks at us and says, "You need to think like him."

Think like him. I shook my head. "I don't know if I *can*."

"Domination. That's what makes him happy. He'll come in and toy with you if he thinks you're scared."

"So sit here and look scared?"

She nods. "Like you've been crying."

So we practiced. Where we'd sit, *how* we'd sit, the sad and sorry faces we'd make. Boo-hoo-hoo.

Then we practiced the break—how Marissa'd open the valve and I'd blast with the hose. Lena's job was just to get up the steps without fainting. She said she could handle it, but I wasn't sure. And Marissa was pretty nervous about her second job—conking ol' Snakeface on his head with the half brick that was left. And if she couldn't get in close enough, I told her to pitch it at him. She only had one chance, but if she delivered a strike, well, it wouldn't take three to call him out.

And we all agreed—if any of us could get free, we wouldn't wait for the others, we'd run for help.

We went through the drill about five more times and

then all of a sudden Lena said, "Ssssh!" with her finger to her lips.

There were footsteps, all right. Outside, getting louder and louder. Then some familiar baggies shuffled past the vent, followed by some smaller feet.

"He's got somebody with him," I whispered.

Lena just nodded and lay down like she was sleeping. "Stay cool."

Marissa and I did our best to look like a couple of sad and sorry weaklings, sniffing and making our breath all hiccuppy and pathetic. But it was hard because my heart was popping around like a string of firecrackers, and my hand was shaking in my mitt.

"Oh, God," Marissa whispered, "I'm not ready for this."

I tried to sound lighthearted as I smiled at her. "Sure you are, Cavegirl."

"But what if he—"

The door creaked open.

"Marissa—focus! He's the strike zone. He's yours!"

Easy for me to say, shaking away in my mitt.

Little Feet came down first. And even though he had a shirt on, I recognized him—the boy who'd given us away to Sonja. Lena was right—he'd recruited a baby.

Only this baby was carrying a gun.

It looked huge in his hand, heavy at his side. And he was trying to act tough, but he looked like a bush-league bat boy playing in the majors.

"Them two," Snake Eyes says, pointing to Marissa and

me. It was the first time I'd heard his voice. It was sort of high. And airy. And at that moment, very scary.

It wasn't hard to play up the fear, believe me. Marissa and I whimper, "No . . . no! Please!" and my hand is shaking on the hose, hidden behind me.

Snake Eyes steps down alongside him, with this crooked, evil grin growing on his face. "Beg me," he says. But I guess he started smelling something fishy because all of a sudden he steps aside, saying, "Do 'em," to the baby.

The gun comes up, shaking like crazy. And for a split second I can't tell who's more afraid, me, staring at the killing end of a gun, or him, looking at me from behind it. Marissa dives for the valve, I roll to the side, and before ol' baby banger can blink, he's hydroroasted.

The gun goes flying. The baby does, too. Just screams up the steps like his diaper's on fire. And before Snake Eyes can finish shrieking, "Get back here, punk!" I turn the hose on him, right in his face.

He drops to the ground, covering his head and screeching words they don't *begin* to cover in Spanish class. And I'm yelling, "Now!" to Marissa so she'll bean him with the brick, and "Run!" to Lena so she'll get out of there, only Marissa's just standing there staring at Lena.

I keep blasting on Snake Eyes as he tries to roll away, working around him so he can't run up the steps. And that's when I see Lena, standing with her arms straight out, the gun leveled on one scalding, screaming snake.

"Lena, no! Just get out!"

She stands there, rock steady, her finger on the trigger.

"No, Lena! Think about your baby! He needs you!"

She's frozen with anger, glaring at him.

"You're free! Go! If you shoot him, you're right back where you started!"

She blinks, then seems to snap out of a trance. And after calling ol' Caesar a string of things that, believe me, Ms. Pilson's never taught us in *English* class, she smacks him, *thwack,* on his piping-hot pinhead with the butt of the gun.

He slumps. Then falls forward. And since he's not moving at all, I kink the hose while Marissa shuts off the valve.

We all stand there for a minute, waiting, and finally, Lena says, "He's out cold." So I grab the roll of duct tape and say, "Marissa, take Lena and get the police. I'm going to tie him up."

"Are you *crazy?* I'm not leaving you here!"

"Lena, go! Get the police."

She shakes her head and says, "I think I'm safer with *you.*"

I laugh, "That's a first," then start wrapping him up. But Lena stops me and says, "We gotta tie him *to* something."

"Why?"

"Believe me. He'll find a way out."

"But—"

"The wheelbarrow," she says, like I've got no choice.

"Okay...but how?" It seemed crazy to me, and really,

I just wanted to get *out* of there. But then I notice she's got this look on her face like she's about to bust up. And I have no idea what she's thinking, but she says, "Please? You wouldn't let me shoot him—let me do this, okay?"

"Well, what?" I ask.

"You'll see. It'll make him a laughingstock. He'll have no power. He'll be done."

I went along with her, and it was amazing to me how the girl who could barely stand a little while ago was lifting and strapping tape and moving like she was Hercules.

She wanted him in the wheelbarrow. She wanted his arms strapped over his head to the handles. She wanted his ankles strapped down by the wheel. She wanted his mouth taped closed.

I didn't see how this was going to rob ol' Caesar of his power, but then when Lena smiled and waved us over to the sacks of EZ-CRETE, well, I smiled right back.

Marissa says, "You're kidding, right?"

Lena shakes her head. "You don't understand. He'd have power. Even from jail. If you've got a rep, people fear you. They do what you say. This," she says, "will finish him."

EZ-CRETE's heavy. And dusty. But the three of us got both bags emptied on him and then ran water-heater water all over it. Then, even though the directions said you could just pour EZ-CRETE in a hole and add water, we took turns stirring the two together with that good-for-*some*thing paint stick.

And let me tell you, we giggled.

A lot.

And in no time, we had one bad-boy serpent, boiled and bound and setting in cement. And from the look in Lena's eyes I could tell—she was finally free.

TWENTY-SIX

Lena managed to hoof it out of Tigertown on her own, but once we hit Morrison, she just crumbled. And I couldn't tell exactly what she was crying over as she dissolved on the curb, but I could tell it wasn't over anything simple.

Like wanting clean clothes.

Or needing real food.

Or getting to a doctor to treat what had to be a nasty burning rash.

No, these were complicated tears. Ones I couldn't claim to understand.

Marissa and I huddled up and decided we needed to get her to the hospital right away. So while Marissa ran off to get her bike, I sat on the curb with my arm around Lena, thinking about all the things she'd been through. How she'd grown up with a tyrant of a father and a mother who drank. How she'd probably gone looking for family—for protection—only to lose herself to a gang.

And I wondered what it would be like to be a widow at fifteen.

To be a mother at sixteen.

And I thought about Tippy, growing up the same way.

Repeating history as she got older. I could just see it happening. I mean, how could she stay sweet and innocent when the world around her was so cold and hard?

But of all the complicated thoughts running through my head, the one I finally whispered to Lena was "I think you're amazing."

She just shook her head.

"Really, you are. You broke out. You got away from all that. I mean, the only reason you came back was because of Tippy's birthday, right?"

She looked at me, wiping some tears back. "How'd you know that. You seen her?"

I nodded. "She's fine. She's...well, Social Services is taking care of her because your parents, um..."

She spit in the gutter. "Those dogs!"

"Well, your dad's been arrested because he attacked a police officer and—"

"It's about time!"

I decided to steer away from talking about her parents. "Well, Tippy's seriously in need of a new Barbie, so I'm sure she'll be happy to get the one you bought her."

Her face turned soft. "She's a little angel, you know?"

"I could tell."

We were quiet for a minute, then I said, "Anyway, I do think you're amazing. I've never been so scared of anyone in my life. And you stood up to him." I started laughing, "You cemented his tush to a wheelbarrow!"

She gave me a little smile. "With a little help from some real friends," she said, then laughed out loud. "Do you think he's set up yet?"

"He's going *no*where," I laughed, then added, "Nowhere but jail."

She nodded. "I just want my baby. I just want to feel safe. I just want a sane life, you know?"

"I know," I said, and really, I did. Not about the baby. No way. But the rest of it—about feeling safe and wanting a sane life—I completely understood that.

And maybe I've got a lot working against that—like a mother who's not actually *in* my life, and no father I can point to, and an address that I can't exactly share with the police—but I do have friends. True friends. And best of all, I have Grams.

Grams.

The thought of her made my heart do a loop-de-loop. Did she still hate me? What in the world was I going to do to get her trust back?

Marissa came riding up all out of breath, saying, "Ready?" So we got Lena on the handlebars and the two of them wobbled down the street as I ran alongside. And I'm sure Lena was thinking of nothing but surviving Marissa's wild ride as we jetted past the high school fields, but Marissa and I couldn't help being distracted by softball because the tournament was still going on.

"Next year," Marissa vowed, "nothing's going to stop us. I'm going to pitch, you're going to catch—that cup will be *ours*. We'll be eighth graders. Bigger, stronger, faster, smarter!"

"Well, hopefully smarter."

"And next year we'll have alibis!"

"Next year we won't need 'em. Next year, I'll cement Heather Acosta's tush to a wheelbarrow if I have to!"

We laughed and took one last look at the fields as we passed by. "Yeah, next year," Marissa said with a sigh. "We'll be down there. Under the lights."

We decided a police car could get us to the hospital a lot faster than Marissa's bike. Especially since we were going right past the station. So we went inside and the first thing Debra the Dodo said was "Sams! The big man's been lookin' all over for you. He's worried sick! He's on the west side now, scourin' the streets for you!" Then she noticed Lena. "Oh, honey," she says to her. "You need some new clothes. And a shower. Bad."

"We've got to get her to a doctor, Debra," I told her. "She's been locked in a basement for days...."

Debra practically pinches her ski-slope nose and nods. "Uh, who exactly is she?" she asks, like Lena's not even there.

"Pepe's mom!"

She lets go of her nose. "Pepe's mom? Seriously?"

Lena nods. "But his name is Joey." She looks at me. *"Joey."*

"Sorry. I've got to reprogram myself."

She turns to Debra and says, "When can I see him?" Her eyes are suddenly brimming with tears as she whispers, "I want to see my baby!"

"Oh honey, he is *fine*. And yes, yes, let me get things

rollin'." She eyes me. "First call, though, is to the big man. Then off to the hospital."

"Um, Debra?"

"Yes, hon?"

"Is there a phone I can use? I, um, we'd like to call home."

"Yes, yes!" She waves an arm. "Come on back. You know your way around!"

She buzzes me in, and I head straight for the phone I'd used before and dial Grams. Seventeen rings later, I hang up and call Hudson's.

He picks up on the first ring, and as soon as I say hi, he calls, "It's her," over the mouthpiece.

"Grams is with you?"

"Yes. Are you all right? We went down to the tournament and heard about the fiasco. That policeman friend of yours was there, too. All anyone knew was that one of your teammates had been abducted and that you'd taken off running down Morrison. I must say, you've had us *all* worried."

"I'm fine. We're fine. And I'm sorry I worried you." I hesitated, then added. "We, um...we found Pepe's mom."

"You *did*? How in the world...?"

"It's a really long story, and we're taking her to the hospital, but I'll come over as soon as I'm done. Can you keep Grams there?"

"Sure." I could just see him, winking over his shoulder at her. "I think I can manage that. Say, why don't I fix us

270

all supper? We have a lot of talking to do, and that may be a nice way to do it."

"Is Grams still ... mad?"

"Hurt more than mad, dear. And worried, of course."

"Well, tell her not to be, I'll get there as soon as I can."

I got off the phone feeling a whole lot better. And then, sort of on a whim, I punched in the McKenzes' number. When the recorder clicked on, I said, "Hey, this is Sammy, calling from the doghouse. Just wanted you to know that Marissa'll be home soon. Bye!"

I went back into the lobby and told Marissa what I'd done, and she said, "Why?" like I was crazy.

I shrugged. "You were grounded, remember? What if they decided to check out the tournament, too?"

"My *parents?*"

"Well, what if they did and you weren't there and you weren't at home and nobody knew where you'd gone?"

"Oh, right. Thanks!"

Just then Officer Borsch comes barging through the door. "I've been looking all over hell and gone for you!"

Debra leans across the window and says, "He's happy to see you, Sams. That's his way of expressin' it."

"Sorry, sir," I said.

"Sir? What's this sir stuff?"

I just shrugged and changed the subject. "This is Pepe's mom. She needs some medical attention and some clean clothes."

"You're Lena Moreno?"

"Lena *Martinez*," she corrects him. "I don't care what no one says. Joey and me was married."

"But...you're wanted for murder, you know that. You turnin' yourself in?"

Before Lena can say anything I start jabbering away a hundred miles an hour about how Snake Eyes framed her, and what a monster he is, keeping her tied up with duct tape in a basement with black widow spiders dangling around everywhere, and how *he's* the one who murdered Joey, not her. And then I tell him how he recruited some ten-year-old to shoot *us*, only we blasted him with hot water and scared him off and then melted down ol' Caesar's crown and knocked him out and tied him up and sank his sorry backside in cement just to make sure he didn't Houdini his way out of the basement.

And when I finally come up for air, all he says is "You did *what*?"

So I start explaining all over again, only he cuts me short and says, "Wait! Are you telling me that Raymond Ramirez is setting up in a wheelbarrow of cement?"

The three of us nod, and I add, "He'll be fine, Officer Borsch. He'll have a little trouble peeing his pants like I'm sure he'll want to when he wakes up, but he'll be fine."

He shakes his head like he cannot believe what he's hearing, then says, "Where? Where did all this happen?"

So Lena tells him the street and describes the Palace, and Officer Borsch says, "We should send a unit over there right away, but...I'd also really like to see this for myself."

"No hurry," Lena says. "Let him set for a while."

Officer Borsch eyes her. "We're going to have to take you into custody, you know."

She nods. "I can face it now. But please, when can I see my baby?"

"Let's get you over to the hospital. I'll try to arrange a visit over there." He turns to Marissa and me. "Something tells me you're coming along."

I grin at him. "Only 'cause I know you'd be lonesome without us."

"Hrumph," he says, but underneath it, he's smiling.

When we get to the hospital, I help Lena fill out about a ream of paperwork while Officer Borsch fills out a police report. So while I'm asking Lena questions, Officer Borsch is asking all three of us questions, and poor Lena's drooping like a wildflower in the desert sun, waiting for someone to cart her away.

Then she sees him, across the room, in the arms of a woman in uniform.

The Barf Bomber himself.

The Sultan of Scream.

The one and only, unforgettable Poopy Pepe.

Lena cries out and tears stream down her face, and when they let her hold him, she buries her face in his neck and just bawls.

And I can't stop the tears from running down my cheeks, either, because even though I know that life for them isn't going to be smooth or easy, even though Lena's got a lot to get through before she's really free of the past—the two of them are back together.

Right where they belong.

TWENTY-SEVEN

Grams and I have an agreement. I tell her the truth, the *whole* truth, and she trusts me and tries not to worry. It seems like a simple deal to make, but it sure took a lot of crying on both our parts to get there. And let me tell you, we didn't use any dainty lacy handkerchiefs to dab our eyes, either. We honked through a big box of Kleenex and some toilet paper besides.

Grams is trying to trust Mrs. Wedgewood, too, although that doesn't come real natural to her. But I guess Mrs. Wedgewood overheard our fight and had a thing or two to say about the way Grams is raising me, which made Grams wonder about *my* mother and where she had gone wrong raising *her*. So I think the whole child-rearing thing's confusing for Grams, which makes me wonder—if you still don't have the answers at her age, how in the world do you make sense of raising a kid when you're sixteen?

Anyway, Lena was right about Snake Eyes. I guess four beefy cops were slightly creeped out by rafters full of crunchy exoskeletons and decided to carry Two-Ton Tushy up from the basement, wheelbarrow and all. They parked him in front of his palace and chiseled him free.

And for a neighborhood that's closed up its windows and rolled up its heart, Officer Borsch said there were a whole lot of spectators present.

Officer Borsch also told me that hot water makes EZ-CRETE set up fast and hard, so by the time they'd chipped him out of his diaper cast and treated his burns, well, let's just say there's one mini macho man from the west side who's got a new reputation he's *never* going to live down.

And while Lena's not exactly living it up, she and Pepe have found a home. I guess the minute Joey's mom found out the truth, she wanted nothing more than to see her grandson. She wound up posting bail for Lena and inviting them both to stay.

I don't know what's going to happen to Tippy. Officer Borsch says it's under review, whatever that means. And Lena says she's got plans for her, whatever *that* means. At least I know there are people looking out for her, and she's now got a Barbie with all its parts.

I haven't seen the Gangster Girls around, and that's just fine with me. I did ask Officer Borsch to maybe talk to someone at the high school about them, though. I don't know about the other two, but Sonja could probably use some help switching colors. You know, maybe get her back into *school* colors. Back into softball. Because she'll sure never make it around the bases with the team she's *been* playing on.

And speaking of losing teams, this past week at William Rose Junior High has been real interesting. Bullfrogs aren't very good at admitting they're wrong. Or saying they're sorry. What they do instead is not look at you. Or they look at you like, Hey, it wasn't *me* talking trash behind your back.

Right.

So I just added I TOLD YOU to the top of my shirt, so it now reads I TOLD YOU WE DIDN'T DO IT, and wore that for the first couple of days.

I don't exactly know what's going on with Mr. Vince. He's been Mr. Grovel all week, so I think he's trying to work his way out of some steamin' hot stew. Maybe they'll get rid of him before I get him for history next year.

As Ms. Rothhammer says, "Hope springs eternal."

And Heather. Heather! She's been absent all week. Ms. Rothhammer won't confirm that she's been expelled, so maybe she's just been suspended. All Ms. Rothhammer will say is that they're "seeking professional help" for her.

Professional help. Shoot, give me a wheelbarrow and a couple sacks of cement—I'll save everyone a whole lot of time and money.

The only thing I haven't been able to figure out is what to do about Casey. I mean, I still can't quite believe he turned Heather in. But *why* did he do it—that's what I want to know. Did he do it because it was the right thing to do?

C'mon. He's an eighth grader. How likely is that?

Did he do it because he hates his sister? Could it be as simple as that?

Or did he do it because he likes me? And if he *does* like

me, is it for *me?* Or is it because he knows that liking me will drive his sister crazy.

And then there's that little matter of my skateboard. What's up with that? Why doesn't he just give it back? Ask him nice? Get real. But Marissa thinks he's just holding on to it as a way of holding on to me.

I don't know, and not knowing is driving *me* crazy.

It's also making me mad. Not because he said I had to ask him nice, but because of how suspicious I am. Of him. Of his motives.

Of everything.

And I know what this comes down to—trust. But that's something I've locked away for so long, I'm not really sure I know how to reach it.

I've *got* to with Grams. But Casey? How could I ever trust *Casey?* He's the biological equivalent of Heather Psycho Acosta, with a minor chromosomal twist.

Still. I do have to thank him. I mean, if he hadn't shown up with that sports bag—if he hadn't broken from the pack to do the right thing—I'd still be the Loser. And believe me, that's one reputation that makes breaking out of a diaper cast look easy.

Besides, Hudson says that the longest journeys start with the first step, and maybe thanking Casey is like that. And after Snake Eyes, baby bangers, and gangster girls, how scary can Casey be?

So here goes. I'm taking a deep breath, see? And I'm going to try that first step forward.

I guess we'll see just where it takes me.